THAT SUMMER

Jo Huddleston

Book #1 in the Caney Creek Series

Sarah —
Enjoy all your
Summers.
JHuddleston
Phil. 2:5

ISBN 13: 978-1-9392190-3-9

Published by Sword of the Spirit Publishing
www.swordofspirit.net

DEDICATION

To the memory of my daddy.

ACKNOWLEDGMENTS
Thanks go to

My first readers, Carrol, Paige, and Vickie, for their feedback.

My publisher and editor, Donald J. Parker, who saw merit in this novel and, with his writing expertise, made it better. I thank him for his patience with me throughout this publishing process.

Members of American Christian Fiction Writers for their support, especially Ane and Bonnie, for allowing me to ask my questions to which they responded.

Those who gave their endorsement and support to this novel.

My ancestors who allowed me to listen to their beautiful stories.

My family's support.

Questions for Reflection and Discussion
For individual or group use
That Summer by Jo Huddleston
Please see Jo's website, www.johuddleston.com

Praise for *That Summer*

"Sweeping from the early days of the Great Depression to the 1950s, Jo Huddleston's debut novel is a memorable story of the heartbreak and happiness one man encounters as he struggles to find the true meaning of faith and family."
AMANDA CABOT, author of *Waiting for Spring*

"As surely as Caney Creek runs through the town, the story of *That Summer* swept me back to the pre-depression era, a time of hope and opportunity. Following Jim's ambitions, this book examines the effects of following self versus following God and the sometimes maddening, sometimes inspiring results."
CHRISTINA BERRY, award-winning author of *The Familiar Stranger*

"A compelling and poignant tale with characters destined to capture your heart."
LAURIE ALICE EAKES, author of *Choices of the Heart*

"*That Summer* is a wonderful romance set in the Southern Appalachians during the Great Depression. Jo Huddleston understands the people of that time and place so well she pulled me right into the story and didn't let me go until the end. Highly recommended!"
CARA LYNN JAMES, author of *Love on a Dime* and *A Path Toward Love*

~ ~ ~

"Behold, I stand at the door and knock: if any man hear
my voice, and open the door, I will come in to him,
and will sup with him, and he with me."
Revelation 3:20

PART ONE
1928

Chapter 1

Sanford County, Tennessee
August, 1928

The back of Poppa's big hand smacked across Jim's face and flung him against the splintered timbers of the barn wall. "What're you doin' outside when you ain't finished your chores?"

"Uh . . . me and The Twins was just foolin' around, Poppa."

Poppa scowled at his son. "Well, you best get that hay pitched down for the mules. The Twins need to draw water for the animals and shuck corn to feed the hogs."

Jim stood and tried not to think about how much his face hurt. "They're comin'. We'll get to it all, Poppa. We'll finish before dark."

John Lee Callaway's hand curled into a fist at his side. "You'll do it now! Don't you sass me."

Jim watched Poppa's temper build. His face flushed. His dark eyes withdrew beneath heavy brows and his fury spewed out misdirected or unmerited. When Jim saw the storm rise in his poppa's dark eyes, he knew he'd better get the chores done or feel the sting of Poppa's backhand again.

"No time for loafin'." Poppa glared at Jim. "Loafin' won't pay the rent. Quit shunnin' your work, or you won't never amount to nothin'."

"Yes sir, Poppa. I promise I'll do better." Jim obliged Poppa with words he wanted to hear.

Jim grabbed the hay rake. He'd had about all of this he could take. No matter how hard he tried, he couldn't please Poppa.

He rubbed his stinging cheek. He would've thought he'd been used to this by now, but he wasn't. His face still hurt, but it hurt a lot worse on the inside. Not that he's ever let his father see that side of him. The crops hadn't brought in what Poppa had counted on, and Poppa always took it out on him. But better him than his younger brothers. He lived for the day he could leave all this behind and make his own decisions. Make his own way.

Recovering from his poppa's slap, Jim steadied himself against the mules' stall. The mules' long ears twitched and their eyes widened and rolled toward the commotion. The pervading stench of animal sweat caused a wave of nausea to punch Jim in the stomach. He pulled his lips into a tight line to keep from retching, and then climbed the crude wooden ladder to the barn loft to throw hay down for the tired mules.

"Twins, come on," Jim shouted out to his brothers as he shoved the rake into the pile of hay and hefted another load. "Poppa says it's time to get to work."

Robert and Richard rushed into the barn, leaving the rusty hoop they'd played with to roll and wobble away to its death. Jim gave them a warning nod to get busy.

Robert pointed to Jim's face. "Did Poppa hit you again?" he whispered.

Jim wiped his mouth with the back of his hand and saw the blood. Jim nodded and spoke in a low voice, "Get to your chores before he gives you the same."

They grabbed the water buckets and headed for the well in the backyard. Jim knew The Twins would stay at arm's length from Poppa and his bad temper as if he were a coiled rattle snake.

When Jim finished pitching hay, he left the barn. He squinted up at the lowering sun to see how much daylight they had left. The scarlet fireball almost touched the rooftop of their modest home and within the hour would settle against the cornstalks on the far side of the house. By the time they finished their work and made their way toward the house the sun would slip below the west edge of the field for the night. Then they would get some relief from the summer heat of the day.

~ ~ ~

The next morning, the savory smell of frying ham nudged Jim into a new day. He blinked against the predawn gray stabbing at the window. The curtains his momma had made from empty cotton feed sacks hung limp and offered little hindrance to the impending sunrise. Increasing light reached with long, bony fingers to push away the night's rest.

Jim rolled over to turn his back to the morning's first light, but flinched from the pain that riveted his shoulder and cheek. Now wide awake he touched his sore lip and his mind replayed his poppa's outburst last night before supper, and the force with which his shoulder had landed against the barn wall.

As hard as he tried, Jim couldn't understand his father these past few years. Why had he become so volatile? Jim remembered a kinder Poppa. When he was a little boy, Jim would climb onto his father's lap and snuggle close. Poppa would cross his long legs and Jim would "ride the horsey," sitting astride Poppa's swinging foot. He recalled how his father would throw back his head and fill the house with his infectious laughter.

Of late, though, Poppa had begun to brood. He spoke in an abrupt manner to family members and showed impatience with their efforts. Criticism became his trademark. Jim dreaded Poppa's sour attitude that dampened the mood of any room he entered.

Thinking now of more recent times, Jim's festering anger rose like bitter bile, burning his throat. Guarded anger against Poppa. Anger at the family's frugal lifestyle, at the way they had to scrimp to exist. At all their back-bending work with nothing to show for it. Anger at the shield of humility behind which his momma always seemed to cower.

Jim often spoke to his momma about this. "I wish you could find some way to take up for yourself. I hate to see you the butt of Poppa's harsh demands of obedience."

"Jim, we've hit on some hard times lately and we should support your father." She continued shelling peas, not meeting her son's gaze.

He pressed her on the situation. "But you didn't cause the hard times, Momma. He should treat you better."

Elizabeth Callaway would only reply, "Jim, the Bible tells wives to submit to their husband's leadership."

Some leadership, when a husband treated his wife and children just a little better than his farm animals. What kind of God expected people to bear up under a Poppa's high-strung behavior?

Now it was time to get up and start all over. Try to keep the weeds from overtaking their Appalachian crops. Tenant farming taxed the body and mind. Old Man Thomas came as regular as the seasons to collect his rent money. Jim could recall few frills. A new pair of shoes before the winter snows exploded from the clouds and an apple or orange found in a sock hung by their meager fireplace at Christmas.

On Saturdays in the spring and summer Momma and Poppa took vegetables from their truck garden, along with any extra eggs, into Newton and sold them to the town folks. The money they made had to get them through the winter when the garden grew barren. Even so, with all their hard work and scrimping, Mr. Thomas still owned the thirty acres they worked, and the house and barn.

Despite his throbbing shoulder, Jim shrugged into the long-sleeved shirt he wore yesterday and snapped his faded bib overalls across his broad shoulders. He pushed his feet into his high-topped leather work shoes covered with yesterday's copper-red dust.

Jim reached back into his bed and shook his sleeping brothers. When he walked by the other bed in the room, he tousled his sisters' hair and drawled, "Get up. Almost breakfast time."

The heat from the wood fire in the cast-iron cook stove met him at the kitchen door. The midday August heat he'd be working in later today would be even hotter. He started to complain but decided against it. If his momma could prepare their meals in such smothering heat, he could endure the discomfort for a little while.

"Good mornin', Momma. Smells good in here." She returned her son's hug with one arm and continued to stir bubbling gravy with her other hand.

"Do you feel good this mornin'?" she asked her firstborn.

"Yes, ma'am," he fibbed and bent down to kiss her smooth cheek, careful not to let Momma see his injured cheek. She hadn't seen the violent display of Poppa's temper last night in the barn, and Jim didn't want to upset his momma by telling her.

She had enough on her, caring for the other four kids and seeing to the needs of her demanding husband. Now the new baby was due soon.

"Here, let me take up the gravy, Momma." He wrapped a towel around the handle, lifted the heavy cast-iron skillet, and turned toward the kitchen table. With a large metal spoon he raked the steaming pale gravy into the bowl his momma had set out.

"Thank you, Son." She tucked a loose strand of auburn hair back into the plain bun she wore on top of her head and bent over to look inside the oven. "The biscuits are almost done. Go tell the others breakfast's ready."

Jim turned toward the door and collided with Poppa coming into breakfast.

His father started to say something until his gaze fell to the bruise marring his son's cheek. For a flickering second Jim thought he saw regret in his father's eyes and that his father was sorry. But then just as quickly, that guard came up and his father was "that man" again.

"Whoa . . . watch where you're goin'!" Poppa ducked his head to clear the top door frame. "You tryin' to knock me down?"

I wish I could. "No, sir, sorry." Jim moved from the room, out of his poppa's reach.

~ ~ ~

Elizabeth Callaway made sure her family started each day on a full stomach. As she put food on the table, her back ached due to the child she carried. Her husband wanted this new child to be a boy so he could work him on the farm. Elizabeth wished for a girl. John Lee would be kinder to her than to a boy. She also felt heavy inside with the weight that had nothing to do with the new life growing inside her. A slight tremble coursed through her as she thought of sleeping next to the man she called her husband. Any tenderness she ever felt for him had died away long ago, like the land they tried to farm.

Before anyone ate, Elizabeth nodded to Jim, who sat to her left, and he offered up a short blessing on the food. As soon as the prayer was over, the boys shoveled their food into their mouths. Breakfast never lasted long.

She glanced at her husband of twenty years—one year of which had been worth remembering—and saw again that he did not bow his head or close his eyes. Elizabeth was thankful that he allowed her to lead the children in the ways of the Lord and say grace at his table. But for a long while he had not joined them.

Elizabeth looked with affection at her family seated in the dining room around the large pedestal table. She passed the platter of fried eggs, seeing the sparkle of question in her daughters' eyes.

"Poppa, have you made up your mind, yet? Can we go to the fair next month? Can we go, please?"

"I don't know yet, Shirley Ann. We'll see." Her father smiled in thought.

John Lee looked at his older daughter. At fifteen, Shirley Ann was a jet-haired beauty. Elizabeth often heard him say, "As pretty as any girl in the Sears and Roebuck catalog." All her children except little Emmajean and Richard had John Lee's dark good looks, the coal-black hair and black eyes.

Jim bit into a steaming buttered biscuit and waited for Poppa to say more to Shirley Ann. Her two oldest usually stuck together. But, Elizabeth knew if Jim tried to side now with his sister against Poppa, Jim would probably say the wrong thing and get in trouble again.

Her husband's decision pleased Elizabeth that every autumn he took the family to the Sanford County Fair. However, he always left them in doubt about the trip until the last minute. He claimed all kinds of reasons why they might not get to go. This year, it was not having enough money.

"But, Poppa." Little Emmajean pleaded with her eyes for a trip to the fair. Elizabeth smiled toward Emmajean. Eight years old and baby of the family, she had more luck than the rest of them when it came to getting their poppa's good favors. The other children teased that it was because she looked just like Momma, with her dark auburn hair and apple-green eyes.

"We'll see." Poppa put down his fork with a clatter, signaling that the fair trip discussion was over.

Robert and Richard continued to eat their breakfast in silence, untypical of ten-year-old boys. The Twins' manner was to listen and not speak, unlike their two sisters. While Robert resembled his poppa, Richard got a little bit of her dark auburn hair, his a reddish-blond. Still, Elizabeth was proud that two of her children looked a little like her.

Glancing at John Lee, Elizabeth knew that now, for sure, he had ended the conversation. She noticed that Robert and Richard remained quiet. Elizabeth never revealed that she knew they didn't want to be the object of Poppa's familiar ridicule yet again. They, like Jim, had felt the sting of his venom that he spewed toward others of late. Elizabeth's heart hurt for her boys but she didn't try to interfere with John Lee's discipline of them.

"Sun's gettin' up. It's time we got to work, boys."

Elizabeth cringed when John Lee scraped his straight-backed chair across the bare plank floor and stood from the massive round oak table. Breakfast was over, whether you'd finished or not. John Lee and his three boys grabbed their frayed bright green John Deere caps from nails driven in the wall beside the door and tugged them onto their heads as they stepped outside.

~ ~ ~

Jim and his twin brothers followed Poppa to the barn, some two hundred yards behind the house. They left an uneven path of footprints on the dew-bathed grass. Jim rubbed their old coon dog's back as it bounced along with them, scattering the yard chickens as he ran on ahead then returned, wanting to play. But as the sunrise's pink glow outlined the spiny ridges above their Tennessee valley, just the day's sweaty labors filled Jim's mind.

Reaching the barn, Poppa didn't have to urge the boys to begin their chores. The three of them knew what was theirs to do and they knew to do it as right as they could. They did not want to help unleash his rage.

Jim had learned their father's work ethic for survival. You didn't work the land, you didn't eat. Jim and his brothers were raised to be mountain-tough, which helped them eke out a living, with little else besides work to do with their time. Except to go into town for the county fair once a year.

Chapter 2

Louisa Lynn Johnson stared at the meal. She sat at the small square pine table with her dad and stepmother. She looked with disappointment at the table: Greasy, overcooked chicken.

Louisa lived in the Appalachians where jagged peaks towered above deep gorges, some that leveled into green open spaces. She wished she lived in one of those lush valleys but instead her home sat in a small, narrow hollow that branched off one of those clearings. Her dad's crops and animals didn't flourish as did those in the fertile dells. Often Louisa likened herself to those crops and animals because young girls didn't do well living back in gloomy isolated hollows. She yearned to exchange her life there for a more attractive one in town.

"You need to eat your breakfast, Baby Girl." Her dad moved her thoughts back to breakfast.

Louisa thought her dad was the kindest man that ever lived. A giant of a man, tall and broad shouldered, yet he moved with catlike agility and grace. Louisa knew him as a gentle man and even-tempered with her and his few farm animals. She would watch when he robbed his bees of their honey, wearing no protection from their stings when they landed on his hands and arms. Louisa guessed the honey bees, like her, knew him as a man who nurtured rather than destroyed.

"Dad, I ain't . . ."

"Louisa, we don't use that word anymore. She knows better, Aaron." Mavis adjusted the napkin in her lap.

Louisa saw her dad's watchful stare. "Okay. I mean, I'm not hungry."

When Mavis married their dad three years ago and came to live in their house, Louisa and her sister had shunned her as an outsider. They hadn't welcomed her with an attitude to show she had a rightful place in their little family, where they'd had their dad all to themselves.

Louisa knew Mavis had taught eighth grade in Newton before marrying her dad. Soon after moving in, she had suggested to the girls that if they spoke English, she would help them to speak it correctly. Louisa didn't like a live-in school teacher who corrected her.

At least Louisa was glad that Mavis saw to it that the family went to church every Sunday, the girls in their best dresses, their blond hair brushed to a high sheen. Also, that the girls did not forget what their mother had taught them about sewing and washing and ironing.

Louisa and her sister found it difficult to accept the fact that their dad had married Mavis less than a year after their mother died in the birth of her stillborn baby. However, despite their disapproval of his quick marriage or his choice, their loyalty remained with their dad.

Last month, Louisa wept when her older sister, Callie, found work in Newton then moved into Miss June's Boardinghouse in town. Without her sister in the house, loneliness crowded in on her. Louisa already craved to leave their hollow and join her.

"Louisa, go on and eat, now. Don't upset your dad."

"Dad, I ain't . . ." Then glancing again at Mavis, "I mean I'm not upsetting you, am I?"

Louisa noticed that her dad sent a slight smile toward Mavis then with his napkin rubbed the biscuit crumbs from his generous mustache. "No, honey, you're not upsettin' me. I guess you do get tired of the same eats every day." He patted her arm with his weathered hand, and then continued tackling his overcooked chicken leg.

Louisa knew that although her stepmother was an accomplished school teacher she just couldn't cook. She tried, but the meals she prepared often resulted in food not fit to eat.

Their dad's good-natured ways worked with Louisa and her sister because they strived to please him, even adored him. His one discipline Louisa could remember was a tap of his fingers on her shoulder. Louisa was proud to be the daughter of this man with handsome blond good looks and gentleness.

Their house in Maple Hollow was little more than a shack, its unpainted exterior seasoned to a dull gray. But it was the only home Louisa knew. She would have been embarrassed to bring a friend home with her. But she never saw any friends except at school.

The house stood just thirty feet from the narrow dirt road that ran through their hollow. Louisa had watched when two buggies met and one of them had to pull off to the side of the road for the other to pass by. No way out existed from the east end of the hollow.

The few passersby Louisa saw were the mail carrier and the Kincaids, whose place was the last one in the hollow. Once a month the peddler's rolling store—an old school bus—would come by, go on up to the Kincaid's, and then pass by again, leaving the hollow. Because Louisa never got into town, her excitement peaked as the time neared for the peddler to bring the store to them.

The peddler allowed her onto his bus through the rear door and permitted her to look at and touch the variety of goods, which he had stacked on the wooden perimeter seating: staples like flour, sugar and coffee. Louisa sometimes even found things like hair bows and combs. She would watch her dad examine the peddler's few farming tools and things traded by other people, like eggs and vegetables in season. Some had traded in chickens, which Louisa saw kept in wire cages lashed onto the back of the bus.

But this morning Louisa continued with her fried chicken. She wanted to please her stepmother because that's what her dad wanted her to do. She even tried to talk the way Mavis instructed. But a stepmother wasn't like a real mother. A youth when her mother died, she had little remembrance of her. Oh, how she wished she could be with Callie in town.

After breakfast, her dad reached over and pushed her blond hair, damp from the heat of the house, back from her face.

He looked at his daughter's pale blue eyes. "Remember, the county fair's comin' next month."

Louisa brightened, clasping her hands beneath her chin. "Will we get to go, Dad? Will we, really?"

"I think so. And we'll get word into Miss June's to your sister so she can go with us."

Louisa jumped up from her chair and leaned over to throw her arms around his neck. "I knew you'd find the money for us to go. I just knew you would."

Chapter 3

Elizabeth sat in silence as John Lee parked the battered pickup truck in the dusty field on the outskirts of Newton. The hurdy-gurdy music from the merry-go-round filled the air. Emmajean sat on Shirley Ann's lap in the front seat between their parents and the three boys sat in the truck bed, against the back of the cab. The younger children were about to burst with excitement. Elizabeth knew that only little Emmajean could get by with her exclamations of joy without Poppa shushing her quiet.

"Oh, Poppa, look! I can see the colored lights."

"Sure can, Little Lady. But you don't go runnin' off by yourself. You stay with your momma. Hold her hand tight, now."

"Yes, Poppa. But won't you walk with us too?"

Ignoring her question, he pulled on the emergency brake and dropped the switch key into the watch pocket of his clean overalls. Elizabeth and the children followed him to the main gate leading into the fairgrounds.

"Boys, get back to the truck by ten o'clock on the dot. Shirley Ann, you go with your momma, do as she says. Here, Elizabeth, give this to the children." He placed some coins into his wife's hand and turned to walk away from the family.

"Poppa, won't you walk with us?"

He pulled his hand free from the grip of Emmajean's little fingers, walked on ahead and was soon swallowed by the crowd.

Elizabeth handed out the change John Lee had given her. Robert and Richard needed no more permission to dash down the midway past the games and spinning rides, toward the flashing lights of the side shows.

"Momma, I'll walk with you and the girls." Jim fell in step with them.

"Jim, you go on, now. I told Shirley Ann she could meet up with her girlfriends and I'll stay with Emmajean. We'll just take our time. I want to see who got blue ribbons for their canned goods."

"Momma, you know Shirley Ann's lookin' for Henry Frank Stevens. She's not wantin' to spend time with no girlfriends."

Shirley Ann swatted at Jim. "You shut up now." Jim expecting her reaction, shrunk back out of her reach.

"You know it's the truth. You're struck on old Henry Frank and his big ears and I reckon he'll be lookin' for you too."

"Momma, don't listen to Jim."

Elizabeth watched her two oldest children pick at each other. She told them often she wanted them to enjoy their youth before responsibility set in. When life would require them to grow up before they might want to.

Elizabeth winked at Jim. "Whatever you say, Shirley Ann. You run on now and meet up with the girls or Henry Frank or whoever."

"I saw that, Momma. Well, see you at ten." Elizabeth watched Shirley Ann's gored skirt of her cotton yellow-flowered dress swirl out as she turned to leave.

"Now, Son, you go on too. You've got more to do than stay with me. Emmajean wants to ride the merry-go-round, don't you, Emmajean?" Emmajean jumped up and down with anticipation. "We'll walk around, look at some of the animals and the produce exhibits. You go on and do what you want to, Son."

Jim pulled on Emmajean's pigtails. "You mind Momma, now, Squirt. Stay with her. Don't go gettin' lost." Then with a look of concern, "Momma, you sure you'll be okay? You know Poppa won't show up again until we meet at the truck."

"I know, Jim. Go on, now. Come on, Emmajean, what do you want to do first? Ride or get some cotton candy?"

Elizabeth didn't look back. She realized that Jim would be watching her and Emmajean till they walked out of sight and his look of pity for her would break her heart. She knew Jim wished he could make her life more bearable. Elizabeth didn't complain about their lack of material blessings or about how all the children had a hard life with no promise of betterment.

Jim was such a joy to Elizabeth. Her firstborn, perhaps her favorite, Jim had stood by her since he was old enough to cling to her skirts. Elizabeth knew that Jim thought he was her shielded warrior but he was just another mouth to feed and another child to clothe with meager resources. She appreciated his kind heart and sensitive personality. The other children were as well-behaved as he was, but Elizabeth leaned toward Jim. Now, at sixteen, he was almost as big as his poppa, and could protect her if necessary from any intruder.

Elizabeth loved all her children and tried not to be partial. A difficult job with Jim growing into a man right in front of her eyes.

Soon he would want to spread his wings and then he'd go. As ready as Jim would be for that day, Elizabeth hoped and prayed she would be as ready when that time came.

Absorbed in her thoughts, Elizabeth walked past the merry-go-round. Emmajean began to pull away from her momma's hand and was loose before Elizabeth realized where she went.

"Momma! Momma! Come look!" Emmajean screamed. She shouted again till Elizabeth turned toward her.

Elizabeth scolded herself for her lapse of attention to Emmajean and joined her. She put on a camouflaged pleasant face that her eight-year-old accepted. Emmajean chose the horse she favored on the merry-go-round. Positioned atop the brown and white animal, she waved at her momma each time the horse circled in front of Elizabeth. Elizabeth labored to keep her mind focused so that she watched whenever her child came into view again and again.

~ ~ ~

Jim watched the milling crowd collect his momma and little sister and move them along. He stood his ground as people jostled against him, around him. Why couldn't Momma's life be easier? With the new baby about due, the winter would be extra hard on her.

He pulled himself back to the present and started down the carnival midway.

"Hey, Callaway! Jim Callaway!" Jim turned to see his best friend, Arthur Gray lope toward him.

It amused Jim to watch Arthur as he moved with a disjointed gait, his arms and legs uncoordinated, puppet-like. Because his height outstripped his weight by thirty pounds, Jim joked that when he walked he looked like a batch of gawky bones and the nickname, "Bones," had stuck. Jim enjoyed time he spent with Arthur, a jovial boy with a full head of untamed brown hair, and not afraid of hard work, who lived with his family on a farm south of the Callaways.

Jim and Arthur were lifelong friends, as were their mothers. Jim remembered them playing together when their mommas visited, picked blackberries for homemade jelly, or attended church functions. Jim envied Arthur for having a father who attended church and acted like he loved and cared for his family.

Arthur caught up with Jim. "What's your hurry? Didn't you hear me hollerin' at you?"

"Sorry, Bones, I've got a lot on my mind, I guess."

"What's goin' on?"

"Same old things, I reckon. My momma fixin' to have another baby. Poppa not watchin' after her." Jim jerked his head toward the edge of the fairgrounds. "Why, right now, I'd guess he's over behind the livestock buildin', drinkin' with his buddies."

"Yeah, I saw some of the men headed over that way a while ago."

"See what I mean, Bones? I'll have to drive us back to the farm. The Twins and me will do good to get him onto the back of the truck."

"Well, he's been like this for a good while now. Why are you lettin' it bother you so much tonight?"

"It's just not gettin' any better. Worse, if anything. I don't know what's eatin' him. He's sure comin' down hard on me and the boys. The least little thing we do sets him off. Poor Momma just watches and prays for him to change. I don't know how much more I can put up with."

"Jim, the Lord won't put no more on you than you can stand. Besides, your poppa's pulled you out of school this comin' year to help him work the place and you'll be around him every day. You've got to find a way to handle that."

"I don't know if I can. I just want to leave, get myself out of this mess. But then, where would that put Momma and the other kids? I'm not sure I could walk out on them like that."

"Jim, you know you've got to honor your poppa. Pray for him to see the Truth. God can change your poppa if he asks."

They walked on down the midway, each deep in his own thoughts, Jim's head bowed toward the ground, until a sudden cheer grabbed his attention. The rowdy noise came from a cluster of young folks gathered in front of a game booth. Curious, Jim and Arthur moved closer.

Jim watched as the boisterous group cheered the efforts of a stout young man throwing baseballs at thick, white opaque bottles shaped like milk bottles. The boy had just knocked down a bottle perched atop two more placed side by side on the ground.

Jim moved closer and watched the young man standing in front of a narrow counter and hurling another baseball at the two standing bottles. The ball grazed against one of them and left it swaying, but both bottles remained upright. The crowd of supporters moaned their disappointment when the young man stepped back in frustration.

"Come on, try it again. You almost made it. Three more balls . . . I'll even give you an extra throw this time," barked the carnival worker.

The young man pulled his pants pockets inside out to show that he had no more money. Just then another boy stepped forward, handed across his nickel and picked up the three baseballs. Jim saw that his aim was good, but he wasn't as strong as the boy before him. He, too, stepped away in defeat.

Jim and Arthur watched several boys try to knock down the three bottles. None had just the right touch to get the job done. Tiring of the repetition, Arthur began to scan the growing numbers who watched the carnival barker relieve the boys of their money.

"Hey, Callaway, look." Arthur poked an elbow into Jim's ribs.

"What?"

"Over there. There! In the green dress. That's Callie. The girl I told you about last Sunday in church." An admiring grin stretched across Arthur's thin face.

"Yeah, I see her." But Jim's gaze had passed beyond the green dress and now rested on the most angelic face he'd seen.

"Didn't I tell you she was pretty? Was I right?"

"Yeah, you're right. She sure is pretty." Jim stood still and leaned forward, captivated by the simple beauty of the girl standing beside Arthur's friend. Her fair skin glowed with a milky smoothness like that of the porcelain doll prizes at the penny toss booth back up the midway.

"Callie's just moved here from Maple Hollow. Somethin' about a stepmother livin' at her house now. So she came to Newton to work at the hosiery mill. I met her when I delivered groceries to the boardinghouse for Mr. Henderson last Saturday."

"Yeah. She's real pretty."

"Jim, are we talkin' about the same girl?" When no answer came from Jim, Arthur discovered the dazed look on his friend's face. "Callaway?"

"I know . . . you're talkin' about Callie. Uh . . . who's that other blond-headed girl next to her? Who's she?"

"I don't know, but somethin' tells me we're goin' to have to find out somehow or another."

Chapter 4

The clank of an occasional toppled bottle didn't register with Jim. He didn't hear the thud of baseballs hitting the tarpaulin draped over hay bales stacked behind the bottles. All thoughts about his drunken poppa, his momma's delivery of the new baby, and even his own weariness from the drudgery of farm work succumbed to the simple loveliness of the blond girl.

Jim followed Arthur as they made their way through the crowd to where Callie and her friend stood. Absorbed in each attempt to win the battle of the bottles, the girls didn't notice them until Arthur spoke.

"Hey, Callie."

Callie smiled at him, but gave no hint of recognition.

"We met at Miss June's." Callie made no attempt at conversation. "Last Saturday . . . when I delivered groceries to the boardinghouse. You sat on the front porch on the swing . . . I'm Arthur Gray."

Callie was as tall as Jim, about eighteen, with an unassuming sweetness about her. "Oh, I'm sorry. I didn't recognize you at first."

It was Jim's turn to poke Arthur in the ribs. "Callie, this is my friend, Jim Callaway."

"Hey, Jim, nice to meet you."

Cheers went up when a bottle fell over.

"Hey, Callie." Jim glanced at the girl beside her.

Discouragement registered on Callie's face at Jim's obvious lack of interest in her. She turned to the girl beside her. "This is my little sister, Louisa."

Louisa smiled at the tall, handsome boy and his friend. When they spoke to her, she lowered her head. But not before Jim looked into her mesmerizing blue eyes, the color of a clear summer sky, and felt them touch his soul. His pounding heart quickened its beat and his hands began to sweat when their eyes met again. Her glance lit up Jim's thoughts and feelings brighter than all the county fair's bright lights. Neither of them could look away, the attraction was so strong.

Jim knew folks who had run off and got married when they were fourteen or fifteen. Jim decided at that moment that Louisa would be his girl, even if she was fourteen or fifteen.

The moans around them signaled another victim had lost to the standing bottles.

Arthur attempted to break the trance that surrounded them. "Callaway, why don't you show this crowd how to knock down milk bottles?"

Jim continued to look at Louisa and she at him, promise showing in her eyes. He tried to turn away. But it was no use. She oozed an innocence that grabbed him and demanded his silent vow of commitment.

And that's how Jim and Louisa began. Two unspoken promises.

~ ~ ~

"Jim . . . the bottles. Why don't you try your hand next?" Arthur pushed Jim toward the counter where the carnival worker extended his dirty palm to collect Jim's nickel.

"Bones, I watched this game at the fair last year . . . they ain't real milk bottles," Jim protested. "They're not glass and they're weighted and you got to hit them a certain way. Just one way you hit them will they all three fall down."

"Yeah, yeah, I know, Jim. You're the one who can do it then. Go on, try it."

Jim looked at Louisa, searching for approval or encouragement to do the impossible. She offered him a smile. That was all he needed.

Swish. The first ball blazed to the right of all three bottles and left them standing. Jim hung his head then prepared to throw again. The next ball caught the base of the top bottle and launched it backwards into the tarpaulin.

Jim straightened to his full height of almost six feet and stepped up to the counter again. He knew he needed raw strength to knock over the last two bottles and that he had that strength from years of working the farm. Silence fell over the onlookers.

Jim drew back his arm and heaved the one remaining ball on its way. It hit on the nose between the two bottle necks and pushed them each aside. Both bottles fell without a sound to the ground.

Jim turned to Louisa. Her misty blue eyes shone with delight and she clasped her hands beneath her chin.

"We have a winner!" shouted the barker. "Here, boy, here's your prize. A fuzzy teddy bear for your girlfriend."

He didn't have a girlfriend. What would he do with a little teddy bear?

"Hey, Jim, who gets the teddy bear?" It was Arthur, teasing him about giving away his prize.

Without thought, Jim stepped toward Louisa. He extended his arm and held out the brown teddy bear. Their eyes met and it was as if Jim gave a gift of gold and diamonds. Without a word between them, Louisa took the plush bear from Jim, their eyes never leaving one another.

Chapter 5

Recollections of the family trip to the county fair helped Jim battle the dreary days of fall and winter. For days afterward Jim listened to his brothers and sisters tell over and over the fun time they had at the fair: The Twins had spent all their money on the sideshows, willing to believe that a man could in fact swallow a sword. Jim was attentive as Emmajean told him she had ridden the merry-go-round, ate sticky cotton candy, and won a tiny rubber doll at the fishing booth. Jim had teased Shirley Ann about how she and the Stevens boy walked the dusty midway until time for the Callaways to meet back at the truck.

Jim had met a blue-eyed girl named Louisa. He could retrieve the memory of Louisa over and over like someone rereading old love letters.

Weeks afterward, Jim sat in church, not listening to the preaching but remembering the girl he'd met at the Sanford County Fair. The girl named Louisa with the luminous eyes. Louisa, who had his prize teddy bear. Who had his heart.

~ ~ ~

Every Saturday morning, Jim envied his friend Arthur who rode into town with his daddy to work for Mr. Henderson. He delivered groceries for Henderson's General Store for part of the day. By late afternoon when his daddy had finished his errands and business in town, they rode back home together.

Then, every Sunday at church Jim urged Arthur to give him an update: Yes, Callie's still at Miss June's Boardinghouse. Yes, sometimes she mentions her sister, Louisa. No, Callie doesn't ask about Jim.

"But, Jim, you just met Louisa that one time at the fair," Arthur tried to explain. "I see Callie just about every Saturday so I have a chance to talk to her."

"Yeah, Bones, but I don't get into town. Poppa keeps me on the place doin' whatever he don't want to do. Or watchin' after the other kids, when Poppa and Momma both go into town."

"There's no way you can get him to let you go once in a while?"

"Looks doubtful. Unless I just up and go. And if I did that you know I'd get the razor strop on my backside when I got home."

"Jim, I've been prayin' real hard for your poppa. I know you're tired of the way he treats you."

"Yeah." Jim sighed, a faraway look in his eyes. "I'm mighty tired of it."

~ ~ ~

Winter hit early and hard in their little valley of the Tennessee Appalachians, knocking the wind out of their hopes for better weather. Jim worried when winter's cold proved difficult on his momma and her new baby. Now three months old, Ollie wasn't a healthy baby. And Jim saw that his momma took extra long to regain her strength after the lengthy labor before this child joined the family.

Jim lay still in his bed and listened for whatever had awaked him. It must have been the cold of the unheated room or the baby's cries from his parents' bedroom. He slid deeper beneath the muslin sheets layered over with quilts, and shifted to find warm spots his own body had made. Robert and Richard crowded toward him from either side to share what heat their three bodies generated. Jim tugged the covers close under his chin.

Enough moonlight shone through the window curtains so that Jim could pick out objects in the room. He looked across to the other bed and saw Shirley Ann snuggled close against Emmajean's back, their covers clutched around their ears. The small table positioned between the two beds held a dusting of crushed snowflakes that had drifted in through the cracked windowpane.

The baby's cries from the other bedroom continued. No wonder little Ollie cried. She was cold. Jim was cold. The whole house was cold.

Every night at bedtime Jim watched Poppa bury the live coals in the fireplace under a lot of ashes and cinders to bank the fire in the front room. But the fire always burned out before the night was over. When the embers died, what little heat the fire gave out earlier seemed to vanish up the chimney. Jim spoke into the chilled room, "Get used to it, little Ollie, it won't get no better."

Jim promised himself, again, that he would be more of a provider than his poppa for whatever family he might one day have. He'd make a better living for his wife than Poppa had done. Jim didn't plan to walk behind a mule and plow on this farm for the rest of his life.

He tried to get back to sleep for the short time left until sunup. He didn't blame the baby for crying, but the cries continued to irritate him. Everything irritated him. He had to get out of there. But how could he leave Momma in the middle of all this? And the kids?

As he had done often over the last several months, Jim contemplated his immediate future. Lying there in the predawn cold, his anger at last burst open like a lanced boil, freeing the pus within. He'd just have to go. The others could leave as they're able. Shirley Ann would no doubt marry Henry Frank before long. Then The Twins would watch after Emmajean. They all would just have to get out as they saw fit.

~ ~ ~

Winter's hard freezes continued into early March. Jim hated when the ground began to warm and the thaw turned the roads into muddy ruts.

Jim stared out the raised window at the budding dogwood trees standing steadfast among the staunch oaks and maples in the churchyard. Springtime and the renewal of all living things in nature strengthened Jim's resolve toward a renewal of his own. His attention was not on the sermon but on his plans for Friday morning.

~ ~ ~

Later, outside the church, Jim confided to Arthur. "Friday's the day. I aim to do it."

"Do what?"

"I'm leavin'. I'm goin' into town. Get a job."

"How are you goin' to manage this?"

"I'm just goin'. Don't you say nothin' to nobody. I didn't tell yet. I'll get together some of my things and hide them under the bed. Then Friday mornin' I'll leave with the kids when they go to school and I'll just keep on goin'."

"What will your poppa do when he finds out?"

"I know what he'll *want* to do. I'm hopin' Momma can keep him from comin' after me. But if he comes lookin' for me, I'll just not go back. It's high time I got out on my own. Wish me luck."

"I will, Jim. But you're goin' to need more than luck. You're goin' to need the help of the Good Lord. I just hope and pray He approves of what you're fixin' to do."

"I'll see you in town on Saturday when you deliver for Mr. Henderson. I'll look you up."

~ ~ ~

Thursday night after supper, Emmajean and Shirley Ann helped Momma clean up in the kitchen and then left to do their school lessons. Jim went out to the kitchen to talk to his momma before she joined John Lee in the front room.

Elizabeth lifted her apron off over her head and went to hang it on a nail next to the cook stove when Jim walked into the kitchen.

She turned to him. "Jim, your mind was a hundred miles away at the supper table. What's troublin' you, Son?"

"Not much, Momma."

"I believe somethin's been botherin' you for a while now. Can I help you at all?" She tucked that stubborn strand of hair back into the bun on top of her head.

"No . . . no, Momma, I'm okay. Just got a few things on my mind, that's all. Nothin' for you to worry about." Why was this so hard to do? Why didn't he just tell her what he planned to do?

"Son, there you go again. Your mind's wanderin' away."

"Momma, I'm sorry. I guess I might as well just tell you."

"Tell me what, Jim?" A worried look crossed Elizabeth's face and settled in her eyes.

"Momma . . . I'm goin' into town." There! He'd said it.

Elizabeth sat at the kitchen table. "What do you mean?"

"I'm goin' into town. I'm goin' to get a job."

"Son, are you sure? Have you thought about it long enough?"

Jim searched his momma's face. Why didn't she cry, try to change his mind? His decision couldn't make her happy. He took a seat beside her.

"Momma? Don't you want me to stay?"

"Jim, I would want to have you with me always." She took his hands in hers. "But that's not God's plan. We raise our children to go out on their own someday. I just hope this is the right time and right way for you to do it. I've been knowin' you've wanted to leave for some time now."

"You have?"

"Yes, Son, I see how your poppa's been treatin' you the last little while. You long to be free of his overbearin' ways. I understand that. You've turned seventeen now, older than I was when I married your poppa." She reached out and brushed his straight black hair out of his eyes.

"Momma, if anybody can understand, you can. I don't like the way he treats us kids and I can't stand watchin' you have to live like you do sometimes. I wish you could go with me."

"Jim, my place is here, takin' care of your poppa. And the other children, more than ever now with the new baby. But don't you worry about me. The others will help. They'll watch out for me like you've always been good to do."

Jim smiled at the courage his momma showed.

He watched as Momma searched his face and his strong resemblance to his poppa. But even though Jim looked like his poppa, Jim prayed he never took on the recent ways of his poppa.

"When are you goin', Son?"

He dreaded to tell her. "Tomorrow."

Momma caught her breath. "Do the others know?"

"No, I'll tell them tonight after we all go to bed. I'm not tellin' Poppa. I hope that don't make it too hard on you."

"You'll have to do it the way you think best."

Jim could imagine his poppa's unbridled outburst when he couldn't find him tomorrow.

"Do you have any money? You'll need money."

"Yes, Momma, I have some money left from what you've been givin' me along from your egg money. I've been savin' for this."

"I'm glad. You're seventeen and a boy your age needs a little pocket money. Son, where will you be stayin'?"

'I don't know yet." They both stood.

"Let me hear from you when you find a place."

"I will, Momma. Once I start drawin' a paycheck, I'll send you some money along. Maybe that'll make up my part of the rent for not bein' here to help work the place. You take some of the money I send and buy you things you might want."

"Son, don't forget to take your Bible. Find you a church to go to on Sundays. And, Jim, remember to pray and let the Lord direct your steps."

"I will, Momma, don't you worry." He squeezed his momma's small frame to him. She returned his embrace as her tears dropped onto the coarse broadcloth of his shirt.

~ ~ ~

On Friday when the Callaway children left to walk to school, Jim took another minute alone with his momma. He leaned down and kissed her on the cheek.

"I'll write and let you know where I'm stayin' as soon as I get settled. Take care of yourself, Momma. And this little one too." He gave the baby in her arms a pat on the head.

"Son, you be a good boy like I've raised you to be. I'll be prayin' for you every day."

Jim shouldered the burlap sack stuffed with his few belongings. He eased the weathered door closed behind him and stepped into another cold April morning. When he looked out past the big black oaks, Jim saw Poppa at the barn stomping into the watering trough to break up the thin ice that had formed overnight. Jim stood on the doorstep and watched his poppa blow into his cupped hands to warm them, ready to start the day's work.

Jim slipped along the side of the house and around the corner until he was out of Poppa's sight. Then he darted across the front yard and turned down the muddy road to catch up with his brothers and sisters.

~ ~ ~

Jim could feel a smile spread across his handsome face in spite of a nip in the air.

He walked the mile to the schoolhouse with his brothers and sisters. When they reached the wooden steps, Jim watched as boys and girls of all ages walked past them and moved up the steps into the school. Robert and Richard in turn pumped Jim's hand. "Way to go, Jim. Wish it was us."

"Good luck. You're our hero. You're getting' off the farm and goin' into town."

"Jim, town's so far away, I'll never see you again, will I?" Emmajean puckered up to cry.

"Squirt, when I come back in a while, I'll bring you a surprise. And watch the mailbox for a letter. Scoot on, now, into the schoolhouse." She turned and walked up the warped steps with Robert and Richard.

Then it was Shirley Ann's turn. "Jim, you're for sure goin'. I can't believe it's happenin'. I'm proud for you."

A maelstrom of emotions filled his head and heart. The strong pull to stay fought against the powerful urge to leave.

"You go on then. We'll get away some day. You just wait and see, our day will come. You go on, now, Big Brother. Make it work out for you." And with that she turned and ran into the schoolhouse, tears moist in her eyes.

Jim watched his brothers and sisters disappear into the three-room schoolhouse and wrestled again with his mixed emotions. He looked back toward their farm, the towering mountains he loved rose in the distance. These Appalachian foothills were his home, as close as family. But Jim couldn't put up with his life any longer: his family, his poppa, strangled the life out of him and strapped him down to the farm as sure as the mules' harnesses tied them to the plow. Jim longed to break free of his invisible bonds, to make a new life and do it all by himself.

Jim knew that as hard as Shirley Ann tried, she wouldn't be able to keep her mind on the lessons this morning. Jim stood in front of the schoolhouse with regrets of leaving a burden on Shirley Ann. She would be the oldest at home, and Jim laid the responsibilities for her brothers and sister onto her small shoulders.

~ ~ ~

At last, the tears dried on Shirley Ann's full cheeks. She dabbed at her eyes with her fingertips and determined to meet the obligations that had now passed to her by way of family hierarchy.

Then, as Jim had done during church last Sunday, Shirley Ann did that morning. She looked out the window and daydreamed about what might be. Outside of her family, Henry Frank was the dearest person in her life. He just might be the dearest *one*. Henry Frank hadn't spoken the word marry to her yet, but she could see in his eyes that he was just about ready to do so. Then she would leave the farm as Jim had done this morning

Shirley Ann saw the questions in Henry Frank's glances toward her. No one knew she had just said good-bye to Jim. Henry Frank wouldn't understand her downcast eyes until recess when she could talk to him. Then he *would* understand. He understood Shirley Ann to the core. She knew it and he knew it. She couldn't be as open with her private life as she could be with Henry Frank, and he with her.

Chapter 6

Elizabeth lifted the cast-iron tea kettle from the cook stove and poured boiling rinse water over the just-washed breakfast dishes stacked in the dented dishpan. She felt the steam rush across her face and dampen her hair. Then she heard John Lee outside when he scraped his muddy shoes against the bottom porch step. When he burst through the back door, he brought a whirl of cool mountain air inside with him. Elizabeth's fear coiled deep inside her but never revealed itself on her face.

"Where's that lazy Jim? I been waitin' up at the barn for him to come on."

Elizabeth watched John Lee walk over to the cook stove and extend his hands, palms down to capture the heat. He looked around the kitchen for Jim.

"Wait'll I get my hands on him. He'll wish he'd come on when he was supposed to." He blustered toward the children's bedroom.

"He's not in there." Elizabeth tucked a stray damp hair back into her bun.

John Lee swung back around the door and looked at her in surprise. "What do you mean, he's not in there? He's layin' in bed all right. I'll roust him up."

In less than a minute, she heard his footsteps return toward the kitchen. "He's not in his bed. Where is that no 'count boy?"

"He's not here."

"I can see that for myself, Elizabeth." He waited for her to explain.

With no other choice, Elizabeth braced for the worst. "Jim's gone."

She stood mute as John Lee waited for her to offer more explanation.

Please, God, give me strength for what I have to do.

"Elizabeth, as my wife, you're obliged to tell me what's goin' on. Where's Jim?"

"Jim's left." Elizabeth saw the now-familiar storm roll in John Lee's dark eyes, the eyes she remembered from the first part of their marriage as full of love and kindness.

"Where'd he go and when's he comin' back?" he growled.

"He's gone into town. He ain't comin' back, leastways not back here to live." Running the risk of losing her own safety, she added, "You done run him off, John Lee."

For the first time in a long time, she attempted to stand her ground with John Lee. This was her son they talked about. Her son and his desires that he'd acted upon. Elizabeth braced herself for the jolt of pain from the thunderous clap of his hand against her face like she'd seen him deliver to the boys.

Elizabeth looked at John Lee's clenched hands, his knuckles whitened. She winced as he took a step toward her, the tensed muscles tight in his square jaw. Her feet remained planted.

~ ~ ~

Elizabeth met John Lee's narrowed eyes and could see they were full of hatred. She realized he had lost control of the situation but had no one to take his hate out on. None of the children were home, and she hoped he wouldn't hit a woman.

Without another word, John Lee spun around and stormed outside, slamming the door with such force that it hit the door jam and swung back into the kitchen. Elizabeth hurried to the door to see him sulking toward the barn. She closed the door then sat at the kitchen table and tried to decide what she would do when he returned. Several minutes later she heard hoofbeats and pulled the curtains aside to look out.

Elizabeth saw John Lee as he raced up the dirt road on the bare back of one of the mules, the reins slapping from side to side on the animal's hind quarters. She watched until they disappeared around the bend, the old mule plodding as fast as possible beneath the weight and lashes of his master. Elizabeth breathed easier and her trembling subsided when she saw that the object of her husband's outburst was the mule and not one of her children.

~ ~ ~

John Lee was at his brother's place by the time he realized he'd ridden the mule too hard, too long. Lather collected on the animal's sweaty neck and the small blanket John Lee sat on was soaked through. Steam rose from the mule's hot body into the cool mountain air.

He found his brother near the barn. John Lee looped his mule's reins around a post of the split rail fence and propped one work shoe on the lowest railing. In silence, the two brothers took tobacco pouches from their overalls and rolled cigarettes.

John Lee scraped a wooden match across the bottom of his brogan. When it burst into flame, he extended it toward his brother. Orrin leaned into the flame, inhaling to bring his cigarette to life. John Lee did the same then fanned the match back and forth to extinguish the flame.

After a while, Orrin broke the silence. "Somethin' the matter, John Lee? Somebody over at your place sick?"

"No. No, Orrin, nobody ain't sick."

John Lee was relieved when Orrin didn't push him for conversation. John Lee's cigarette dangled from the corner of his mouth. Squinting against the smoke, he looked at his brother.

"Jim's left and I don't know what to make of it."

"John Lee, I been tellin' you to let up on them boys. You've even got your big girl scared of you. They're all goin' to leave you soon as they can see a way out."

"Orrin, what can I do? Where'd I go wrong?"

"You didn't used to be such a hard man, John Lee. Nobody can't see no love in you nowadays."

"I love my family. Why, I'd die for Elizabeth. She knows I love her and the kids."

"You're tryin' to hold onto them with a selfish love. You don't love them with the love of God."

"Now, Orrin, don't start in on me again about God. I've told you and told you I got no use for all that holy stuff." He threw his cigarette to the ground and crushed it with the toe of his brogan.

John Lee felt comfortable talking over his concerns with Orrin. But now and then John Lee resented it when Orrin seemed determined to preach to John Lee. No matter how John Lee tried to stop him, Orrin could bring God into their conversations before he knew what happened.

John Lee could feel his aversion to God rekindled each time Orrin brought Him up. He'd held his resentment toward God since he was ten years old, the same age as his own twin boys. In recent times it seemed he could feel the resentment grow stronger.

Over time, he'd allowed his hostility to simmer but his memory remained clear. For a time now that hostility had begun to overflow. John Lee looked out across Orrin's field of winter wheat and still saw the rushing currents of the river and felt the cold water splash his face.

John Lee's daddy and mother had sat up front in the wagon and he and Orrin in the back. His daddy had reined in the two

31

mules to give them a rest before he pushed them across the most shallow, narrow location in the roaring waters of the Big Stone River.

"You boys hold on back there. Old Big Stone's for sure rollin' today."

"Giddyap." His daddy had coaxed his mules and they made their way into the water. "Easy now," he encouraged his animals when the cold water touched their bellies.

Then their forward progress halted. The mules' muscles strained but they couldn't pull the wagon any farther.

John Lee's daddy looked down into the swift, clear water. "A wagon wheel's stuck against a big river rock. You boys scoot up here real close behind your mother while I try to get us on across." He had moved the mules backward and then forward in an attempt to free the wheel. The wagon wheel lurched up to the top of the rock just to slide off its side.

All of a sudden the wagon tipped to the right, throwing John Lee's mother into the icy water. She caught onto the sideboard of the wagon bed. Her long dress whirled in the rushing water around her and weighed her down as the current pulled her legs out behind her.

"John Lee, grab holt on to your mother, Son. Hurry!"

John Lee remembered he reached over the sideboard and held onto his mother's arm. When she let go of the wagon, he grabbed her hand.

"Daddy, help me, . . . I can't."

"Yes, you can, Son."

His daddy fought to control the mules and right the wagon. Just as John Lee was about to pitch over the sideboard into the water he felt his daddy's hand grab his leg. His mother's hand slipped out of his smaller one.

The strong swells of the Big Stone carried her downriver and out of his sight. Why would he have anything to do with a God that tore his mother from his life before his very eyes?

"John Lee, I was there on the river that day too." Orrin brought John Lee back to the present. "And I didn't even try to do nothin'." Orrin threw down his own cigarette.

"You was too little."

"You always have an answer, but you've got to let it go. You can't keep on punishin' yourself and those around you, your family, for the way Mother left us."

When John Lee remained silent, Orrin continued. "Our mother's at peace in heaven. She wouldn't want you turned bitter like this. Why can't you believe that? It's past time you got rid of that wrath toward God you carry around all the time."

"I can't! And I can't see how you do it, neither."

"Do you think I like it any better than you do? But I've got past it. Didn't do it on my own, though. I did it with God's help—His strength and love. God wants to forgive you for your bitterness, but you have to ask Him."

John Lee pulled his heavy brows together in a questioning, silent plea for peace.

"John Lee, you could love that family of yours better if you'd love them God's way. And they wouldn't be afraid of lovin' you back if you did that."

Today John Lee thought about it a while longer than usual. Then he untied his mule and started for home. He didn't ride the tired animal but walked ahead of him, not holding the reins tight, the animal trailing behind him.

Chapter 7

Still outside the schoolhouse, Jim turned away from the purple haze settling over the mountains. He tugged the wool collar of his plaid mackinaw tighter around the back of his neck and pushed his bare hands deeper into the pockets. He walked an hour on the twists and turns of the rutted road down out of the hills. Leaning into the biting wind, with no going back, Jim reached the paved two-lane road to Newton at Maynard Junction.

The cool mist of the mountains behind him, he walked out into the morning sunshine on level ground at the junction. He had more spring to his step, like a man just released from prison and walking through the big gate behind which he'd been serving his time. Jim turned his coat collar back down and unbuttoned the coat. The welcomed warmth thawed his body and soothed his troubled mind.

He began the fifteen mile trek north to Newton. When an occasional vehicle passed, Jim put his thumb in the air asking for a ride. After a while a car stopped and the man gave Jim a cursory glance. "How far you going?"

"I'm goin' all the way to Newton."

"Young man, why aren't you in school today?"

"My poppa . . . he took me out of school this year."

"Then, why aren't you home helping your poppa?"

"Uh . . . he sent me to town to buy some things he needs."

Jim knew the driver doubted his explanation for being on the Newton road alone, but he let it go and they rode in silence the rest of the way to town.

~ ~ ~

"How's this, young man? I'll let you out here by the courthouse."

"Yes, sir, this is fine. I'm much obliged for the ride." Jim slammed the car door and waved.

Forlorn, Jim stood on the sidewalk a few minutes to get his bearings. He stood in front of the Sanford County courthouse where it faced south and covered a square block in the middle of town. In awe Jim looked at the impressive two-story structure. Finished in aged red brick, the top of the broad steps up to the entrance supported four white columns that stopped at the second story overhang. Jim saw a few cars parked around the courthouse, angled toward the sidewalk like ants around spilled honey. The clock on the courthouse steeple claimed his attention as it struck three o'clock.

Jim dropped his burlap sack at one of several wooden benches along the sidewalk that surrounded the courthouse yard. Relaxed, he sat alone and ate the biscuit with ham Elizabeth had stuffed in his coat pocket that morning.

The weight of his isolation settled around him like a heavy fog. The ham and biscuit that had smelled so good this morning swelled as he chewed it, until he could almost not swallow. Well, he'd made the big trip. He was in town and tried to push the farm into a distant memory.

He forced his gaze away from the southern direction toward the farm as he took a long look around. He saw street signs and a red wooden stop sign stood at intersections on all four corners of the courthouse square. Raymond Street ran from east to west in front of Jim, and on the east corner where it dissected Polk Street stood a cramped two-pump Texaco gasoline filling station, its round red and white Texaco star logo perched atop a free-standing post.

Jim took in the Bank of Newton across the street on the west corner of Raymond and Polk Streets. The bank impressed him as it covered most of that side of Raymond Street and shared the block with Cummings Drugstore. On the east side of the courthouse to his left across Polk Street Jim saw Henderson's General Store with barrels of flour and sugar stacked in front. Single and doubletree harnesses, mule collars, and plow blades filled window displays. His friend Arthur Gray worked at Henderson's on Saturdays.

Next to Henderson's he saw Arnold's Dime Store. To the west on his right Montgomery's Dry Goods shared the block with Goldberg Jewelers. Jim noticed that navy blue awnings faded from sun and weather hooded all the store fronts. He turned all the way around and spied a three story building identified on a sign as The Blanchard Hotel. It loomed on the north side of the courthouse and claimed the entire block.

In awe, Jim looked again at Newton's commerce and entertained his first doubts. Had he thought this through well enough? He could be back at the farm, in his momma's kitchen savoring the aromas from her cook stove.

What had Jim gotten himself into? Poppa wasn't so bad, if he stayed out of his way. Had God meant for Jim to put up with it all a while longer?

~ ~ ~

Jim bit off another mouthful of his ham and biscuit as he saw two town ladies approach. They walked along the sidewalk in the spring sunshine in the direction of Montgomery's Dry Goods store. When they were still a half block away, Jim saw them look at him on the bench and ease to the outside edge of the walkway. Jim guessed they didn't see someone in town during the week like Jim with his mismatched clothes, his too-short sleeves and his homemade haircut.

It was obvious to Jim that the ladies did their best to ignore Jim but seemed compelled to stare at his uncommon sight on a weekday in their town. Jim noticed them look with disdain at his pitiful bundle on the ground at his feet. Jim tried to scoot the burlap sack beneath the bench, and as he did so, noticed his muddy shoes with their broken and retied shoestrings.

When Jim looked up again, the ladies were straight in front of him and picked up their pace to get by faster. As Jim watched them walk past him one of them turned back to take one last glimpse of him and examined him from head to toe.

Well, she'd know him the next time she saw him. But from the looks of both the ladies he figured they hoped they wouldn't meet up with Jim again.

He wondered again what kind of mistake he had made. Should he just go on back to the farm? No, he'd done some big talk back home and to Arthur. He had to get that job at the mill now.

One day the town matrons wouldn't look down their noses at Jim. No, sir, they'd have to look straight at him because he aimed to be one of them. He'd be just as good as they think they are. One day, he would. He in truth would.

Determined not to return home a failure, Jim stood and brushed the biscuit crumbs from his lap and his hands. He raked his mackinaw sleeve across his mouth to remove any crumbs there and ran his hands back through his hair.

He pulled his burlap bag from underneath the bench. Jim strode across the tender spring grass and reached the sidewalk at the northwest corner of the courthouse. He followed Long Street north until it ran into the Knoxville Road. Jim reached the mill in fifteen minutes.

He stood before the black and white painted sign in front of the mill that proclaimed, "Southeastern Hosiery." He stared at the sign until it seemed to flash "Success Here."

Jim cleaned off his shoes the best he could in the grass and entered the one entrance he saw. He glanced from side to side when he entered a quiet room about the size of the Callaway's entire farm house. Three desks stood in the room, one right in front of him, and the front of a desk faced him from either side. From the Sears catalogs at home, Jim thought he recognized a manual Remington typewriter atop each desk, settled amid stacks of papers.

Jim saw no one occupied any desk but could see a narrow hallway to the right behind one of the side desks. While he decided whether to start down the hall in search of someone, he heard heavy footsteps from the hallway. Jim's lofty presence startled the man who emerged into the reception area and he looked around for help from someone who should have been at the desks. He straightened to his full height of at least five feet ten inches. He smoothed back his thinning sandy-blond hair, cleared his throat, and walked to where Jim stood.

"Can I help you, young man?" His shirt collars curled up, and his thick neck strained against his bow tie.

Under the scrutiny of the stranger, Jim stammered, just about unable to speak. Then Jim reached deep inside himself, stood as tall as he could. "I'm lookin' for a job at the hosiery mill."

The man sat behind the desk that Jim faced and continued his assessment of Jim. "We're not hiring today, son." He had a tinge of sympathy in his voice.

When Jim turned to leave without further question, the man called him back. "What's your name, son?"

"Jim. Jim Callaway. I'm John Lee Callaway's oldest."

"I'm Fred Jacob." He extended his hand. Jim took the small, fleshy hand and relief washed over him. Someone in town indeed wanted to shake his hand!

Jacob detected the solid strength of Jim's firm handshake and noticed the calluses, evidence of a man unafraid of hard work.

"Jim, we may be hiring on some next week. On the loading dock. It's hard work."

From the top drawer of the center desk, Fred Jacob withdrew a sheet of paper. He handed it across to Jim. "Here, take this job application. Fill it out and come back first thing Monday morning. When you get here, go through this front parking lot and around the side of this building you'll see the loading dock." He motioned with his hand to the left.

Jim thanked him, pumped his hand up and down, and turned to leave. When he started to push through the outside door, Jacob called after him, "By the way, you must be eighteen to work the loading dock. There's a lot of lifting out there and a body must be grown and strong." Jim nodded back his agreement and left the building.

~ ~ ~

After another two hours he'd found a place to stay: a spacious upstairs room in Mrs. Gertrude Hall's two-story house on Collins Street about three blocks west of the courthouse square. Jim saw that the yard looked neat and well cared for, and he used a short sidewalk to cross the grass and get to the small porch across the front of the house. He thought of his home back on the farm when he saw the afternoon sun reflected on the shiny clean upstairs windows. On down the street, Jim spied a white church steeple stretching toward the clouds.

Jim liked his new landlady as soon as he met her. She asked about his family and when she learned his mother and daddy were Elizabeth and John Lee Callaway, she beamed that she knew of them and right away showed him a vacant room. She seemed to Jim to be a fair lady, and she acted like she was genuine when she welcomed Jim to her house. Jim was amused with Gertrude Hall's abundant laughter that pressed her plump cheeks up against her eyes until they became mirthful crescents and sparkled with each smile. He wanted to live there because her house smelled of fresh baked bread and desserts. Jim saw from the look of Mrs. Hall's thick waistline that she must sample everything she cooked.

"This old house moans and groans a lot more since Arliss passed on two years ago." She removed loaves of bread from the oven. "I'm just glad to let out some rooms to you nice young men. Arliss and I never had any children, so I mother all of my boarders and love every day of it."

"You're a lifesaver, Mrs. Hall." Jim put his three dollars for the next week on the kitchen table. "I sure needed to get settled in before night."

"I know of your fine mother, Jim. I'm happy to help out one of her children. You must pay me every week, have no women friends in your room, and there won't be any problems."

"I've got me a little money saved up that'll do for a while."

"I'll be cooking you two meals a day, breakfast and supper, except no Sunday supper—that's the day I rest like the Lord wants me to. I'll pack your lunch box once you start to work." It sounded to Jim like Gertrude was content with feeding others and eating her delicious meals. "I don't do clothes but I know a lady who will do your laundry and ironing. Her charges are low and she does a good job. Just let me know when you decide you want to get in touch with her."

"I aim to get a job down at the hosiery mill. I'll be goin' to check it out Monday mornin'."

"Oh, Jim, I hope getting a job will be that easy. Just going over there, I mean." Gertrude turned the loaves out onto clean dish towels she had placed on the table. "I've seen many young men come through this house in the last year or so. They all had dreams about that big job and all that money. But then I've seen many of those same young men go away, no dreams left, when they weren't hiring down at the mill. They just drifted in and soon drifted out."

"I got my feet on the ground, Mrs. Hall. But I do have me some dreams."

"You have dreams too, do you? What dreams, Jim?"

"Well, for starters, gettin' into town like I done, bein' on my own. Then gettin' that job and that money you talk of. Someday I want me a wife and kids." He thought about Louisa and how her sky-blue eyes had penetrated his heart. "I'll treat them so good, they'll think they've gone to heaven. I aim to have me a nice house and pretty clothes for the women in my family. All the good things, you know."

"You have some mighty high dreaming there, Jim Callaway." She sliced the hot bread. "The good things are nice, for sure. Remember, though, you're certain to have to take some of the bad along with the good. Heaven's not here on earth."

Jim sat at the round kitchen table and spread butter and molasses on the warm bread Gertrude offered him. He took a big bite, not arguing with her advice, like he didn't hear a word of what she'd said. His mind turned his dreams over and over.

Dear Lord, please watch over this young man, Jim. He stands at a crossroad in his life as he craves to be grown-up. He'll need your help to keep his feet on the ground and headed in the right direction. Place your road signs on the paths he takes, whether they turn out to be smooth or rocky ones.

~ ~ ~

Hunched by their small fireplace that evening, Elizabeth couldn't find any warmth from the glowing fire. John Lee sat in the other straight chair across from her, their conversation sparse. Jim was gone, his comforting presence absent.

Then John Lee burst into talk. "Elizabeth, I'm sorry the way I lost my temper and stormed at you this mornin'."

Surprised at John Lee's kind words, Elizabeth nodded at him.

"I rode the mule over to Orrin's. He always can calm me down."

"It's good you and your brother can talk about what bothers you."

"I just shouldn't of took my anger out on you. I sure wish Jim had of talked to me before he left. Did he say why he wanted to leave and live in town?"

"John Lee, he's almost grown. He's got dreams. I guess he wanted to see how it was to live in town. You know, it is different there, a different kind of people."

"I sure hope all this works out for him." John Lee stared into the fire's flames, pensive. "Him bein' our oldest, I guess it's not possible he'll come back home to live."

"I think you're right on that."

Elizabeth turned up the wick of the oil lamp again. But tonight the lamp had dimmed and refused to shed light on the loss of their son.

~ ~ ~

Despite the early spring wind that whistled outside the window, Jim's new upstairs bedroom offered unfamiliar warmth. A room of his own. And what a room! It was as far across as half the farm house and the ceiling was upward to nine feet. His one window looked across the front yard toward Collins Street and had a pull-down shade and sheer blue curtains. For the first time in a long time, Jim had a big double bed all to himself. He plopped onto the bed, let out a loud sigh and stretched his long legs until they pushed against the footboard.

Although relaxed, sleep wouldn't come. He couldn't will his eyes to stay closed. The faces of his family marched across his mind. He imagined the kids back home in the hills, shivering in their unheated bedroom and his baby sister whimpering in her cradle. Jim dealt with guilt at his own comfort.

His thoughts shifted to his sisters. Emmajean, sure she'd never see him again. He hoped she'd not cried herself to sleep. And Shirley Ann, anxious for her turn to follow Jim's lead. Then the boys who were stronger than the girls, but so quiet. How long can they survive staying at home? How long can they hold up against Poppa's mistreatment?

They'd all encouraged him at their good-byes this morning outside the schoolhouse. That's the kind of family they were, proud for their brother's big chance, though they all wanted to come with him.

And what about Momma? Jim tried to push away the thoughts of what his poppa's behavior had been when he'd found out his son had left. His son? He treated Jim more like his field hand. That's all he seemed to be to his poppa.

Jim wasn't proud of leaving his momma to fend for herself with the help of fifteen-year-old and eight-year-old girls, and two ten-year-old boys. But he couldn't think too much on those back at the farm if he wanted to make it for himself. It was just him now he had to watch out for. Just him and he would do a good job of it.

Chapter 8

As spring unveiled herself the next morning, Newton enjoyed her endowment of welcomed sunshine. Jim went to find Arthur where he worked at Henderson's General Store. Men from all over Sanford County came into town for supplies on Saturdays so Jim waited across the street from the store for Arthur to show up.

Jim didn't want to run into his poppa today, so he stayed out of sight of the places where he thought John Lee might go. Maybe he'd see Poppa some weeks later, when Poppa had cooled down and had a chance to realize Jim had left for good. Maybe then Jim wouldn't dread a face-to-face encounter with his poppa. But not today.

Jim saw Arthur jump out of his daddy's truck and lumber into Henderson's front door. Jim yelled across the street but didn't get his friend's attention.

Jim stayed put until Arthur came out a short while later with bundles that he loaded onto Mr. Henderson's delivery pickup truck. Jim sprinted toward the truck as Arthur climbed into the driver's seat.

"Bones, was Poppa in the store?"

"No, I didn't see him. You lookin' for him?"

"Lookin' for him so's I can stay out of his way. Where you goin'?"

"I'm takin' these groceries and things around town. Come on, go with me."

Jim looked around and hoped his poppa didn't see him then hopped into the truck next to Arthur. Jim had been to Newton some, but just for things like the county fair and to Mr. Henderson's store to get shoes. He'd never had the time or need to learn his way around the town.

"How did it go yesterday, leavin' home and comin' into Newton?"

"Pretty good, I reckon. I didn't see Poppa before I slipped off. I wonder how he acted when he found out I was in truth gone? Hope it went okay with Momma."

"Yeah, your poppa can explode real easy." Arthur turned the truck north at the corner. "Where you stayin'?"

"I've rented a room in Mrs. Gertrude Hall's house. Bones, my bedroom is almost half as big as our whole house on the farm. My room was warm last night, not freezin' like the bedrooms at home."

"Did you look for a job yet?"

"Yeah, before I got me a room, I walked out to the hosiery mill to find out about a job."

"How'd that go?"

"Well, I met a Mr. Fred Jacob and he was real welcomin' to me. He gave me a job application to fill out and bring it to the mill first thing Monday morning. Maybe I'll get hired on then. Where're we headed?"

The delivery truck bumped along the streets and Jim listened as Arthur introduced him to the residential parts of Newton. Jim waited in the truck when Arthur made two stops for small deliveries at houses on Avery Street. Jim took in the quiet street and discovered it hugged the base of the hillside around the east side of town.

Jim paid attention as Arthur told him that between Avery Street and the hillside, Caney Creek followed its crooked path then it flowed past Buford Park and on to the Big Stone River. Jim noticed that most of Newton's homes on the east side stood along a pattern determined by the route of Caney Creek. He saw that the houses sat back on their lots, near the creek, and had front yards as big as gymnasiums.

Arthur drove farther away from town. "Mr. Henderson delivers to folks who can't get to his store and live just a few miles from town. We'll get back to town in time to eat a bite for lunch."

Jim lost his bearing as Arthur delivered to several places out of town but soon recognized buildings they had passed earlier. Arthur pointed out the moving picture show located around the north corner from the Blanchard Hotel. "Cost you a quarter to see the picture show in there, but they don't get in a new show but every now and then. It's somethin' to do, though."

They returned to Henderson's store. "I think my boss will give us something for lunch." After Mr. Henderson cut a wedge of cheese from the hoop he kept underneath the glass counter and gave it to them, the boys shared it while they sat on a bench in front of the courthouse.

"Arthur, I'll miss you after today. I'll have nobody to count on for advice next week when I set out to the mill for work."

Arthur nodded at Jim as he chewed the cheese.

"My first goal is getting' hired at the mill. I hope it happens quick. I don't know how long my money and me will hold out without work."

~ ~ ~

After they ate, Jim helped Arthur load the pickup truck with more deliveries. "This sure looks like a lot more than you took this mornin'. Who needs all this stuff?"

"Most every Saturday afternoon I take big orders to the Blanchard Hotel and to Miss June's Boardinghouse. It takes a little longer for me to get these last two delivered."

Jim realized the hotel was the building he'd seen when he first arrived in town the day before. Closer to the hotel, it seemed even bigger than it had looked to him from the courthouse yard yesterday. Jim felt important in Arthur's delivery truck, learning about the town. He waited in the truck while Arthur carried things into the back entrance to the hotel.

After the hotel, Jim recognized they were back on Raymond Street, headed east out of town. Then Jim saw the boardinghouse. "Good gracious." Jim took in the white frame house, its many tall windows shuttered in black three stories above the southwest corner of Avery and Raymond Streets.

He looked at the long, deep porch, enhanced by its white banisters and baluster posts, like sentries between the outside world and the young ladies who lived inside. He saw the many yellow buttercups that had pushed out of the earth on both sides of the front walk to the house to find fresh air and sunshine. He wished his momma had flowers in her yard.

Again, Jim stayed in the truck as Arthur parked in front and carried the groceries around back to the kitchen door. Nervous, Jim imagined unseen pairs of eyes peering at him from behind lace curtains. When Arthur rounded the back corner of the house to return to the truck Jim noticed the front porch stirred with a dozen young ladies of all descriptions.

He watched as the girls spilled out of the house like salt from a shaker and positioned themselves across the porch. Some of them relaxed in white, roomy rocking chairs, legs crossed at the knee, a pretty foot waving in the air while others lounged lady-like on the wide porch steps. He spied two long-legged girls on the porch swing. The swing's chains squeaked a little as they pushed back and forth.

Not bold enough to look straight at any of the girls he was aware they all looked at him. Arthur returned to the truck and grinned toward the array of femininity, more accustomed to the company of females than Jim.

"This is where I met Callie." Arthur searched the porch and saw her on the swing. He started toward the house before he remembered Jim. He jerked his head for Jim to follow. Jim hung back and walked behind his friend up the broad front steps. He didn't dare meet anyone's eyes, ashamed of his lack of good clothes to match this occasion.

The boys made their way to where Callie sat on the porch swing as it swayed at a snail's pace. Jim leaned back against the banister, content to remain in the background, and Arthur and Callie fell into comfortable conversation. Jim wanted to ask Callie about her sister, Louisa, but couldn't get the words past his lips.

When Callie introduced Jim to the other girl in the swing, his words choked into silence. The girl tried her best to coax Jim into conversation, but without success. When the girl gave up and left the swing, Arthur winked at Jim and slid his lanky frame onto the swing to replace her and sat beside Callie. Jim marveled at how smooth Arthur worked it so he could sit beside Callie in the swing.

After what seemed an hour to Jim, but in reality was ten minutes, Arthur stood to go. "I'd better get back on the job or Mr. Henderson will be wonderin' what's takin' me so long on these deliveries."

Callie offered him a smile and walked with them down the steps into the yard.

"See you next Saturday, when I bring the groceries."

"Bye." Callie turned to Jim. "I'll tell Louisa I saw you."

"You will?" Jim stammered. "Tell her I'm stayin' in town now."

"I'll tell her."

On their way back toward town Jim looked puzzled. "Bones, how do you do that?"

"Do what?"

"Talk like that to Callie without no trouble. And in front of all them girls to boot."

"You keep comin' by here on Saturdays with me, you'll get the hang of it. It's just natural."

"Natural maybe for you." Jim looked straight ahead through the windshield and squinted against the afternoon sun. "The only girls I've ever talked to are my sisters. And they don't count."

Discouraged, Jim watched Arthur throw back his head and laugh. "Just keep your eyes and ears open, you'll learn a lot. It'll get easier. I promise. Just give yourself time, Callaway."

~ ~ ~

After supper that evening, Jim offered to help Mrs. Hall clear the table. Her other boarders had migrated to the front porch to smoke, not even carrying their own plates to the kitchen. They must not have grown up in a big family like Jim's or they would be accustomed to help around the house, even in the kitchen. Jim was never ashamed to help his momma with her housework.

"I'll take you up on that, Jim. If you start your job at the mill, you'll do well to drag home and eat before your bed hugs you into sleep for the night. You won't be so anxious to help clear the table then."

"You may be right but I'm used to hard work. I'll still help you some even then." Jim carried the empty milk pitcher and some glasses from the dining room table.

After they washed and dried and put away the dishes, Jim stood at one end of the long table and positioned the tablecloth as his landlady straighten the lace tablecloth at the other end.

"Jim, I'd be happy to have you attend church with me in the morning. It's just two blocks on out Collins from here.

Jim hadn't thought about church tomorrow. He wasn't sure how people would treat him, after the actions of those two ladies Friday afternoon.

"I guess I won't go, Mrs. Hall. I don't have a suit of clothes. I wouldn't be dressed proper."

"Jim, what you have on won't matter to God. What matters to Him is what's in your heart. Your clothes are clean, they'll do just fine."

Jim continued to beg off as he had already forgot his momma's words when he left home yesterday morning. "Not this time. Maybe some other Sunday."

~ ~ ~

Jim didn't attend church Sunday morning or Sunday night, the first time he'd missed services since he could remember. However, he couldn't enjoy the day's leisure. Instead, he struggled into the evening about what Fred Jacob told him when he'd left the mill Friday. His momma had taught him right from wrong as she'd read in the Bible and one of those wrongs was lying. At home things went smoother for him when he was honest with her.

"I'm not a kid anymore," Jim spoke into the empty room. "I can't tell the truth about my age tomorrow at the mill or I won't stand a chance for a job." Jim pondered how to fix this problem.

"Even if I just turned seventeen, I could pass for eighteen. I'm big enough. I'll just say I'm eighteen. What will it hurt?"

He licked the lead end of his pencil and wrote the numbers one-eight on the application form in the space for his age. With that decision wrestled down, Jim went on to bed so he'd get up the next morning on time. He planned to get to the mill early, first thing, like Fred Jacob had said.

~ ~ ~

Monday morning, when Jim shaved his young face in the bathroom down the hall, he looked at his image in the cloudy mirror and decided that money from his first paycheck would go for a haircut in a real barber shop. His momma did the best she could do with her boys' haircuts, but Jim still thought he looked like someone had set a bowl upside down on his head and cut every hair below the bowl. "Yes, first thing will be a genuine haircut."

Back in his room, Jim dressed in a clean pair of dungarees and a denim long-sleeved shirt. He looked in the dresser mirror and ran his hands through his shiny black hair then smoothed it down with the fine-toothed end of his comb. He put the comb in a shirt pocket, went down the stairs, heard Mrs. Hall in the kitchen, and slipped out the front door.

When Jim reached the mill, he rounded the north corner to locate the loading dock. The huddle of men he saw at the dock in the morning's first light both surprised and discouraged him. At six thirty, Jim had wanted to be first in line. Instead, he waited behind at least two dozen able bodies already there on the ground below the four-foot-high concrete loading dock that stretched forty feet along the outside of the mill's back extension.

The men stared at Jim when he joined them, their conversations muffled and their breath frosted in front of their faces. Then the lone door to the left of the loading platform opened.

Two men burst through the door and stopped in front of the group. One of them held a notebook, a yellow stub of a pencil jabbed over his ear. Jim paid close attention as the other man spoke in a loud, harsh voice, all businesslike.

"You men here about jobs?" Everyone nodded, some shuffled their feet.

"I'm Gus Yearout, the foreman here on the loading dock. We need two more workers. This here's Ralph Sloan from the personnel office up front." He waved his hand toward the man with the notebook. "Give him your name and he'll give you an application form to fill out and leave with us. We'll be in touch with you when we decide who to hire."

Sloan hunkered down on the loading dock so that he could just about meet them eye to eye as each man took his turn. When

Jim reached the platform, he took his piece of paper from his mackinaw pocket, unfolded it, and handed it to Sloan. He smoothed the paper out across his notebook and glanced over it before his eyes locked with Jim's.

Accustomed to working men, Sloan almost dismissed Jim, seeing his youthful face. "Where'd you get this?" He held up the application.

Jim licked his dry lips. "Fred Jacob gave it to me on Friday when I talked to him."

"Fred Jacob gave you this?" Sloan exchanged glances with Gus Yearout. "Where'd you see Fred Jacob?"

"I guess it was the front office, around up there." Jim pointed around the corner of the mill.

Sloan stood while he and Gus talked in hushed voices. Then he motioned for Jim to stand off to the side until he finished with the rest of the crowd. Jim wondered if he'd done something wrong. He worried they would doubt his age, but so far they said nothing about it.

Jim saw some of the men drift away with their applications and others laid their papers on the smooth concrete platform and began to complete them.

"You men leave your papers with Mr. Sloan here, soon as you finish. We'll get in touch. Callaway, come over this way with me." Gus walked toward some steps at the left end of the loading platform near the door he'd come through earlier. He waited at the top of the steps by the time Jim climbed them up to the platform.

They shook hands and Gus saw right away as Fred Jacob probably had that Jim was strong enough to work the dock.

"Callaway, you've never worked loading before, have you?" Gus looked at Jim's application form.

"No, sir."

"You don't have to 'sir' me." Gus continued to look from Jim to his application form.

"Do you think you're up to this work? It's not easy. Matter of fact, loading shipments on these trucks is everything but easy." He gave a quizzical look at Jim.

"Yes, sir . . . I mean, yes, I can do it. I know I can."

Gus looked as though he thought better than to hire Jim. "Well, if Fred Jacob sent you then you must be okay for the job. When can you start?"

"Right now, I reckon."

"Good. Come on in here with me. We've got time to go over some things before the shift starts."

Without anymore talk between them Jim could tell that Gus thought Jim had favor from Mr. Jacob and Gus didn't like it.

That first day of work at the hosiery mill was more of a test of Jim's mettle than any day he'd spent on the farm with his poppa.

Gus had some of the other men switch work between the loading dock and bringing stock out from the production floor. But he kept Jim at the trucks all day. Lifting and hoisting.

Gus worked right beside him and Jim watched Gus match him box by box, which strengthened Jim's determination by the hour.

Jim hadn't expected to start work the very first day and so hadn't brought food with him when he left Mrs. Hall's before breakfast that morning. When the men broke for lunch he grabbed a bottle of Coca Cola from the cooler and gulped it down in four big swallows.

At day's end, the walk back to his room took Jim longer than it had that morning. He saw Mrs. Hall at her kitchen window as he dragged up the front steps, and she met him at the door.

"My goodness, Jim, where have you been all day? Have you eaten? When you didn't come back by dinner time, I worried about you. Aren't you just about starved?"

"Yes, ma'am, I am pretty hungry." Jim grinned. "I got me that job, Mrs. Hall. I've been workin' all day."

"I'm glad for you, Jim." Her plump cheeks rose as she smiled. "Come on in now and let me warm you up something to eat."

"Thank you, but I guess I'm just about too tired to eat right now. When I put in long days on the farm, most of the time my chores changed from job to job, not in one place all day. On the loading dock today, the work was not that much harder, but steadier, with no chance to look up at the open sky and the purple mountains. I never thought that a box full of socks could weigh so much. Let me go upstairs and wash up and rest a bit. I'll be back down after while."

"I'm proud of you, Jim and mighty happy you got hired on at the mill"

"I stood toe to toe with the boss and pulled my share of the load all day."

He'd put in a day's work in town. Honorable work. He grinned at his reflection in the same cloudy mirror he had used that morning, now satisfied with himself. He splashed water on his face and pushed his hands back through his hair. "I got me that job." He looked at his reflection. "Nothin' can stop me now."

Chapter 9

Friday, May 10, 1929

Dear Momma,

I hope these few lines find you well. How is Shirley Ann and The Twins? How is Little Ollie and how is Squirt? I'm doing fine. Momma, I got me a job at the hosiery mill working on the loading dock. We move boxes full of socks onto trucks for shipping. The work's not too hard and my boss is a fair man who don't mind hard work neither. I've got a room at Mrs. Gertrude Hall's. She's a widow woman and says she knows of you. She goes to church every Sunday. I like her cooking but not as much as yours. Her house has a dining room about as big as our whole house. And she's got running water and two bathrooms inside the house. One of the bathrooms is upstairs down the hall from my room. What about that! I guess Poppa was pretty mad when he found me gone. I hope he wasn't too hard on you for it. Bones will help me watch out for Poppa around town on Saturdays but I ain't seen him yet. I work five days a week and most times a while on Saturday mornings. They pay me a dollar a day, so here's a few dollars. I hope it comes in handy for you. It's hard to believe I've already been in town a month now. I've made me some friends, men I work with and here at Mrs. Hall's. The folks here in town are real nice to me. Don't worry about me, Momma. I'm fine and I'll take care of myself. I remember all you told me and I'll be good. I'm reading my Bible like you said. I'll write again soon.

Your loving son,

Jim Callaway

Not all the folks here were nice to him, but Momma didn't need to hear that. Jim had soon learned that two kinds of people lived in Newton: the mill workers like Jim and then Mr. Jacob who runs the mill and the other town people who run the stores and the county offices. And they seemed to live in different parts of town. He wished they wouldn't look down their noses at him like he's not as good as they are. *Someday I will be. Just wait and see, I will be.*

When he started to address the envelope to his momma, Jim glanced to the top of the dresser where his Bible lay. No need to tell Momma he hadn't picked it up since that first day he'd arrived. He wouldn't tell her anything that might trouble her. What she didn't know, she couldn't worry about. He added the address on the envelope and stood.

Jim walked over to the dresser and stared at his Bible a long time. He picked it up and turned it over in his hands then opened it. He looked in the front where Elizabeth had written: To my firstborn Jim. From Momma.

Maybe I'll start readin' the Bible some along, like Momma told me to do. It would please her. But I'm just so tired every day when I at last get home from work. Then on Saturday afternoons I visit with Arthur and Callie and on Sunday I need time for myself to rest up for the next week.

He shut the black book, eased open the top dresser drawer, gently laid the Bible inside, and closed the drawer.

Chapter 10

For weeks, on Saturday afternoons Jim had told the men no who worked on the loading dock. "No, not today. I believe I'll go straight on home."

"No. I don't believe I'll go with you for a drink after work."

"No, drinkin's not wrong, I just don't want to go."

But Momma thinks drinkin' is wrong, Jim reminded himself.

"Besides," he'd asked them, "how do you get drinks in broad daylight? I hear revenuers have been all over Sanford County for months bustin' up stills."

"It's all in who you know, Jim." Martin Roberts laid a hand on Jim's shoulder. "The stuff we drink don't come from no mountain stills. Some's smuggled in here, some from Canada, and some comes up from Nassau in the Bahama Islands. Come on, you owe yourself a treat!"

What Jim didn't say to his coworkers but what he wanted was to ride with Arthur while he delivered groceries to Miss June's.

Now here he was, going with the crowd to Duke's for a beer on Saturday after the mill's whistle signaled time to quit work at noon. He'd just drawn his pay when they clocked out at the mill and he could afford the twenty cents a glass. If he went with them today, maybe they'd drop the subject every Saturday. His momma's words to pray and let the Lord direct his steps sounded less than an echo.

Jim rode in the back of the pickup truck with Timothy O'Neill and Scott Nelson while Charley Snider rode up front with Martin Roberts. The air refreshed his tired body. Dust billowed up over Jim and his friends when the truck slid to a stop in the almost filled parking lot. Duke's Café was just north of the Newton city limits on the Knoxville Road. Jim had never been this far north and for certain had never been to Duke's.

They all climbed out of the truck, their fatigue from working long hours this week forgotten. Jim stayed close to the other men but still hung back so he could watch and follow what they did. Just like Arthur had told him to keep his eyes and ears open to learn how to talk to the girls at Miss June's, Jim did the same now.

Martin Roberts led the way through the café and on to the back. They turned left into a narrow hallway and stopped at a closed door that Martin tapped on twice. A panel behind an iron grill opened to reveal a cautious face. Jim heard Martin's gruff voice exchange a few words with the lookout on the other side.

"Come on, fellas." Martin swung his head for them to follow him into the back room.

Once inside, Martin pulled Jim aside. "Now Jim, because there's a respectable café out front, we have to speak easy so we won't be heard and bother their customers." Jim nodded his head to indicate he understood.

A cloud of blue cigarette smoke gathered against the back room's low ceiling. The difference of the bright May sunshine and the inky interior of Duke's back room caught Jim by surprise. Before he got his bearings in the crowded room, he stumbled into chairs and people. By the time the waitress set their frothy glasses of draft on the table, Jim's eyes had begun to adjust to the dim lighting.

Duke's back room had no windows and Jim squinted to see on his right that a long smooth bar and tall stools lined the length of the room. Round wooden tables with chairs sat at random over the rest of the room.

"What about this, Jim?" Scott Nelson adjusted his ample body onto a narrow chair. "You ever been to a place like this?"

"Yeah." Jim didn't want his friends to think him a greenhorn.

"Now, Jim, your eyes are as big as saucers." Timothy O'Neill pushed his red hair out of his eyes. "I know you've never seen the likes of Duke's before."

Charley Snider snorted with Timothy and Scott. "Drink up, boy, it'll take a load off. Make you feel good." Charley held out his glass toward Jim in a toast then swigged half of his beer before he took a breath.

Martin Roberts, the oldest of the group, sat beside Jim. "Boys, leave Jim alone. He's come with us today, so now let him be."

Following his friends' lead, Jim brought the glass to his lips. The beer's pungent odor assaulted his nostrils and his head snapped backward. A quick look around the table told him everybody gulped down their own beer and hadn't noticed. He held his breath and drank the cold liquid. The biting taste was as bad as the smell but he forced himself to swallow it.

Martin Roberts, quiet but observant, kept an eye on Jim. He saw that once Jim got past his first few swallows, the beer went down easier and Jim seemed more relaxed.

Jim soon discovered Charley was right. His body had changed for the better, not as tired. Their waitress set a second round of drinks on the table. Her arm brushed against Jim's shoulder when she put his drink in front of him. She smiled down at Jim. "Hey, Cutie. First time I've seen you in here." Flattered by her attention, he returned her smile and admitted, "Yeah, it's my first time here."

They started to tease Jim again and Martin kept them from getting out of hand. Although this time, Jim, more relaxed, went along with their teasing better than before. That was easy. Arthur said talking to the girls would get easier if he just kept his eyes and ears open.

~ ~ ~

Martin Roberts stopped his pickup by the curb at the side of the courthouse. Jim unfolded his tall frame and slid over the side of the truck bed.

"'preciate the lift, Martin." Jim tried to steady himself upright.

"You get to your place okay from here?"

"Yeah, this is good. Just a few blocks . . ."

Martin watched Jim reel toward the sidewalk. "Be careful, Jim. See you Monday."

The first beers of his life had taken away his steadiness and Jim moved like he walked on air a few inches above the ground. He stepped high across the walkway and sat on the nearest bench in front of the courthouse. He'd get his bearings soon and make his way to Mrs. Hall's.

After a few minutes to pull himself together, he stood to start for home and noticed his momma walking north on the far side of the courthouse square. Thinking she was in town shopping, he first tried to catch up with her. Then he saw her stop at the rear of their old truck parked between other farmers' vehicles. She was there to sell her eggs and early vegetables to the town people.

Forgetting that the strong smell of alcohol and cigarette smoke was all over him from being in Duke's, he started toward her. She saw him from a distance and a smile broke across her face. Then her smile faded when John Lee appeared from the front of the truck. Jim stopped in his tracks and his momma turned her back to him.

She was telling him not to come any closer. It wasn't time to be around Poppa yet. He watched his momma count out eggs into a small paper sack for a lady in a gay frock, a ruffled umbrella above her head to ward off the late spring sunshine. The lady paid Elizabeth for the eggs.

Jim was certain that if his momma didn't have the eggs she wanted, that lady would be walking far away, like those town ladies did to Jim. Momma's faded cotton feed sack dress wasn't as dainty but it was every bit as good as that fancy lady's clothes.

If his poppa wasn't there, he could go to Momma and talk a while. He could cheer her up, let her know about his job. Then he remembered . . . the beers. It would break Momma's heart if she knew he'd even been inside Duke's back room, let alone been drinking. Jim turned and started for home.

Nearing Gertrude Hall's, Jim knew she would be at her kitchen window, and see him staggering up the steps. She came to meet him as he approached her front door.

"Jim, they're working you too hard down at that mill. You were supposed to get off at noon and here it is after five o'clock."

"I'm not too tired." Jim gave her a stupid grin, willing to let his landlady blame his unsteadiness on the mill. He let the screen door slam behind him and enjoyed the relative cool of the dim foyer with its dark, dull woodwork.

Jim's letting the screen door slam shut gave Gertrude a hint that he was not as considerate as usual. Then when he came closer Jim didn't realize she could smell the beer on his breath and the cigarette smoke that drenched his clothes.

"Jim, Jim. What have you done? Where have you been?"

"I've been havin' me some fun. I met a girl too. Even talked to her."

"Jim, I saw your momma in town today. She asked about you. She'd like to see you."

But not like this. The mention of his momma helped to clear the haze from his brain then regret washed over him.

"I saw her too." Jim was unable to raise his eyes to face Gertrude.

He started up the stairs to his room, the sound of his heavy footsteps booming through the house. The image of his momma in her plain dress, selling eggs to the town folks, lingered in Jim's mind well into the night.

~ ~ ~

The next morning when Jim tried to open his heavy eyelids, sharp pain exploded to the top of his head. He pressed both hands across his head as if to keep its contents in place. He'd seen his poppa drag through the house after he'd had a drinking spree the night before, not even giving any of the family a nod. Jim sat up in bed in too big of a rush and then settled back down on his pillow.

He rolled onto his side and that made it easier to sit up and stay there.

Queasiness and a whopper of a headache went along with Jim as he washed his face in the bathroom down the hall and dressed with much effort and in slow motion. Even larger than the pain, shame shrouded him. What would Momma think of him? At that moment Jim made a promise that he wouldn't allow himself to get in this shape again. He had proven his resolve throughout his young life in all he attempted. He was able to set his mind on his purpose and his willpower would see him through to fulfill his obligations. Well, he'd do it now. Jim vowed he would not drink again. He would *not* follow his poppa's example.

Chapter 11

Jim didn't know that Gus Yearout took an instant disliking to him because he thought Mr. Jacob had sent him around to be hired. Jim wondered why Gus worked him extra harder than the others, not realizing he was testing Jim to see if he could do the work. Jim was determined to do everything Gus threw at him without complaining.

Jim's body had filled out during the time he'd worked for Gus. The muscles in Jim's arms and legs stood out more and he'd put on about ten pounds. Gus watched as Jim finished loading boxes from a four-wheeled cart, and called to him before he went back inside.

Two months after Jim started work at the mill, Gus approached him on the loading dock. "Jim, take these filled orders up front." Gus jerked his head toward the door he had come through that first morning Jim saw him. "Give them to Ginger, Mr. Jacob's secretary. You know where his office is, don't you?"

"Yeah." Jim took the papers. He shrugged into his denim shirt, the material sticking to his sweaty back, and tucked it into his dungarees. He moved through the door and headed for the front of the building to find the place where he had first met Mr. Jacob. Jim had not been back since that first morning, but he tried to act like he knew where he was going.

Making his way across the cavernous production floor, he was aware of heads turning as he passed the rows of steady clanking machinery. Jim crossed the noisy room and left through a door he thought would lead to the front of the building. Once he closed the door behind him, Jim welcomed the cool quietness.

He followed the network of narrow hallways until the people he saw no longer wore dungarees and work shoes. Now the men wore stiff white collars and neckties and the few women he saw had nice hairdos and wore dressy shoes. At last Jim found himself in the familiar main outer office and hesitated, wondering which of the three girls was Ginger.

"Can I help you?" The three secretaries gave the good looking young man a thorough looking over.

"I'm Jim Callaway. I'm supposed to give these to Ginger."

"I'm Ginger." She reached for the papers Jim held, as if she had just won a contest and Jim was her prize.

Before Jim could hand the papers to Ginger, the door behind her opened and a young lady glided through. Jim had never seen so fine a lady in all his days. Everything about her was the perfect size and shape and in the right place. Jim gazed at her shiny green long-sleeved blouse, her milk-white skin, her strawberry blond hair and her spirited sapphire eyes.

She entered the room talking over her shoulder to someone still in the other office. Turning, she saw Jim at Ginger's desk and stopped not three feet from him.

"Well, well, well," the fashionable young lady spoke with a flowing Southern accent, pinning Jim with those sapphire eyes. "Why haven't I met *you* before? Daddy," she tossed over her shoulder, "come introduce us."

A short, stout man scurried out of the other office and rushed to her side. Jim recognized the man as Fred Jacob.

"Caroline, this is . . ."

"Jim Callaway, Mr. Jacob," Ginger offered to her boss.

"Yes, yes. Jim Callaway it is," Mr. Jacob's eyes showed a flicker of remembrance. "I believe I gave you a job application in here a while back. By the looks of you I'd say things must have worked out all right for you."

"Yes, sir, Mr. Jacob." Jim shook hands with the older man.

"Daddy!" Impatience colored Caroline's Southern accent.

With equal impatience, Fred made his introduction of the young people. "Jim, this is my daughter, Caroline. She's home for the summer from Atlanta. She's just finished her first year at Agnes Scott College."

Jim didn't notice the three secretaries withdraw like wilting flowers in July heat as Caroline took center stage. He didn't know she thrived on attention and attracted it like nectar draws bees.

~ ~ ~

Without Jim's invitation, Caroline felt drawn to Jim. She became lost in his gorgeous eyes as dark as midnight and noticed his glossy black hair falling onto his forehead. His height towered over her despite her wearing high heels, which further pleased her.

"Where have you been all my life, Jim Callaway?" Caroline surprised herself with such audacious words.

The crimson blush started on Jim's neck and moved over his face. Seeing she had flustered him without effort, Caroline continued.

She was emboldened by her own daring. "I thought I knew everybody who worked here at the mill. How did I miss you?"

Again, she had disarmed Jim and put him at a loss for words. He handed his papers to Ginger, wanting to get back to the dock.

"Ginger, where have you been hiding Jim?"

"No place, Caroline. Jim's just been here a short while . . . and you've been away at school."

"I'm here now," Caroline purred, with shocking comfort in her improper approach to Jim.

Fred Jacob sought to stem this onslaught of Jim and took his daughter's elbow. He steered her toward the front door. "Come, Caroline, we'll be late meeting your mother for lunch."

"Bye, bye, Jim. I'll see you again real soon." Caroline threw him a confident smile. She didn't take her eyes away from Jim and exited through the double glass doors with her daddy.

And that's how Jim and Caroline began. A ticking folly.

~ ~ ~

"I guess I'll be gettin' back to the dock now." Jim sounded almost apologetic after Caroline Jacob left the building.

"Don't let her get to you, Jim. She may be the boss's daughter, but you stand your ground."

"The boss's daughter?"

"Yes. Mr. Jacob. He owns the mill. Didn't you know that, Jim?"

~ ~ ~

Caroline and her daddy met Mrs. Jacob at The Blanchard Hotel dining room. Caroline had spent most of the morning at her daddy's office while her mother shopped and after lunch the ladies would go home together.

The spacious dining room sprawled across the hardwood floor, a welcome breeze parting the sheer curtains at the windows. Seated at a square table covered with a crisp, white cloth, one tall candle, and gleaming crystal, Caroline started the conversation with her parents. "Now, Daddy, tell me about this Jim Callaway."

"Not much to tell, Caroline. He walked into the office a couple of months ago looking for a job. Said he was John Lee Callaway's son. I liked his determination, and he looked like he wasn't afraid of hard work. We hired him. That's about it."

"What department?"

"The loading dock, I believe."

"Is this Elizabeth Callaway's son you are talking about?" Mary Jacob asked. "The egg lady who sells on the courthouse square on Saturdays?"

"Yes, he's Elizabeth and John Lee's oldest."

"Oh, Caroline, not those poor, poor Callaways! There are plenty of young men anxious for your company. Remember who you are!"

Mary Jacob fixed her husband with a warning look, and Fred cleared his throat. "Caroline, your mother's right. You need to see young men from more prominent families."

Caroline knew her daddy saw nothing wrong with her being sociable with Jim. But she had seen him many times agree with her mother to keep peace in the family. Caroline was aware that her mother was more class conscious than her daddy. Caroline was sure her mother had married her daddy because he had inherited the hosiery mill from his family.

Now urged by her parents not to see Jim, Caroline's rich blue eyes sparkled with an increased assurance. Without another word of discussion, she smiled at her parents and took another sip of her iced tea. Caroline saw the shared glance of relief her mother gave her husband.

~ ~ ~

Jim didn't know Caroline stretched the social boundaries her mother had set for her when she directed undue attention to him. Jim, in his backwoods naiveté, didn't understand what was happening. Two days of the next week, Caroline visited her daddy's office. Instead of parking her car at the front, closer to his office, she parked in the lot on the north side of the mill. Jim stared at the owner's daughter riding in her brand-new 1929 two-toned Buick Roadster. Such a car was alien to Jim's world of hard work, long hours and low pay. He delighted in watching Caroline Jacob sashay across the parking lot, the sun bouncing off her bobbed, strawberry blond hair. Jim pondered why she parked in full view of the loading dock when out front would have made more sense.

"Jim, there's your new girlfriend. She's looking this way. Wave to her, Jim," heckled Timothy O'Neill.

Gossip traveled through the mill faster than the white water rapids on the Ocoee River. The day after Caroline's return from school, all 180 employees speculated what was in store for Jim Callaway.

"Not *my* girlfriend, I guess she's lookin' at you, Timothy." But he felt the heat of blush move across his face. He recalled the casual way Caroline had spoken to him in the office and Ginger's warning not to let her get to him. What had Ginger meant? Why *does* Caroline park near the loading dock? Maybe if he didn't pay attention to her, she would lose interest. He didn't want to disappoint his momma by getting involved with Caroline because her family was above the Callaways.

Chapter 12

Earlier, Louisa and her sister had swept the dirt front yard where little grass grew, sending small twigs and pebbles dancing in the dust before the broom. Now they walked across the narrow road back toward the house, each carrying a bucketful of spring water that spilled pure and cold right out of the side of the mountain. The spring then flowed on to Caney Creek.

Reaching the yard, Louisa saw her dad sitting underneath a large shade tree whittling on a small black walnut branch.

Callie had caught a ride yesterday afternoon from town with Arthur Gray and his daddy and had stayed at the house overnight. They went to church that morning and now Callie helped Louisa with her chores before she walked out of the hollow to catch the bus back to Newton.

"What are you girls jabberin' about?"

"We're catching up, Dad. Callie's not been home in a good while."

They took their water buckets to Mavis in the kitchen and came back outside to join their dad. He clicked his pocketknife shut and tilted his wooden cane-bottom chair back on two legs to lean against the walnut tree.

Louisa, shifting from one foot to the other, punched Callie to urge her into their plan. Her eyes pleaded for Callie to tell Dad.

"Dad," Callie began. "Louisa and I have been talking about maybe she could live in town with me this summer."

"Dad, it won't cost you any money for me to go live with Callie." Louisa argued her case. "Callie says I can sleep with her and she'll settle with Miss June for my meals out of her paycheck from the mill."

"I don't know, Baby Girl."

"It'll do Louisa good, Dad. School's already out and this will give her a good break before she starts to high school in the fall. She can learn a lot, being around other girls at Miss June's."

"Please, Dad," Louisa begged. "I'll be good. Callie will take care of me. I'm big enough, Dad. I'll be sixteen in August, you know."

He clicked his pocket knife first open and then closed a few times before he spoke. "Well, if it really means that much to you, Baby Girl," He tested her.

"Oh, it does, Dad." Louisa clasped her hands under her chin in delight. Then she threw her arms around his neck and covered his cheeks with little-girl kisses.

"Better hurry then, and get your things bunched together. I'll walk you and Callie out to Chestnut's fillin' station to catch the five o'clock bus into town. You'll get on in town before dark."

~ ~ ~

He settled his girls in the first seat behind the driver. Louisa heard her dad ask the driver to look after them. She watched out the wide back window as the rumbling bus wheezed back onto the two-lane Newton road, covering her dad in a blanket of diesel and dust as he watched the bus leave.

"I can't believe Dad let me go so easy."

"Dad's pretty smart, Louisa. He knows you're not happy there with just Mavis and him. Stuck up there in Maple Hollow, you'd never see any other young people now that school is out. He let you go because it's best for you. But I mean for you to go back when school starts at the end of summer."

"I will, I will," Louisa squealed. She couldn't suppress the smile spreading across her face.

"Callie," she continued, "Will that Jim Callaway still come by Miss June's on Saturdays, do you think?"

"Maybe. Sometimes he comes with Arthur to deliver our groceries. He used to come by every Saturday but now Arthur comes alone sometimes."

Louisa smiled and warmth moved inside her.

Pleasure lighted Louisa's face at the mention of Jim's name. But Louisa hadn't heard about Caroline Jacob flirting with Jim from the parking lot and that Jim was yielding to her attentions. Louisa's hopes were high for something to develop between her and Jim. Callie might have a tough time protecting her little sister from heartache this summer.

"Louisa, don't set your sights too high where Jim Callaway's concerned. You've not been around many boys, except at school. You can't act possessive around them or sometimes they'll run the other way."

"Possessive?"

"You know," Callie tried to explain. "If you see a boy you like a lot, you can't . . . he's not like your bantam hens at home . . . he's not something that belongs to you. You haven't spent any time with Jim. You've not known him very long at all. "

"But, Callie, he gave me his prize teddy bear last year at the fair. Doesn't that stand for something?"

"Louisa, you haven't been counting on that all this time, have you? He may have forgotten all about that bear he gave you."

"He's not forgotten." Louisa continued staring out the front window of the bus, watching the landscape hurry by. "I've not forgotten and he's not forgotten, either." Louisa remembered when her eyes had met Jim's and a silent promise of commitment passed between them. She was as sure of this as she was that her dad's mountain spring would never run dry. She just needed to move to town, close to Jim, to nurture and cherish that vow. To let Jim tell her he hadn't forgotten.

~ ~ ~

Just visible from the highway, The Evergreen Café sat back from the Newton road among the tall, sturdy pines and delicate mimosa trees. The restaurant catered more often than not to folks from nearby Chattanooga. None of Newton's citizens ventured this far south for meals. Sure that word would not get back to her parents that she was seeing Jim, Caroline had begun bringing him here for supper every Sunday evening when even the Chattanooga crowd was small. Her mother thought she was with friends. However, Caroline imagined her daddy suspected she was seeing Jim only because her mother *didn't* want her to.

Caroline had picked up Jim at Mrs. Hall's and they'd been at The Evergreen for three hours now, sitting in a back wooden booth. Most times she carried the conversation, but Jim had begun to talk easier around her. He was comfortable now in her presence and blushed less and less when she lavished him with her attentions. He didn't withdraw any more whenever she reached across the table to hold his hand.

Even Caroline couldn't completely understand what had come over her. Mrs. Jacob awaited Caroline's entrance into the summer social circles of Newton, mixing with the boys and girls of the Jacobs's friends and business associates. Caroline's acquaintances telephoned her and sent invitations, but she couldn't muster up interest enough to make a date to see them. Thoughts of Jim Callaway filled her dreams at night and her fancies every day. Caroline had never reacted this way before. Was it the challenge of something new and untried, to befriend Jim Callaway? Or was she bored with the usual and wanted to take a chance on a relationship with someone her mother most opposed? Whatever the situation, Caroline's excitement soared, looking forward to the rest of the summer with Jim Callaway.

"Caroline, it'll be dark before long. Don't you think we'd better start back? I don't want you to get in trouble with your folks by bein' gone too long."

"Jimmy, I won't. Daddy knows I'm a good driver and he keeps the car in good running order."

"I know that."

"Don't pout, now." She reached her hand across the table and stroked his cheek. "I suppose you're right, though. I do need to get you back. You must go to work in the morning while I can stay in bed and get my beauty sleep."

After paying the bill, Caroline led the way to her car. With Jim in the passenger seat, she pulled out onto the highway and steered the car north toward Newton. Nearing Newton, they overtook a Red Star Lines bus. At the first stretch of straight road, Caroline pushed the accelerator to the floor to pass the bus.

~ ~ ~

Callie heard a car horn's blare and looked down from her seat on the bus just in time to see the little Buick passing below her window. She saw Jim Callaway's muscular arm, bent at the elbow and resting in the frame of the open car window. Callie didn't have to guess who he was with. Everyone in Newton knew who drove the little two-toned Buick Roadster.

Callie glanced at Louisa who was still captivated by the rolling hillsides passing by the front windows. Going to live in Newton, her expectations to see Jim Callaway rose, visible in Louisa's glowing face and straight back as she sat on the edge of her seat. Nothing could dampen her spirit. Callie was glad Louisa didn't recognize the car speeding on ahead of the bus.

How would she keep her little sister from heartbreak? It was sure to happen if she clung to these dreams about Jim Callaway. Callie had even heard Louisa thank God for bringing Jim into her life. She knew that Louisa was sure God was directing her life to mesh with Jim's forever. Callie wondered about that, but then God often did work in mysterious ways.

Chapter 13

"Bones, I thought you'd never finish high school but here you are strikin' out on your own, like me. I'm glad Mrs. Hall said you could move in this big old room with me. We've put another big bed in here for you. Okay with you if we share everythin' right down the middle?"

"Yeah, fifty-fifty—the dresser, the chifforobe, the desk—we won't have no problems. You're like a brother, Jim. We'll do all right."

"You start full time at Henderson's General Store on Monday?"

"Right. Daddy won't have to bring me into town on Saturdays and take me back home anymore. I'll be right here in walkin' distance of the store." Arthur hung three shirts in the chifforobe and moved underwear out of his suitcase to the bed. He placed his Bible on top of his side of the dresser, picked up the underwear, lay across the double bed and stretched. He looked up at the tall ceiling, smiled, and let out a whoop. He still gripped a bunch of underwear in each hand, both held high above him.

"Here . . . I cleaned out the second drawer for you." Jim pulled out the drawer to show him. "You won't much enjoy walkin' to work in cold weather but it's not bad this time of year. I walk in to the courthouse square every mornin' to meet Martin Roberts and ride out to the mill with him. He lets me out there after work and I walk on back home."

Arthur jumped off the bed and went to deposit his underwear into the dresser drawer Jim had opened. "You ever thought of buyin' a used car?"

"Bones, I'm not rich . . . not yet. I can't afford a car."

"I aim to buy one soon as I save up enough money. From what I hear *you* don't need a car. Is it true what I'm hearin'?"

"What're you hearin'?" Jim stood looking out the window across the front yard to Collins Street, remembering Caroline Jacob and her Buick Roadster.

"I hear you're bein' chauffeured around town by Caroline Jacob. That true?"

"So, what if it is, Bones?" Jim shot Arthur a smirk. "What if it is?"

"Nothin', I guess. Be careful, Jim, she's not our kind. She'll have you thinkin' and doin' things you've never dreamed of. Things you might regret."

"You think I don't know what's goin' on? Well, let me tell you, I do." He wagged a finger at Arthur. "It's nobody else's business, okay? Let it be!"

The silent gauntlet lay between them. Would it sever their friendship, wedging them apart? Arthur and Jim, lifelong friends, might get along now no better than fire and ice.

Chapter 14

A sudden breeze carried away the heavy heat for a brief moment and then died down. A late June dry spell had taken hold of Newton and with it an oppressive heat had settled over the town. The porch swing glided back and forth, stirring up a gentle draft that cooled Callie's and Louisa's bare arms.

"Callie, you get Jim to invite Arthur and you take me. That way we can all be together at the mill's Fourth of July picnic."

"I don't know, Louisa."

"Oh, yes, you do know! You have to get this done, Callie. Arthur and I can't go because we don't work there, but you and Jim can ask us to go and it'll be okay."

"Louisa, I'm not sure . . . "

"I know . . . you still don't want me to be *possessive*. You think I'm chasing after Jim. I've told you, Jim and I, we've got this thing. We don't even have to talk about it. It all started last fall at the county fair. You were there. You know what I mean. You shouldn't fight something that's in God's plans."

~ ~ ~

Saturday afternoon, when Jim and Arthur came around to the boardinghouse, Callie noticed that Jim did look at Louisa in a special way. Something of a promise brightened their faces when they talked. At times, Louisa and Jim seemed unaware of their surroundings, deep in conversation. But it troubled Callie to think that he continued to spend time with the Jacob girl.

"So, we're all set for July Fourth then. Hey, Callaway, how about it?"

"What's that?"

"The mill picnic. We're all goin' together? Right?"

"Sure. You and Louisa can go as our company. Callie and me will take you two along. Since the fourth falls on Thursday, Mr. Jacob is goin' to close the mill at noon and give us the afternoon off." Jim squeezed Louisa's hand.

"Bones," Jim continued, "get Mr. Henderson to let you off Thursday afternoon and you come by here to get Louisa. Callie and me'll walk over from the mill and meet y'all two at the park."

~ ~ ~

It was almost noon, but work had slacked off a good while ago. The mill's annual Fourth of July picnic gathered the employees' families at Buford Park like no other day of the year. The park was the perfect setting for a picnic of this size. The area spread out across a grassy, flat area with a sloping section that was ideal for the fireworks show. The mill was Sanford County's biggest employer, and the workers appreciated the way Mr. Jacob looked after them. He went to great effort to see that there was food and fun for everyone.

Jim stacked the last boxes brought from production. Since the mill closed at noon, he'd pulled his cart just inside the dock doors and Timothy O'Neill began pulling them down.

"She's already here for you, Jim, boy."

"Who's that?"

"You know who. The little Buick sedan's been in the parking lot for fifteen minutes now. She's waiting on you."

"Not me. Not today." Jim's thoughts went to Louisa who would be waiting with Arthur at the park. He wished for the hundredth time that Louisa were out of high school. Jim had decided he wouldn't try to date Louisa until then. He'd promised himself that and he intended to keep his promise. But a picnic wasn't a date, he'd decided.

"You're wrong this time, buddy. Look over there." Timothy stopped the last door halfway down, nodding toward the parking lot.

Not content to wait in her car any longer, Caroline walked toward the loading dock, her mission obvious to all. Her skirt flapped around her knees as she hurried closer to Jim. He stepped out to the dock's edge just as Timothy pulled down the door behind him, closing off the stacking room.

"Jimmy, don't you know Daddy's closing the mill for the picnic? It's time to quit. Come on down here."

Jim jumped off the dock onto the parking lot. Caroline brushed her cheek against his. "That's more like it. Now let's get on over to Buford Park." She looped her arm through his.

"Caroline, I can't. I've got to meet Bones and . . . "

"Oh, hey, Daddy," Caroline called when Fred Jacob drove in no hurry across the parking lot, waving to her. "Mother said tell you she'll be all ready when you get to the house."

Caroline straightforward defied her parents' request for her to date other young men. Her daddy would tell her mother he'd seen her with Jim. Then he would convince Mary Jacob that he saw no harm in their daughter spending time with Jim now that everyone knew him better. Caroline turned back to Jim. "Excuse me, Jimmy. Now, what were you saying?"

Mr. Jacob might not like it if he saw Jim turn down Caroline's invitation. And he looked straight at them. Jim couldn't afford to get on the bad side of Mr. Jacob. He could fire him quicker than he hired him.

Jim walked beside Caroline toward her car, giving in to her insistent tugging, under the watchful eye of her daddy.

~ ~ ~

Callie watched for Arthur and Louisa to arrive at the park. She enjoyed the noontime sunshine unfettered by clouds warming her arms. She spotted Arthur and Louisa entering the park before they saw her. She dreaded Louisa's questions about Jim. It would shatter Louisa if she learned the truth. Callie went over in her head what she'd planned to say.

"Hey, y'all two been here long?" Arthur reached for Callie's hand.

"Is Jim not with you? I thought everybody got off at twelve today."

"We did. Jim had to tie up a few loose ends. He'll be along in a while." Callie and Arthur shared an expressive glance suggesting that Jim must be with Caroline.

"Well, it's his bad luck. Let's get on with the eatin'. Looks like Mr. Jacob has lived up to his reputation and spread on the food again this year. Come on, let's get started."

Arthur grabbed Louisa's hand too and pulled the girls along. Although half-dragged along by Arthur, Louisa looked from left to right and searched the crowd for Jim.

Callie looked over the picnic tables laden with baked hams, chicken and dumplings, corn on the cob, sliced red tomatoes, fried okra, slaw, mashed potatoes, gravy, biscuits, cornbread, fried fruit pies, and cakes from coconut to chocolate. Never before had she seen as much delicious food for one meal, or smelled the many flavors floating toward her as they approached the long tables.

"Maybe I'll go on and fix Jim a plate." They lined up to get their food. "That way we can all sit together to eat and Jim won't have to wait in this long line."

~ ~ ~

Caroline parked her Buick at Sanford Park. "Jimmy, I'm not hungry right now. Let's don't go get our food yet. Besides, look at the long lines. You're not too hungry, are you?"

"No, I guess not." Jim saw his friends in the distance. He recognized Arthur's willowy gait as he and the girls walked away from the food tables. "What do you want to do if you don't want to eat now?"

"Let's go down to the creek. It'll be cooler there. We can wade in the water." Jim followed Caroline along the narrow footpath toward the shallow creek, which was shielded from the park by a thick stand of hickory trees and dense underbrush.

The noise from the picnic faded as they neared the bubbling creek. Streaks of sunlight squeezed through the overhanging trees and glittered on the cold water gurgling over smooth stones. Caroline hurried and sat on a log, kicked off her shoes and began to remove her thick, cotton stockings. Embarrassed, Jim looked away when she pulled up her skirt and peeled off the stockings.

"Why, Jimmy, whatever *are* you blushing for? Have you never seen above a woman's skirt hem? Bless your heart, Jimmy. Come here."

She didn't wait for him, but jumped up from the log and came to hug his neck. "You are the dearest boy. I do declare, you are precious. Look, they're just plain old legs." She reached down with one hand and hiked her skirt above her knee again.

The heat of blush stirred throughout his body, not just across his face. When Caroline reached up and put both her arms around his neck again, he returned her embrace. The warmth that ran the length of his body was not from the torrid July day but from her nearness. He liked this uncomfortable awareness well enough to want to become better acquainted with it.

Jim tried to think about something, anything else besides beautiful Caroline clinging to him. His momma didn't raise him to behave like this with a young lady. He urged his mind to think on Louisa's sweet innocence but Caroline's nearness pushed the thoughts away. Jim's human nature replaced his resolve to do what was right. There on the moss-covered bank of Caney Creek, hidden by the stand of lush hickory trees, Jim surrendered to a smiling Caroline Jacob. His last rational thought was that no one could see them. No one would ever know.

~ ~ ~

The three friends ate in the shade of a small water oak tree. Less talkative, Louisa had picked at her food. The plate she had

71

prepared for Jim sat beside her on the grass, covered with an army of scurrying ants.

When the games started at two o'clock, Louisa watched children in the three-legged races squeal as they ran and fell and got up to run some more. She saw even grown men shouting out as they hopped along in the sack races. She looked out across the field where a game of softball claimed a good audience.

Noises of fun were a distant background to Louisa's thoughts. Where could Jim be? Maybe something had happened to him. She hoped he wasn't hurt. He told her he'd be here, so Louisa knew he would show up.

Louisa tagged along with Arthur and Callie for the rest of the afternoon. She watched the softball game for a while and sat on the swings with Arthur and Callie to watch some races. When dusk neared Louisa and her friends gathered for the fireworks display.

The edge of the park dropped to a natural sloping bowl and they sat on the grass near its top. The land leveled at the bottom of the slope where a man stood on a small stage elevated about a foot above the ground announcing the winners of the races, the softball game, and pie-eating contest. Visible between the trees beyond the bowl flowed a thin ribbon of Caney Creek. The first burst of fireworks lighted the evening sky with blazing reds, whites, and blues and cast a brilliance across the crowd. That's when Louisa saw him.

Chapter 15

Jim stood below them near the stage. Before Louisa got very excited she saw that a beautiful girl with strawberry blond hair held his arm. He must just be helping her to find a place to sit. Then Louisa saw the girl say something into Jim's ear and throw her head back in laughter. Jim even laughed along with her, looking into her face, which was inches from his.

Louisa grabbed her sister's arm, squeezed it hard and didn't let go. "Who is she?" Louisa never took her eyes off the couple.

Callie's gaze followed Louisa's. As much as Callie had tried to avoid this moment and dreaded its coming, she had to tell the truth. "Caroline Jacob. Her daddy owns the hosiery mill."

When Arthur heard Callie mention Caroline Jacob, his head jerked in her direction. He and Callie had agreed they wouldn't tell Louisa about Jim seeing Caroline, hoping Caroline would lose interest in him before Louisa saw them together.

"Callie, did you know about Jim and her?" Louisa asked, pinning Callie with her glare.

"Yes."

"Yes? You knew he was seeing her and you didn't tell me? You let me go on about Jim and you knew all the time he was seeing . . . what's her name, *Caroline Jacob*?"

"Louisa, I tried to warn you . . . I didn't want you to be hurt."

"Well . . . I'm not hurt . . . Jim will have a good explanation."

"Louisa," Arthur said, trying to soothe her mood, "she's the boss's daughter. Jim didn't have much of a choice. If he turned his back on her, old man Jacob was sure to fire Jim."

Louisa turned away from Callie and Arthur as more fireworks streaked upward and splashed across the night sky. Their light sliced the darkness and reflected against the tears easing down Louisa's cheeks.

~ ~ ~

After the fireworks, Arthur walked both girls back to the boardinghouse and then left for Mrs. Hall's.

"I'll just sit here on the porch swing a while," Louisa told Callie. "You go on in if you want to. I'll wait for Jim to come by. I'm sure he has an explanation for not being with us at the picnic."

"Louisa–"

"No, I'm going to wait," Louisa interrupted. "You go on in. I'll be fine."

Louisa waited until Miss June shooed her inside at ten o'clock.

~ ~ ~

Jim stood at his bedroom window and watched Caroline's car drive out of sight. Then he crept down the stairs and stayed quiet as he slipped out the front door so he wouldn't awaken Mrs. Hall. He crossed the yard in long strides and broke into a run when he reached Raymond Street.

He ran the quickest way he knew: three blocks to town, on past the courthouse square, not stopping until he could see Avery Street. He slowed to catch his breath. Reaching the corner of Raymond and Avery, he looked up at the boardinghouse and stopped in his tracks. The porch light didn't burn and no one moved about outside. Jim walked close enough to see that the porch swing was empty and the front door shut to safeguard the girls inside. Shades had been drawn and light from within showed through just a few of them. Even as he watched, some of the shades went dark as the boardinghouse residents began to turn in for the night.

He'd wanted to explain to Louisa, try to set things right with her. He turned to retrace his steps back to Mrs. Hall's. Instead of running as before, Jim slouched past the courthouse without even hearing the clock toll eleven.

Chapter 16

Sunday, August 11, 1929

Dear Momma,

Sorry I've not been writing you like I ought to. I hope this finds you well. How is Robert and Richard? How is Shirley Ann and Squirt? I hope Little Ollie is doing okay. I saw you in town the other Saturday. I would have come over to talk to you, but I saw you had a buying customer and Poppa was there too. I didn't want to cause you no trouble by me and him maybe getting into a fuss. You looked pretty, Momma. Here's a few more dollars from my work. I still like my job and they treat me good. The mill owner had a big Fourth of July picnic for all the workers. Bones and me went with the Johnson girls from over in Maple Hollow. The food was good and so was the fireworks. I'll try to write again real soon. You take care of yourself and tell the others hello for me.

Your loving son,

Jim Callaway

Jim read over what he'd written. Why did he lie to his momma? She trusted him and would believe anything he said. But if she knew the truth about Jim, she wouldn't like it, and she'd worry her mind about him. The way he lied in his letter, his momma won't know about him being with Caroline or having gone for a beer with the guys after work that one time. He couldn't explain to her about Louisa Johnson, so young and pure and innocent. Caroline couldn't hold a light to her. Jim was relieved Louisa didn't know about Caroline. He didn't want to hurt Louisa's feelings.

What would Momma tell Jim to do? He was afraid he would lose his job if he didn't please Caroline, but he wanted to spend time with Louisa. He wanted to wait for her to get older when they could go out together. But Caroline was fun to be with too. She treated him like a king, taking him around in her car, and holding his arm when they walked. She was nice and pretty too. *Oh, Momma . . . .*

Pushing aside the guilt that swelled inside his chest, Jim addressed the envelope and slid the letter inside.

Chapter 17

Packed boxes lined the stacking room ready for transfer out to the loading dock for the next trucks. Jim pushed his empty cart against the wall and walked outside. Wiping sweat from his brow with a red bandanna, he sat on the edge of the concrete dock and let his long legs dangle over the side.

Timothy O'Neill saw Jim sitting there. "Jim, no quitting yet. We've got to get these boxes moved real quick."

"You do it yourself. I'm tired . . . I've been liftin' stuff all mornin'."

"You and the rest of us," Scott Nelson chimed in. "Come on, lend a hand."

"No! I'm through for now. Leave me alone!"

That sent Timothy's temper flaring. "O-o-o-h, you too good to work with us common folks now, aren't you? Did Caroline tell you not to work too hard?"

"I guess when you date the boss's daughter you can just work when you want to," Scott added.

Gus Yearout, the foreman, noticed the raised voices and stepped out onto the dock to see what the racket was all about. He started to break it up then waited.

Jim looked at Timothy with a sneer. "Maybe I can."

"And maybe you can't." Timothy's face turned red to match his hair. He took a step toward Jim.

"You goin' to make me work when I don't want to?"

"Yeah, I think I am."

Jim stood and moved toward his friend, fists poised in front of his face. "You and who else?"

"Now, boys, that's about enough." Gus stepped between them. "Both of you, get back to work. Now! Go on."

Timothy and Jim glared at each other, fists clenched, but backed away and walked toward the stacking room. Jim had lost much of the respect he'd gained from the others who worked on the dock. Much of the time Jim didn't put in a full day's work for a day's pay. All Caroline had to do was pull up in the parking lot and Jim would clock out for the day, leaving the work to the rest of them. Since she was the boss's daughter, none of them, including Gus, tried to stop it.

Because they couldn't stop Jim's foolishness with the Jacob girl, they let their resentment build. Often lately, that resentment surfaced like it had just now between Jim and Timothy. Nobody liked a bully and for sure one that received special hiring treatment from the big boss and one that went around with his daughter.

~ ~ ~

The four of them lingered on the front porch of Miss June's, not wanting to lose a precious Saturday afternoon comfortable enough to enjoy the outdoors. The first frost was just a couple of months away. Then the biting cold of winter would howl down from the heights of the cobalt Appalachian Mountains and grip Newton. The carefree days of summer would be replaced by effort to stay warm and healthy enough to survive the winter.

"Enjoy these last few weeks of good weather," Arthur said. "Won't be long till the cold will push us inside to sit by the fire."

Talk of the weather continued between Arthur and Callie and Louisa. Sitting alone on the top porch step, Jim remained quiet and almost inattentive as if their conversations imposed on him.

"Jim?"

"What, Louisa?"

"Are you okay? It seems like something's on your mind."

"No, nothin'."

Jim didn't say anything more that afternoon.

~ ~ ~

That night as they dressed for bed, Louisa asked Callie if she'd noticed anything different about Jim that afternoon.

"Now that you mention it, he stayed so quiet. What's wrong? Do you know?"

"I've got a good guess. I think it's that Caroline Jacob."

"What's she done, now?" Callie pulled her long gown over her head.

"I just think she's making Jim into what she wants him to be. She's changing him. If I didn't know him better, I'd think he was putting on airs. I aim to tell him how awful pride can be in God's eyes. Caroline will be leaving soon, going back to college at Agnes Scott in Atlanta. She can't run his life from way down there."

"Well, neither can you. You'll be back with Dad, going to high school."

"No, I won't, either." Louisa rushed to brush her hair, letting out her frustrations.

"But you promised Dad you'd come back home when it was time to go back to school. He wants you to finish high school like I did."

"I'm not going. I'm staying here. I'll hire on at the hosiery mill like you. I can see Jim just about every day then. I'll turn him around, get that Caroline out of his head. I'll help him see God's ways again."

~ ~ ~

A week later, Jim arrived home from work, and the sweet smell of cinnamon rolls and baked bread met him at the front door. He found Gertrude bustling around in her kitchen. On Saturday afternoons, Gertrude stayed busy baking and delighted in offering Jim fresh goods from the oven.

Gertrude turned the cornbread from the black cast-iron skillet onto her hand and then laid it onto a plate. She cut it into pie-shaped pieces and placed the plate on the kitchen table in front of Jim. He sat, took a wedge, and began to crumble the steaming bread into a tall glass.

"Jim, I don't believe you've been home to see your family since you came to live here. When are you going back to visit them?"

"I don't have a car to go in, Mrs. Hall, you know that." He smiled up at her, but all the while thinking about how he'd rather spend his Saturday afternoons with Louisa and his Sundays with Caroline than go visit at the farm.

"There's folks going down toward Chattanooga every Saturday. Somebody'd be glad to give you a ride as far as Maynard Junction. You could walk to the farm from there."

"I guess so. I need to give myself a while longer to get settled in my job and all. I'll go soon." Jim used a spoon to push more chunks of cornbread down into the glass.

Gertrude Hall watched Jim pour cold sweet milk into his glass till it covered the cornbread. "Folks at church say they saw you with the Jacob girl at the mill picnic last month. Is that right?"

Jim tried not to resent Mrs. Hall asking about his private business. She'd been too good to him for him to act that way. "I guess they did see me with Caroline Jacob," he answered. Then he couldn't refrain from adding, "Does that bother you, Mrs. Hall?"

Gertrude dipped flour from the meal chest into a deep bowl. "Well, yes, Jim, it does bother me some. What do you know about this young lady?" Before he could answer, she continued. "Caroline Jacob has never seen the likes of you, Jim. She's used to boys of her own class, ones with family money and position."

"Maybe so in the past, but right now, she wants to spend time with me." Jim had an arrogant edge to his voice. He spooned out another mouthful of cornbread and milk.

"So, what about this young girl over at Miss June's, this Johnson girl? I hear tell you go over there just about every Saturday afternoon to see her. Does she know about Caroline Jacob?"

What was this woman? A mind reader? How did she know this very thing was on Jim's mind? He began to get uneasy with all of Mrs. Hall's questions.

"Don't you worry about me and my women," Jim had an unfamiliar sly smile on his face. "I've got everything under control, Mrs. Hall."

"Jim, you may think you have control of everything. You don't." Gertrude began to sift the flour into another ample bowl and a white cloud rose as it fell through the sifter. "God planned your every day before your momma ever birthed you. You just haven't decided to go along with God's plans for you yet. But, son, that's what you need to think about—turning loose of things and giving in to God. He'll guide you the way that's best for you."

Jim continued eating, not looking up at his landlady.

"Jim, your mother raised you by the Bible. You know what's right, but you're enjoying your freedom out from under your folks' roof. Be careful you don't leave God out too long. You get into the Good Book, Jim, and you'll see where it shows us how to behave. Remember, the main thing is to please God."

"I 'preciate the cornbread and milk." Jim stood without finishing. "That was good. It'll hold me till supper, I guess." He left the kitchen and took the stairs up to his room two at a time.

Arthur was still at work at Henderson's and once inside their room, Jim closed the door and leaned back against it. Mrs. Hall was right. He wasn't being true to his own. He needed to go see the folks. His momma wouldn't approve of his behavior . . . he was treating Louisa awful by running around with Caroline.

Then he heard the familiar car horn honk from the street out front. He stepped over to his open window and looked down. Caroline stood on the running board of her sedan and waved across the roof of her car to him. Then she motioned for him to come down to join her.

She was like a narcotic to Jim. He was addicted to her charms, her beauty, her money, and her family's position. The sight of her pushed aside all thoughts of Mrs. Hall's gentle reproofs. He even forgot it was almost time to meet Arthur at Mr. Henderson's store and walk over to the boardinghouse to see Louisa.

Chapter 18

Sunday, August 18, 1929

Dear Dad,

I hope you're all right. I hope Mavis is too. Callie and I are well. I like staying with Callie. Dad, I'm writing to let you know that I won't be home to start high school. I've decided to stay here with Callie. I got a job at the hosiery mill. I work in the boarding room where Callie does and I like my work. I hope it won't bother you too much my not coming back home like I said I would. I'm sorry if this hurts you. I guess it's just time for me to get out on my own like Callie's done. Dad, I know you wanted me to finish school so I could make my way in the world. But I don't need more education to work here at the mill. The work's not too hard and they pay pretty good. Southeastern Hosiery is a big place and I'm mighty glad to be working there. I hope you can be pleased for me. I'll be good and Callie and I will watch out after each other. Tell Mavis hello. Take care of yourself.

I love you,

Your Baby Girl, Louisa

Chapter 19

"You stay away from that boardinghouse while I'm gone, Jimmy."

"Caroline, why do you have to go back to Atlanta?"

"Jimmy, it's my second year of college. Daddy wants me to finish and that takes four years to do. Don't pout, now. I'll be home for Christmas."

"What about between now and Christmas?"

"I'll write you. But don't get to missing me so much that you spend all your free time around all those girls at the boardinghouse."

"I won't do that." Jim already thought of Louisa.

They were at The Evergreen Café for their last Sunday evening supper before Caroline was scheduled to leave for school. After she paid the cashier, they walked hand in hand to her car. Before Jim opened the door for Caroline to get in, he turned to her and kissed her cheek.

She reached up and brushed his straight hair back from his face. "Time will fly by, Jimmy, and before you know it I'll be back for three weeks at Christmastime."

"Time will fly by for you, down there with those rich guys in Atlanta. You won't be lonesome."

"Why, Jimmy, are you going to be jealous?" she smiled.

"I already am." He put his arm around her waist and pulled her toward him.

Chapter 20

Reaching home after work, Jim stood for a while under the ancient oak tree in Mrs. Hall's front yard before going inside. Work had been demanding that day, and he stretched some tense muscles. A few leaves trailed to the ground in the gentle November breeze. Caroline had been gone only two months and already Jim longed for Christmastime.

"Jim," Gertrude called, coming out through the front door. "I'm sorry, but I have bad news from your family."

Jim met her on the porch. "What is it?"

"Jim, your mother sent word by the peddler. It's your baby sister. Poor little thing. Bless her little heart."

"What is it, Mrs. Hall?" he repeated, trying to get her to finish. "What about my baby sister?"

"She's died, Jim. The little thing died yesterday. Your mother wants you to come home as soon as you can."

Jim fretted about how he would get to the farm and back if he went. About getting word to Gus, his boss. About missing work if he stayed a few days.

"I'll get word to the mill, Jim. The peddler will wait at the courthouse till dark and you can ride to Maynard Junction in his old bus with him."

"Did he say how Momma was?"

"No. But you go gather up the things you need to take with you. I'll get word to your boss in the morning."

"Yes, ma'am. Okay. It won't take me long." He called over his shoulder as he started up the stairs to his room.

~ ~ ~

When Jim walked into the backyard at the farm, two cars were there and some horses stood tied to nearby trees, their buggies empty. He saw that the church people had gathered to join the Callaways in their grieving. Entering the back door, Jim made his way toward the front room. He walked past the dining room table and saw vegetable dishes, fried chicken, cakes, and pies there, almost resembling a picnic without gaiety. Jim knew the

Southern custom of bringing food to the home where death had occurred never failed. The food appeared without thought or wonder. Jim watched several friends of the family gather around the table and fill their plates. That was expected too. You had to eat if you visited the bereaved.

In the front room some neighbors and church friends stood about, others sat uneasy in the wooden folding chairs brought in by the funeral home. When Jim entered the room, faces wreathed in sadness turned toward him.

The bittersweet reunion with his momma twisted Jim's insides. She clung to him, sobbing both from her pain at losing her baby and from her pleasure of having her firstborn at home again.

"Jim. Let me look at you," she held him at arms' length. Then she pulled him to her again.

"Momma, I'm sorry. What happened to Little Ollie?"

"Last winter was hard on her, you know. She never was strong and couldn't never make her place." Elizabeth swiped tears across her cheeks with her palms. "She tried to fight back but the pneumonia fever overtook her. She lost the fight."

"I didn't know she was ailin'. I should have come around before now."

Elizabeth released her son and stepped back. Jim realized his momma and the children were excited to see him, but the circumstances that brought him home didn't allow for much celebration. He wanted to talk to his sisters and knew they found it difficult to contain their desire to talk to him. Jim returned their grins. The Twins shot smiles across the front room at him. But good manners and respect for the dead dictated their silence while in the room with their baby sister lying in her open casket. Jim's poppa stood in a calm quiet across the room and watched the reunion. He and Jim exchanged a nod without a word of greeting.

~ ~ ~

That night Jim had to sleep in his old place, in the double bed with his brothers. Lying in their beds, all four of the children plied Jim with questions about his life in town. Jim knew they envied him being grown-up and out on his own. Jim basked in their praise and adulation.

Emmajean said, "Jim, you didn't never write to me. You promised you would, but you didn't. Did you just forget about me?"

"Squirt, I'm sorry. I'm pretty busy in town. I work hard and don't have much time to write letters. But I'll try to do better." Jim was glad he'd already blown out the oil lamp light and didn't have to look his little sister in the eye when he lied to her that way. Why did lying come so easy for him these days?

"Jim, I heard about Caroline Jacob," Shirley Ann teased from her bed across the shadowed room.

"What did you hear?" Jim teased back.

"I know you've been runnin' around with her. Arthur's sister told me at school. Sounds like she's a handful."

"Not too much for me to handle. You just worry about handlin' old Henry Frank."

The Twins listened but kept quiet as usual. When the conversations slacked off, Robert spoke up.

"Jim, Teacher told us the other day at school that the country was in for some hard times. Something about stocks in New York City fallin'. Did you hear that?"

"Yeah, I heard. But, Robert, that's up in the north. I wouldn't worry about it none. Nothin' bad from all that will ever get way down here to us in Tennessee."

"But Teacher talked about how those stocks fallin' would have a bearin' on everything, one way or another. Someday they would, she told us."

"I doubt that. Nothin' to worry about, Robert. The hosiery mill and stores in town are still goin' strong."

"I'm glad to hear that." Robert turned over and soon sleep captured him and the other Callaway children.

For Jim, sleep was hard to find because he had no room in the bed to toss and turn. He lay on his back, his hands clasped behind his head, and stared up into the despairing darkness. He hoped his momma had gone to bed to get some rest before morning. Dim light slipped underneath the bedroom door from the next room where two or three people from the church sat up with his baby sister's body. To brighten his mood Jim brought his thoughts around to Caroline. Just thinking of her brought a smile across his face. Knowing he'd see her soon, he gave into restless sleep.

~ ~ ~

The next afternoon after the funeral in the old frame church house, the mourners walked a short distance behind the small casket toward the graveyard out behind the church. Little Ollie's pall bearers had an easy load to bear her body to the open grave. Jim looked around the grave yard. He saw that some tombstones stood erect pointing to the heavens. Other, ancient ones, tilted to their sides, unstable in their purpose to protect graves entrusted to them. The overcast sky void of sunshine further set the somber mood as

Jim and his brothers and sisters followed their parents, ducking under the canvas tent covering erected next to the open grave and taking seats in folding chairs.

After a few short comments by the preacher and the ritual of burial finished, the crowd of friends and family meandered away toward the church. John Lee approached Jim with an outstretched hand.

"Poppa." They shook hands.

"Jim. Good to see you. I hear you're workin' at the hosiery mill."

"Yes, sir."

"You've filled out some. Work must agree with you."

Then John Lee had walked away. Jim let out a ragged breath that his poppa hadn't lit into him about leaving last spring like he did. Jim noticed a hint of favorable change in Poppa but decided it was because of the funeral and the other people surrounding them. Jim guessed that his poppa could behave when he tried.

Three days later, before Jim left to walk to Maynard Junction and then the road to Newton, he and his momma spent some time alone together in the kitchen.

"Jim, I wish you'd come home more. The children need to see you and I miss you."

"I'll try harder. I will, Momma."

"Shirley Ann tells me you have a new girl . . . a Caroline Jacob? She says this Jacob girl's not our kind, Jim. Tell me about her."

"Momma, she's from a fine family. Her daddy owns the hosiery mill where I work. They're good people."

"But what are you doin' with the likes of her? Don't she spend time with her own?"

"Now, Momma, don't go to meddlin'," he teased her. "Caroline and me get along fine. She likes to spend time with me."

With a stern but loving expression on her face, she looked at Jim. "You be careful, Jim and don't fall into ways that you know God don't approve. You be sure to keep the things of the Lord first in your life, Jim. You go on to church and read your Bible regular. You hear me?"

"Yes, Momma, I hear you." But Jim made no promises to his momma before he started walking down the winding road toward the junction and back to Newton.

Chapter 21

When Caroline arrived home from Agnes Scott for the Christmas holidays, she set her suitcases in her room, dashed back downstairs, hopped again into her car, and headed for the mill. Jim welcomed the little Buick Roadster pulling into the parking lot. He jumped off the loading ramp and started toward her car before she stopped it.

"There he goes again," Timothy O'Neill spoke to whoever of the other guys would listen. "She's back and reeling him in. It's pitiful the way Jim runs any time she hollers." There was a chorus of grumbling agreement as the men took on Jim's work another time while he visited with the mill owner's daughter.

"Boy, have I missed you." Jim approached the car as she got out of it.

"And I've missed you." Caroline nuzzled his neck. "Did you behave while I was away down there in Atlanta?"

"You know I did," Jim grinned. He would never tell Caroline that he'd continued to go over to the boardinghouse with Arthur. She didn't need to know that he'd been spending time with Louisa on Saturdays. After all, it was lonesome with Caroline gone and Louisa was such a sweet girl to talk with him and to be his friend.

"I'm out of school three whole weeks." She pulled him close. "I want us to be together every day. And Mother and Daddy said invite you to our house for their Christmas Eve party. They plan a splendid dinner with a group of their friends from town."

"I don't know about that, Caroline." Jim was comfortable with her and also around Mr. Jacob. But he wondered if he could be at ease around her mother and a house full of strangers.

"Yes, you do. You'll be there. I'll pick you up so now you don't have any excuse not to go."

~ ~ ~

Jim had shined his shoes until he could see himself in them better than in the clouded mirror in the bathroom down the hall. He combed his hair away from its middle part and smoothed it down with brilliantine and buttoned the vest of the dark gray suit Caroline had bought him and shrugged into the jacket.

When she honked her car horn, Jim grabbed his new chesterfield from the chifforobe, bounded down the stairs, and flew off the porch to race to her side.

Arriving at Caroline's, Jim was awestruck when he gazed at her two-story home. The matching front windows across the massive brick Federal cast light out across the snow. A tall chimney hugged each opposite end of the house like matching bookends. After they got out of the car at her house, they hesitated in the shadows before going in.

"You look real pretty, Caroline." She leaned into him and he kissed her.

"You'll be the most handsome man in there tonight." She wrapped her fur-collared coat tighter around her. "Here, let me work on that necktie."

"I tried and tried but I couldn't get it right like you've showed me."

"You did fine." She returned his kiss and stepped closer to him, brushing fat snowflakes off his chesterfield's velvet collar. She slipped her arms around his neck. "You look even more handsome in your new coat than you did in the store when we bought it."

"When *you* bought it, you mean. Caroline, we'd better go in . . . your parents."

"They're too busy with all their guests to be looking out here at us." She continued to cling to Jim.

"No, let's go in while I've got my nerve up."

"Jimmy! Don't be nervous. They're just a bunch of old fuddy-duddies. They'll like you. Just be yourself and remember to talk and use the correct grammar like I've been teaching you. After all, what's not to like about you?"

~ ~ ~

Stamping the snow from their shoes, Jim followed Caroline across the porch toward the elegant front door. More light escaped through the overhead fanlight and the sidelights framing the door. They shook off the cold of the December evening and stepped into the warmth of her parents' house. She turned to Jim for him to help her off with her coat, which she laid across the stairway banister together with his chesterfield.

Jim looked at the broad curving staircase that swooped up the right side of the tall foyer. The second story balcony railing sported garlands draped with red ribbons woven in and out of the greenery. He returned his attention to Caroline.

"Is it all right for me to tell you again how pretty you look tonight?" Jim whispered. Her straight, golden chemise with the dropped waistline added to her already hypnotic effect on him.

"Yes, and you can tell me as many times as you want," she whispered back through her smiles she directed toward her parents' guests. The room quieted as everyone ceased their conversations to look at the attractive young couple.

Fred Jacob strode into the entrance hall. "Jim, good to see you."

"Mr. Jacob." Jim gave the man a polite nod of his head like Caroline had instructed him to do.

After they shook hands, the older man ushered the couple into the large living room located to the left of the entrance hall. Stepping into the room, Jim didn't even recognize the quiet undertow pulling him farther away from his humble upbringing.

Gentlemen and ladies filled the room, standing or sitting in small clusters. Jim knew these men were the elite of Newton: the bankers, lawyers, store owners, and doctors. He saw that most of their wives wore festive and fashionable tailored dresses with flashing long strings of beads and large earrings.

In the farthest corner of the room, Jim noticed that the top of the decorated Christmas tree brushed against the high ceiling and carved moldings. Jim could reach the ceilings at home without even getting on tiptoe. He looked around the room where lighted candles, greenery, and sweeping red bows decked the mantelpiece over a crackling fire and more greenery and red bows adorned the many tables in the spacious room. Jim had never seen so many presents as those resting underneath the tree.

He thought about the Christmas tree at the farm with its popcorn strings and no decorations in the house. Not any presents the likes of here.

This was his first Christmas Eve away from his family. Certain they missed him, that familiar faint stab of guilt rested in his chest.

Fred Jacob guided them toward a small group of ladies and singled out one from among them. "Mary, this is Caroline's friend, Jim Callaway. This is Caroline's mother, Jim. I don't believe you've met."

"Ma'am." Jim took the hand she offered. He nodded toward her and just as their eyes met, recognition crossed her face. Mary gave Jim a withering stare.

~ ~ ~

Jim recalled his first day in town last spring. He remembered the humiliation he'd experienced when two town ladies had stared at him with contempt. He recalled how they had eased to the outside edge of the walkway, keeping their distance from him. And Jim remembered like it was yesterday how one of the women had turned back to take one last glimpse of him, from head to toe. He recognized Caroline's mother as that woman. Jim had promised himself then that one day the town matrons wouldn't look down their noses, but look straight on at him. Like now in the Jacobs' grand home.

He was one of them now and they were accepting him into one of the finest homes in town. The lady of the house had offered him her hand and her precious daughter was on his arm. Caroline's mother acknowledging him gave Jim a supreme note of accomplishment.

"Jim . . ." Mary Jacob glanced at her daughter and saw the undisguised love on her face. It was obvious to Mary just how much her daughter cared for this poor boy.

Jim had heard around the mill about Mr. Jacob and his family. Talk was that Mrs. Jacob grew up in one of Newton's respected families but had been rejected by the love of her life. She had then wed Fred Jacob, an acceptable man of a lower class, whom she had never loved as completely or passionately as she had the love of her life. Jim knew that Caroline could have her pick of young men in town and sometimes wondered why she was in love with him. He questioned whether she was following her mother's footsteps by being content with him who was not of her social status.

"So nice to meet you, Jim." She choked the words out without emotion, almost robotic. "Please come in and warm yourselves by the fire. Would you like some punch? We will have dinner in a while."

Jim swelled with pride as Caroline's daddy escorted them around the room and introduced Jim to his friends. Jim shook hands and spoke the words Caroline had drilled into him. Mary Jacob had no chance to poison her guests' thinking with details of his pitiful beginning she had witnessed last spring. And, so, the townspeople embraced him as one of them.

Jim took pride in the way they all accepted him because he knew the Jacob family and escorting their daughter put the chocolate icing on the cake. He knew his foot was in the door in this town now. He was sure he could certainly move up someday. And he'd done it all by himself. Jim could almost taste the success he had been striving toward. He knew it would be just a matter of time.

~ ~ ~

After dinner, filled with baked Cornish hens, dressing, and all the trimmings, Jim was disappointed when the guests separated, ladies retiring to Mary Jacob's sewing room in the back of the house and men returning to the living room. Fred Jacob passed a wooden, nut-brown humidor among the gentlemen and Jim helped himself to a Cuban cigar. Soon a thick blue smoke floated toward the ceiling.

From a small cherry cabinet sitting near the Christmas tree, Fred retrieved a bottle of whiskey and offered drinks. The Revenue stamps and liquor label on Jacob's bottle looked legal to Jim compared to the counterfeit and plain bottles he'd seen at Duke's.

Jim smiled. This was money talking. Someday he'd have fine cigars to pass around, but not the liquor.

Raised voices around him jolted Jim from his thoughts. A heated discussion ensued, centered on the business world. Jim heard terms foreign to him being tossed about the room. Listening, Jim pieced together the essence of the conversation.

Mr. Jacob was talking, "Now don't y'all go worrying yourselves sick over this stock market problem in New York City. My purchase orders at the mill haven't slacked off one bit. And I don't look for them to."

"But, Fred, if people lose their jobs here like they are doing in the big cities up north, they won't have money even for my doctor charges."

"Yeah, and if they don't work, they can't buy groceries or clothes," Mr. Henderson added.

"I told you, don't worry. I'm not looking to have to change anything at the mill. Things are going along as usual, aren't they, Jim?" Fred Jacob included his daughter's friend in the discussion.

"Yes, sir, they are. We're as busy as ever."

"See there, gentlemen, nothing to worry about. We're not up north, we're as secure as ever right here in . . ."

Just then, Caroline appeared at the door to the living room. All the gentlemen who were seated stood and Jim did the same after a slight hesitation. Caroline crossed the room toward him.

"Jimmy, I need some fresh air. Would you please take me outside?"

Fred Jacob nodded in the affirmative when Jim looked to him for permission to fulfill Caroline's request. They left the room, gathered their coats from the foyer and stepped out into the cold, night air. Jim was glad the snow had stopped and the chilled air had quieted.

Thinking she had had enough of the ladies in the sewing room and just wanted to be alone with him, Jim began to steer Caroline toward her car.

"No . . . no, Jimmy. I needed some fresh air. The room started going around and I thought I was going to faint. It must be something I ate."

"What's wrong? Are you going to throw up?"

"Oh, . . . Jimmy, I feel so queasy."

Jim set aside his selfish, amorous attitude and instead reacted with empathy, as he had seen his momma do many times. He put his strong arm around her shoulders and held her close to his side. He took her elbow with his other hand.

"Here, lean on me. Let's walk. Breathe in deep and you'll clear your head."

"It's not my head. I'm nauseated to my stomach." She stumbled as he tried to walk her.

"We ate the same things, Caroline, and I'm not feeling sick."

"I know we did. Jimmy, I think . . ."

Jim interrupted, "Could you smell all that cigar smoke clear to the sewing room?"

"Maybe that's it, but I doubt it. Jimmy, I'm afraid I'm . . ."

He pulled her along. "Let's walk just a little bit more. Is this helping you?"

"I guess. But, Jimmy, I need to tell you . . ."

"Come on, let's walk over this way."

They moved to the sidewalk in front of the house and paced up and back until Caroline felt some better.

Jim walked her a few more trips in front of the house. "Do you want to go back inside, now?"

"I guess so. I'm sorry I took you away from the men. I wanted to tell you–"

"That's fine. They were just talking about business things up in New York City. Nothing important."

~ ~ ~

Later that evening when Caroline drove Jim back to his place, they lingered in the parked car.

"I'm so proud of you, Jimmy. You made a good impression on my parents' friends. I think Mother liked you too."

"She was nice to me. I guess she did." Jim recalled the brief look of shock that had passed across Mary Jacob's face when she had recognized him. He smiled to himself at how Mary Jacob had included him in the evening, in spite of herself.

"And, Jimmy, don't forget to go to Daddy's office when you go back to work after Christmas, like I told you. He may have something special for you. Maybe a raise or a promotion."

"A raise would be great. But a promotion . . . I don't think so. Lots more guys are ahead of me in time on the loading dock. They wouldn't like it if I got a promotion now. They'll get promoted before me."

"We'll see." Caroline put a knowing smile on her beautiful face.

Then she asked Jim to reach behind her seat to get the package there. He had to use both hands to raise the rectangular box brightly wrapped in Christmas paper and bow.

"Open it."

"What is it?"

"Jimmy, it's for you. Merry Christmas."

He tore away the paper and opened the box. Puzzled, he looked inside.

"It's one of Richard Sarnoff's radio music boxes. It's a radio, Jimmy," she explained. "I bought it in Atlanta. Just about everybody down there has one."

"You must have paid a bundle for this. You shouldn't have done that."

"It's okay. I figured since you lived upstairs you should be able to pick up something out of Knoxville or Chattanooga. You can listen to music and news, and get the *Amos 'n Andy* show every week night and *The Happiness Boys* comedy shows on Friday nights. It will help to fill some of your evenings when I'm back at school."

"Don't talk about going back to school, not tonight. You've got more than a week left before you have to go back."

He reached into his overcoat pocket, pulled out a small wrapped box, and turned to her. "Here, this is for you. Merry Christmas."

Caroline opened the package and lifted out a tiny garnet stone hanging on a delicate golden chain.

"Jimmy, it's my birthstone! That's so thoughtful of you. Here, can you help me?"

She turned away so that he could fasten the clasp behind her neck then faced him again. With her arms around his neck, she held him close for a very long time.

"It doesn't amount to much next to your other jewelry, but I thought it would look good on you. It does." He pulled away from her and fingered the small stone lying in the hollow of Caroline's graceful neck.

"It doesn't matter how it compares. This is from you and that makes it the best of all. Merry Christmas."

"Merry Christmas, Caroline." The light from the street lamp cast its dim glow through the windshield and Jim noticed how pale her face was. "You'd better go on home now and get some rest. I'll be back from the farm in a couple of days. Maybe your queasiness will be better by then."

"I don't know . . . maybe."

As Jim turned to open the car door, she grabbed his coat sleeve and held tight, not wanting him to go. He turned back toward her.

"What is it, Caroline?" He saw something in her eyes he'd never seen there before. Doubt . . . fear. "What, Caroline?"

"Jimmy, I just wanted to tell you . . . that . . . Jimmy, I love you more than anything."

She released his coat sleeve and threw her arms around his neck and held on as if Jim was her life boat in a rolling rough sea. After several minutes, Jim pried her arms away and held her hands between them. She looked up at him, unshed tears shining in her eyes.

"Is that what you were trying to tell me earlier tonight when we were walking in front of your house? That you loved me?"

"Yes," she lied. "But I really do love you."

"Caroline, you're the best thing that's ever happened to me."

"Do you love me, Jimmy?"

"Yes, I do." Jim had voiced what he felt in his heart.

Chapter 22

Red and green tissue wrapping paper flew about the room as the family opened Jim's presents on Christmas morning. Emmajean leaped around Jim's neck, thrilled with the jump rope he gave her. Robert and Richard sat on the bare floor in front of the small fire grate comparing the round glass marbles Jim had given them. Shirley Ann blushed when she opened her package to find a little red diary.

"You can write all about Henry Frank in there every night." Shirley Ann blushed even more.

Elizabeth cried over the pretty red cloth her son had brought her. She assured Shirley Ann and Emmajean that she would sew them each a new dress out of the material.

"Momma, there you go, giving away your present. I brought that to you," Jim teased, knowing that his momma most enjoyed her life when she shared with her family and he expected she would do so the rest of her life.

"I'll have enough to make me a dress too. You must have spent an awful amount of money on this."

"Aw, not too much. Montgomery's Dry Goods Store opened me a credit account. I'll have it all paid off before long."

"Oh, Jim, I hate for you to owe people. Please get out of debt when you can."

"I will, Momma. Don't you worry about it. I shouldn't have told you, I guess." Jim looked at his poppa who still held the small package Jim had brought him.

"Go on, Poppa, open up your present," Emmajean urged, trying to help him tear the wrapping paper from the thin, square box.

"It's not much, Poppa." John Lee opened his box of white handkerchiefs.

"I 'preciate this, Jim. Thank you. Your momma saved your fruit out in the kitchen. The other children found theirs in their socks first thing this mornin' when they got up."

"That's good. Thank you, Poppa . . . Momma."

"Merry Christmas, Son."

"Merry Christmas to y'all." Jim looked around the room at his family.

"We missed you last night on Christmas Eve. Why didn't you come on home last night?"

"Shirley Ann, I went to Caroline's house for a party last night. I met her mother and some of her parents' friends."

"Oh, Jim . . . talk about me and Henry Frank! You've got it bad over this Caroline girl. You goin' to marry the boss's daughter?"

"Time will tell, I guess," he hedged, not yet knowing the answer himself.

~ ~ ~

Christmas morning Caroline sat with her parents in their spacious dining room having breakfast. Immersed in her own thoughts and staring out the window, Caroline watched the sun glisten across the frozen glaze of snow that had fallen last night.

Mary passed the platter of fried eggs and sausage to Caroline.

"No thank you, Mother. I'm not very hungry."

"At least fix you some biscuit and peach preserves. And here, drink some milk."

Caroline looked at the foamy milk set before her and her stomach lurched. "Just a cup of coffee, please, Mother."

"Are you drinking coffee now? What will you take up next down there at that school in Atlanta?"

Caroline took a few sips of the dark, steaming coffee, but it didn't settle her stomach. When Mary urged her again to eat some eggs and drink the milk, Caroline put her hand to her mouth and excused herself.

"Now, what is wrong with that girl."

Laying aside his newspaper, Fred motioned toward the upstairs. "Maybe you'd better go and check on her. She didn't feel well last night. She looks a little peaked this morning too."

Fred remained at the dining table and poured himself another cup of coffee. He was still reading the front page of the newspaper when Mary called down for him to come upstairs right away.

~ ~ ~

The two women were in Caroline's bedroom. Fred found his daughter lying on her four poster bed underneath the ruffled canopy, a wet cloth across her forehead, her eyes puffy and red. Mary wrung her hands and paced back and forth.

"What's wrong in here?" Fred saw an obvious problem but was certain it could be resolved. His wife got agitated at the least little problem.

"Caroline has just broken my heart! How could she do this to me? To us? How will we ever hold up our heads in this town again?"

"Now, Mary, calm down, and try to get hold of yourself. It can't be that bad. Does Caroline need to go to the doctor?"

Caroline's sobs burst out loud with Fred's mention of the doctor.

"What's wrong, Caroline?" Fred asked, still standing in the doorway. "Where are you hurting?"

"Fred, she is not hurting anywhere. She has just thrown up . . . she tells me she is going to have a baby! She is already five months along. Do something, Fred!"

"No! My little girl . . . in a family way . . . how on earth did this happen." Fred crossed the room to sit on the bed beside his daughter. He took one of her hands in his and asked her, "Is this true what your mother is saying?"

Caroline nodded, shut her eyes, and turned her face away from her daddy.

"Who was it, Caroline? Who's the boy?"

When Caroline refused to answer or even to look her daddy in the eye, he demanded again, "Give me a name!" Caroline knew that to him the solution was simple: find the boy and get them married.

Mary had seen Caroline's love for the poor Calloway boy on her face last night when she brought him to their home. To cast blame away from her daughter and to prevent her from having to marry into the Callaway clan, Mary turned on her husband.

"You are the one who wanted to send her away to that fancy girls' school in Atlanta." Mary flung the accusation at Fred, but was not finished. "It was your idea to get her educated. Well, it looks like she got educated, all right. Educated in the grown-up ways of the big city and all the men you have thrown her in with," she spat out in disgust. "This is your fault. Now do something!"

Fred patted his daughter's hand, got up, and walked to the window, looking out over his neighborhood where he was respected as a leader in his town. Caroline watched her daddy. She knew their family was welcomed anywhere they wanted to go and she was sure he expected the town's doors would slam shut in their faces if this scandal ever got out.

After several minutes he turned back to the silent room and in an even, unhurried voice, he spoke. "No one in this town must ever know about this." He looked at his only child still lying on the bed. "If you won't give me a name, I have no other choice. Caroline, get up. Pack you some things."

He walked closer to her bed and bellowed at her when she made no move to get up. "Now!"

"Mary, you help her. I'm going downstairs to call my sister Martha in Knoxville. I'll tell her to expect Caroline there this afternoon." He watched as Caroline, bent over with nausea, gathered her brushes and combs and some jewelry from her dresser.

"You'll stay in Knoxville until the baby comes. You'll give it away. Then you can come back home. It will be about the same time you would come back from the end of your school term anyway. Nobody in town will know the difference but that you've been away at Agnes Scott as normal." Fred started out of the bedroom.

"No, Fred, you cannot send her away. She needs me now."

Fred turned back from the doorway. "Don't send her away? What would you have me do? . . . What? . . . You want to hold up your head around here, don't you? What else can I do?"

Mary twisted up her face in anguish and continued to wring her hands. "This is Christmas Day," she cried.

"There's nothing else to do, Christmas Day or not. Caroline may need you now, but she'll have to make do without you. Martha's had babies. She'll know what needs to be done. And she's got the means to care for Caroline with all that railroad money her husband Hensen left her when he died. She'll take good care of our daughter." He left the room to make his telephone call.

When he returned, he'd made all the arrangements for her to stay with her Aunt Martha in Knoxville. He'd told his sister that Caroline would drive up and to expect her by the middle of that afternoon. Caroline closed the two suitcases on the bed and turned to her mother.

"I'm so sorry, Mother. I've failed you and I'm sorry." Still sobbing, she turned to her daddy. "Daddy, please forgive me."

Ignoring his daughter's plea for forgiveness and taking a suitcase in each hand, Fred turned to Mary. "We'll tell anyone who asks that Caroline had to return to school now to get some assignments finished."

Chapter 23

The next day, Jim began to resent the time he spent with his family. The remaining days of Caroline's school break would slip by and he didn't want to spend any more time away from her. He should have returned to town yesterday after the folks opened their presents.

He found his momma in the kitchen cutting up a chicken for dinner.

"Momma, I'll be going back to town now."

"Goin' back . . . today? But you said they shut down the mill all week for Christmas."

"They did. I need to get back though. I've got some things to tend to."

"How will you get back? Arthur and his daddy's not coming by for you till Sunday."

"I'll walk to the junction and then thumb a ride on in."

"Son, you just got here yesterday. Ain't you happy to be here with your family?"

"Momma, I told you, I have some things to do, that's all. I'll stay longer next time."

"You've got yourself into town. You've got a good job and friends. I thought you'd be more satisfied. What's troublin' you, Son?"

"Who said anything's troubling me? Things are fine, Momma."

"I don't know all about your circumstances, but I do know my children. Somethin' is botherin' you."

"I can handle it—don't you worry about me."

"I try not to worry, Son. I try to turn my worries over to God. When I let Him help me carry them, they don't weigh as heavy on me. And whatever's burdenin' you, you can ask the Lord to help you too. God may not change your troublin' situations but He will give you strength and guidance to get through them."

Jim heard his momma's words, but remained silent.

"Jim," she continued, "He'll help you, but you must ask Him and have faith in His love for you."

Her words both settled and unnerved him. What she said ate at him like a gravel in his shoe. She spoke the truth, but right now he wanted to get away from this farm and his family's simple ways. He wanted to get back to Caroline. Now.

"I've got to go, Momma. I've told the others good-bye already. I'll write." And with that he was out the door.

Walking down to Maynard's Junction, his momma's words tumbled around in Jim's head. He knew she meant well. But Jim decided he could run his life now. Everything would be fine when he could get back to town to Caroline. She loved him and he loved her. He guessed he would be there by the middle of the afternoon.

~ ~ ~

"What do you mean, she's gone, sir?"

"She's gone, Jim," Fred Jacob answered.

"But . . . when will she get back? I can wait till she does."

"You don't understand, Jim. You can't wait. She's not coming back."

Puzzled, Jim looked from Jacob to his wife standing in their opulent entrance hall. He looked up the staircase, hopeful that Caroline would appear.

"Jim, Caroline had some assignments to finish at school. She has gone back to Atlanta," Mary said with halfhearted compassion in her voice. "You can see her another time."

"When? When can I see her?"

Neither of them answered and Jim pressed for a plausible explanation. "She wasn't due to go back to school yet. Did she leave me a note?"

"No, Jim. No note," Mary answered.

"No message at all?" he asked.

Mary and Fred Jacob shook their heads in silence. The scene tore the insides from them as well as from Jim.

Resigned to the fact that Caroline was not there, Jim mumbled a thank you to her parents and turned to leave. Fred Jacob followed him across the porch, stopping him at the top step. He put a hand on the young man's shoulder and tried to soften the bad news they had given him.

"Jim, you liking your work down at the mill?"

Jim tried to muster some enthusiasm. "Yes, sir, I sure am. I appreciate you hiring me like you did."

"That's hard work out on the loading dock. A lot harder now that winter's come. Caroline hates to see you having to work out in the cold. She assures me I'm wasting a good mind keeping you working out there with Gus."

"Thank you, sir. You've got a mighty sweet girl, sir." Jim's pride again swelled from within.

"Yes, of course. Nevertheless, I've come to agree with her assessment of your talents. When the mill opens back up next week, don't go to the loading dock. Check in with me first thing. I have some place else in mind for you. We'll see if we can't put that good mind of yours to better use."

~ ~ ~

Walking across town to Mrs. Hall's, Jim searched for answers.

Why had Caroline left earlier than she had to? Why didn't she wait till he got back from the farm? Why didn't she leave him a note? Why? . . . Why?

The weight of his questions scorched his mind as he trudged the last few blocks toward home. Without answers, his burden grew heavy. Remembered words broke through his confusion. *Come unto me, all ye that labour and are heavy laden, and I will give you rest.* He stopped in his tracks and looked all around, but saw nobody near.

Where did that come from? He'd heard the words as clear as if someone spoke out loud.

Come unto me . . . I will give you rest.

He recalled his momma's pleading that morning for him to ask God for help in his circumstances. He continued walking toward home, mulling over what she had said.

But after all he decided he still had things going his way. He'd be fine. He was certain Caroline would write soon and explain all this, he was certain. And it looked like next week he would get a promotion and maybe a raise to boot. Everything would be just great.

His steps got lighter and he held his head higher. All was well after all.

Chapter 24

Christmas had been slim at the Johnson's, but Louisa and Callie hadn't expected presents in return for their gifts to Dad and Mavis. Louisa knew that what material things Dad failed to provide his family he made up for in kindness. Louisa was glad he had showered the girls with love all their lives. And she was thankful that he made sure they knew about God's love for them—His love and care for them wherever they were.

The day after Christmas the four of them sat in front of the coal fire in the open grate. "Baby Girl, tell me, have you decided to stay home and get back in school?"

"Dad, I don't need school anymore." Louisa glanced at Mavis, sure of her disapproval. "I'm working at the mill now."

"I hate to see that—you workin' hard in that place."

Earlier he had told Mavis she was trying her wings and wouldn't be coming back to nest at home again.

"Just don't you forget where you come from, girls. You're from good, honest raisin' and don't you let nobody tell you different. You'll be facin' big choices out there. You meet them head on and choose right. Don't let other folks be makin' up your mind for you . . . on anything. Remember to trust in the Lord."

Callie and Louisa assured Aaron with their agreement. "We will, Dad. You don't have to worry about us."

They hugged all around, including Mavis. After all, she would watch after their dad now that neither of them would be around to do so.

Chapter 25

Orrin's wife answered John Lee's knock at their door and took his coat and cap.

"Do you want some coffee? It's on the cook stove, still hot."

"I'd 'preciate some. It was a cold ride over here."

John Lee found his brother sitting in a straight-back wooden chair close to the fireplace. The snapping fire and hot coffee helped to warm him from his ride in the chilling cold.

"Put your mule in the barn if you're goin' to stay a while. Mighty cold out there . . . looks like we might get another snow tonight."

"I already put the mule in the barn."

"That's good, John Lee. You done turned over a new leaf for the New Year?"

"Maybe so, Orrin. Maybe so."

"Everything all right over at your place? Good Christmas?"

"Orrin, it was a good Christmas. Jim came home, stayed the night. Made his momma and the kids real happy to see him."

"Sounds like you took kindly to his visit too."

"I tried, Orrin. I did try."

"What happened, John Lee?" Orrin asked. "Did you and Jim have another fuss?"

"It went good with my boy. Jim's workin' at the hosiery mill, filled out some. We didn't pass many words, but we got along."

Orrin stayed silent, waited out his brother.

"I've been tryin' to treat the family better, like you said—love them better. Looks like it might be workin' too."

Thank you, God, Orrin prayed within himself.

"Love always works, I believe I said some more things to you, John Lee. You thought about tryin' them too?"

"You mean all that you tell me about God and His forgiveness and His peace? Let me hear some more."

"That's right, John Lee. God offers you His forgiveness for every wrong you've sinned against Him . . . and every sin *is* against God, against His commandments for our lives. His forgiveness is a gift for you when you admit you're sorry about those wrong things you've done."

"Orrin, I am sorry about how I've cursed God all these years and treated my family the awful way I have."

John Lee was near tears, showing sincere remorse and desire for atonement.

"All you have to do, John Lee, is repent . . . be sorry . . . for your sins and ask God to forgive you. He sacrificed his own son Jesus Christ, who took all our sins to the cross. That one sacrifice paid all our debt of disobedience to God."

"Go on, Orrin, please."

Orrin took his timeworn Bible from the fireplace mantel and began to share God's plan of salvation, Scripture after Scripture. John Lee had heard the familiar words when Elizabeth taught their children. This time he was intent on listening.

"*Except ye . . . become as little children, ye shall not enter into the kingdom of heaven,*" Orrin read.

"It's simple, John Lee. With the faith and trust like an innocent child, accept the grace God offers you."

"I can't never be good enough to deserve God's grace. I've been mean to the core."

"It's not a matter of deservin'. Look here, John Lee, would you go to the wash pan and say, 'I can't wash my hands because they're dirty.'?"

John Lee squinted toward Orrin as if he were walking in a dense fog and trying to see beyond it.

"Maybe I understand, Orrin. Go on."

"John Lee, it's time for you to pray for your own redemption. Tell God you're sorry and you need His help to turn away from your old ways. Go on, tell Him."

John Lee tried to speak with God from his heart. He paused.

"Ask God to forgive you through His grace," Orrin prompted. "Ask Jesus to come into your heart. Turn you life over to Him, right now, once and for all, forevermore."

Again, John Lee talked with God, a broken man, tears of repentance streaming down his face. Then he began to laugh out loud. The tears and the laughter mingled as he faced his brother. His eyes sparkled as if blinders had fallen from them. The joy and peace of God's redeeming grace now replaced John Lee's usual scowling expression.

He grabbed Orrin in a bear hug and sobbed onto his neck. A burden had lifted from John Lee—the burden of unforgiven sin fell from his big shoulders.

Chapter 26

A few weeks later, Callie and Louisa, in their upstairs room on a Saturday afternoon, heard a car horn's incessant *ah-ooo-ga, ah-ooo-ga, ah-ooo-ga* and a gleeful voice yelling their names. They rushed to their window to identify all the commotion down on the street.

"Come down here, ladies, your carriage awaits you," shouted Arthur. He motioned from the open window of a fire-engine red Ford Model A, so shiny it gleamed like stripes in an American flag waving in the sunshine. Jim smiled from the opened rumble seat at the back of the car, his coat collar turned up around his neck and his snap-brim cap pulled low on his forehead.

The boys hopped out of the car and met Louisa and Callie on the broad front porch steps. The girls slipped into their coats and Arthur took Callie by the hand. He led her toward the car and Jim and Louisa followed.

"What on earth?" Callie said.

"We got us a car." Arthur's grin stretched across his slender face. "It's used or we couldn't have afforded it. New it would have cost us $385. It's a '27 Ford Model A Roadster—the one with an open rumble seat. And it even has an electric ignition."

Callie and Louisa looked from Jim to Arthur for an explanation. Jim shrugged and smiled again.

"Bones talked me into going halvers on us a car. I'm going to drive it to the mill to work—Bones is close enough to walk to work—and we'll share it on Saturdays and Sundays. And this is it!" He made a grand gesture with his arms, encompassing the car.

"Yeah, neither one of us could ever save up enough to buy one of our own," Arthur admitted.

"She's a beauty. Look at those white walls. What do you think of her?"

The girls joined in the excitement, walking all around the car, opening and closing the doors, looking into the rumble seat, which was open to the brisk breeze.

"Get in. We'll take you for a ride around the courthouse square."

Despite the January chill in the air, Louisa and Jim climbed into the tiny rumble seat and Callie joined Arthur up front. They chugged away amid their fits of laughter, under the envious eyes of the girls at the boardinghouse.

Chapter 27

"My dad says we always have a choice. We just have to be careful what we choose."

Louisa and Jim sat facing each other at a table with a scuffed up Formica top in the mill's crowded employee lunchroom. Louisa couldn't eat. She didn't look forward to this meeting even though she had begged him to eat with her today, making the meeting sound urgent.

She knew Jim was now Receiving Manager for the mill and had a small office of sorts—a converted storage room—near Ginger's desk.

Louisa saw him every day as his new job's paper work took him back and forth across the production floor—from his office to the loading dock—several times a day. Louisa had a view of the entire floor from the boarding room on the mezzanine where she stretched socks onto forming boards, blocking them to size. Because she could do the repetitious chore in her sleep, her work never suffered as she watched Jim's trips across the production room.

Louisa regretted that his new job had added a swagger to his step, and a smirk to his face. She didn't like Jim's sour attitude, which annoyed everybody, including Louisa. Now, in the lunchroom, Louisa was rattling off something about choices.

"What are you talking about . . . what choices?" he snapped.

"Like Dad says, you'd better be careful how you choose." Louisa tried to control her quavering voice.

"What do you mean? I'm not working on any choices."

"Yes, Jim, you are. You must." Louisa's voice filled with compassion. "You're going to have to make a few choices and one is to choose between Caroline Jacob and me."

He blinked with surprise and his face paled. She continued.

"Yes, Jim, I know about Caroline Jacob and you. I didn't at first. When I saw you with her in July at the picnic I gave you the benefit of the doubt, but you never offered an explanation."

Jim sat in stunned silence and when he didn't offer an explanation now, Louisa took a deep breath and spoke again.

"Then when I started to work here I heard everybody talking about the two of y'all. About how she had wrapped you around her little finger."

"But, Louisa, that night after the picnic, I . . . you don't understand . . ."

"I think I *do* understand. Just let me say my piece on this. I may be only sixteen, but I know a thing or two. When Caroline's away at school, you spend more time coming by Miss June's. Then the minute she's back in town she honks her horn and you go running."

"But, Louisa, things may be fixing to change . . ."

"Yes, things between us *are* going to change." Her voice was cool and icy. "I won't be a fill-in for her when she's gone and I won't share you any longer when she's here. You do have to make a choice, Jim."

"But, Louisa," Jim stammered, his half-eaten lunch forgotten on the table between them. "Let me finish . . ."

"No, Jim, I've given you long enough to come to your senses by yourself. Now, maybe I can help you do that. Jim, there's a bond between us, I know. You feel it too, though we've never said the words. Ever since that first time our eyes met, I've promised myself to you. I've thanked God for bringing you into my life. You're truly God's gift to me. I'm certain of that."

That was as close to a declaration of love that had ever passed between them. The discovery left them both breathless.

Louisa took another deep breath, trying to calm her pounding heart and went on. "If you ever come down off your high horse it would work for us. You've got everything all mixed up. You're so full of yourself and your *success*, you can't see the real blessings God has given you—your family, your friends. You'd better be careful you don't leave God out of your life too long."

"Louisa . . ."

She gathered up the remains of her lunch and pushed back her chair with such force it fell to the floor with a clap that caused heads to turn toward her and Jim. Standing, Louisa placed both hands on the table, palms splayed, and leaned across toward Jim, her blazing blue eyes pinning him to his chair. Amid the clamor of the lunchroom, she whispered, "Don't be coming to Miss June's to see me until you make up your mind. Caroline or me."

Jim's dark eyes dulled with confusion and he reached across the table. He had almost touched her hand as she pulled it away and straightened.

Before walking away, she turned back. "It hurts me to say these things to you, Jim. I just pray that the final choices you make won't hurt either one of us as much."

~ ~ ~

That night, Louisa's words robbed Jim of sleep: *Caroline or me.* He tossed in the stillness, trying not to disturb Arthur asleep in the other bed. But he could not get comfortable. He kept seeing Louisa's image as she had looked at him before she'd walked away. Those blue eyes, how the soft finger waves in her blond hair framed her face.

Jim pushed back the covers, crawled out of bed, and tiptoed to stand by the window. Looking down across the front yard toward the street, his mind flooded with Caroline's vivid image. He could see her standing on her little sedan's running board, waving for him to hurry down to join her. Winter had moved into February and Jim hadn't heard a line from Caroline. All his letters to Caroline in Atlanta had been returned and he battled the irritation of rejection.

Passionate memories of Caroline filled his mind. Then Louisa's innocent face appeared, snapping away his daydreaming. Jim wanted the excitement, which Caroline brought into his life.

But without Louisa he was not grounded. She tugged him back every time he had just about pushed God completely away. Jim needed her calm and her faith.

How could he continue without Caroline? The way she called him Jimmy and leaned into him. Not anymore, she didn't. Caroline's absence made his choice easier every day he didn't hear from her. In fact, she may already have made his choice.

Mrs. Hall and Momma warned him about Caroline. Arthur and Shirley Ann too. His family and friends, and he had paid them no mind. Was Caroline down there in Atlanta laughing at how she had played him for a country fool? Maybe he hadn't meant a thing to her all this time. He had begun to care for Caroline. At first it was the excitement of having a girl from town to pay attention to him. The boss's daughter, to boot. He had become accustomed to her. They grew close, spending time together. Jim thought he *did* love Caroline.

A steady drizzle sprayed against the window pane, bringing dropping temperatures and a forecast of more snow. Jim watched the opening of another day by dawn's gray light that outlined his beloved mountains, which snaked along the east side of Newton as far as the eye could see. His simple homeland, his family ties and friends' loyalty pulled at him. That's another choice he must make.

Louisa was right. He didn't need to ever forget where he came from. He didn't need to get above his raising. It was time he made some choices. Right choices, for a change. . . . He couldn't wait to tell Louisa.

~ ~ ~

Caroline stood upstairs at the window in her Aunt Martha's majestic guest bedroom. She pulled aside the heavy drapes and watched the same dawning herald another day. Sixty miles north of Newton, she looked at the stretch of blue-green Appalachian Mountains. Known here as the Smoky Mountains, the distant peaks punctured the morning skies east of Knoxville.

She cinched the belt of her velour robe tighter to help deflect the frostiness of the cold, flat window pane. She could still see Jimmy all dressed up for her parents' Christmas Eve party. She remembered how he'd looked at her with so much love in his dark eyes. She longed to feel his arms around her again. What was he doing right now?

Caroline yearned for Jimmy. A dull, persistent pain tore at her heart whenever she thought of him, and that was all day and all night. She had been jerked away from him as quick as a bolt of lightning. No time to talk with him or even to leave him a note. But then who could she have left the note with? Not with her parents, of all people!

Tears trailed down her cheeks to the corners of her mouth then dripped off her chin. Caroline made no attempt to wipe them away, resigned to the aching sadness in her chest. Yet another night her thoughts had held her a sleepless captive. Grief and guilt battled within her every night and day. When would her tears go dry? And she had to give her baby away or she could never return to Newton.

Later, during breakfast in the dining room, Caroline's Aunt Martha urged her to eat. "Child, you're going to blow away if you don't start eating. You're going to need all your energy in a short while."

Caroline's Aunt Martha watched her from the opposite end of the long cherry dining table, polished and shining like the still surface of a lake on a bight summer day. Caroline recognized much of her daddy in Aunt Martha, the thick neck and stocky body, the sandy-blond hair now streaked with gray, showing its strong widow's peak. Her aunt had a pleasant, agreeable disposition like Fred Jacob. Except on that last day Caroline saw him in December.

But, like he'd said, what else could he do? Her situation had brought disgrace to her parents. Would they ever forgive her? Would she ever be their daughter again?

"Put some nourishment in your body, you're eating for two now!" Martha continued. "This is the one time a lady is allowed to eat her fill. Eat up, Caroline. You don't want to harm yourself or your baby."

Caroline's head snapped up, her eyes widened. She obliged and began eating. Not until that moment had she thought of this circumstance other than *her predicament*. Not as a living, growing baby. Jimmy's baby! She carried part of him inside her and she *would* take care of it.

Yes, she was certain the baby was Jimmy's. She'd enjoyed flirting and flaunting her position with others but only with Jimmy had she known such depth of desire. With Jimmy she had discovered real caring. Only with him had she felt secure enough to share her passions.

Caroline was pleased that Jimmy released her from living up to the image of the little rich girl. She could be herself with him, confident in the attentions of someone who looked past her daddy's money and into her heart instead.

He was a simple farm boy, but she was sure of Jimmy's loyalty. She'd never experienced shame about their relationship when she was with him. Now, in exile at Aunt Martha's, shame and guilt were her companions each day. She was having a baby and she felt sure Jimmy was having fun. Fun with all those girls at the boardinghouse. Maybe that girl from Maple Hollow. And here she was—the only one to suffer the consequences of what they did at Caney Creek. She was such a fool. They both were. She had failed to realize that Jimmy didn't know where she was.

Aunt Martha had followed Fred Jacob's stern orders to keep his daughter housebound. When accompanied by Martha, Caroline could venture out of the backyard. She was to mail no letters and Martha was to intercept any that might come addressed to Caroline.

Caroline was a prisoner who found it hard to believe her jailer had her best interests in mind.

"Now that's more like it, Caroline. You've found your appetite!"

"I'll eat. I can't let anything happen to this child. This child of . . . mine."

"This child of whom, Caroline? Give me a name."

"Aunt Martha, you sound like Daddy. He demanded a name. But I wouldn't give him one. Daddy wanted to go right then on

Christmas Day and snatch up someone and drag him to the preacher to marry me."

"Your daddy was looking out for your future. Yours and the baby's. There's no way a single woman can keep a child and raise it. That's not done. It's impossible. Your daddy wanted to make it so you wouldn't have to give away his grandchild to strangers. Now it looks like that's what's going to happen when you give the baby up for adoption."

"Well, Daddy won't get a name from me. I won't say *I do* to anybody who marries me because he's made to." With a faraway look in her eyes, she added, "Not even if I do love him. I wouldn't humiliate him that way."

"But, child, if you love each other, tell your Daddy who the father is. Then y'all can work it out."

"Aunt Martha, people can count! I'm seven months along already." Caroline spread both hands across her swollen belly. "Even if I went home and we married right now, I'd ruin his good name and destroy his family. Not to mention my own."

She pushed her chair back and began clearing breakfast from the table. "No, I'll just take this punishment from God and try to make the best of it. I'll do what I must do. It'll work out somehow."

Caroline saw pity and concern in her aunt's eyes. "Caroline, sit back down, child!" The urgency in her voice caused Caroline to set down the dishes with a clatter and resume her seat.

"Now listen to me. Do you read the Bible?"

"Yes, ma'am. Some."

"Do you believe what it says?"

"Yes, ma'am, I do."

"Well then, if you do, you should know that God didn't put this situation on you. God isn't out to bring us down. Instead it's our own wrong choices that cause bad things to happen to us. God doesn't want to hurt us but help us . . . if we'd let Him.

"Caroline, allow God to forgive you for your bad judgment and release you from your shame and guilt over this baby."

"Bad judgment is right. Why would God want to help me? I'm impure. I've dishonored my mother and daddy." She dried new tears from her cheeks with her white linen napkin. "I'm no good, Aunt Martha."

"God created you good. Human nature prevails here on this earth and your human nature led you down the wrong path—you and your baby's daddy. One of God's best gifts is forgiveness. We just have to accept it and let Him cleanse us from within. He can redeem you and make you whole again as if you'd never sinned."

"I've read all that, but why would God redeem me after what I've done?"

"God won't condemn you if you pray for His forgiveness. Caroline, can you do that now?"

Caroline bowed her head and prayed. Then she looked up, wonder filling her face.

"Aunt Martha . . . I did . . . God did . . . my heart is lighter . . . God *does* love me!"

She had bowed her head in shame and raised it in the quiet transformation of God's love.

Martha heaved her heavy body from her chair and met Caroline half way around the elegant dining table where they embraced. "Praise the Lord."

Chapter 28

Jim didn't wait until Saturday for his usual visiting time, but rushed over to Miss June's after supper the next day. He wanted to tell Louisa what a fool he'd been and thank her for being patient with him. Driving across town, he rehearsed what he would say. He would tell her he remembered that first night at the fair. He'd say how he, too, had been compelled to make a silent commitment to her forever. The closer he got to the boardinghouse, the more he wanted to smile.

Until Miss June's porch came into view. Jim braked the car to a sudden stop. He got out and stepped behind some holly bushes, their leaves snagging his pants' legs, to make certain of what he first saw. Sure enough, Louisa sat on the porch engaged in animated conversation with Roger who worked in the packaging room at the mill.

Jim's happiness faded and he stumbled backward from the boardinghouse. He turned, got in the car and drove home.

~ ~ ~

Later, as they got ready for bed, Callie questioned Louisa about Roger. "How come, Louisa?" she asked.

"Why not, Callie? When I talked to Jim yesterday he just looked at me, didn't try to stop me from leaving. I thought he'd come after me, but, no, he just sat there. He offered me no explanation whatsoever."

"I'm sorry, Louisa. You were so sure."

"I'm still sure. So, I've just turned the whole thing over to God like I should have done a long time ago. I've asked Him to work things out according to His plans."

"God doesn't need our permission. He always does a pretty good job of straightening out our puzzles."

"I know. I pray that He does so in a hurry this time. My patience is growing thin, and Jim needs help."

Chapter 29

February 23, 1930

Dear Emmajean,

I know you're surprised to hear from me, but I did promise I'd write. Sorry it took me so long. How's school? Hope you're doing well in your lessons. Hope you like school. You stay in school and study real hard. You need to stay there at home as long as you can and you won't have so many worries. The world off the farm is different. Out here sometimes things don't go like you hope they would. So, Squirt, you stay in school and learn. Stay there on the farm where you'll be happy, with people who love you. Momma knows what's best for you so you be sure to mind her. She won't give you bad advice. You stay as good as you are pretty and you'll marry a fine man someday who will take care of you. Tell everybody hello for me. Be good.

Love,

Your big brother, Jim

Chapter 30

Dogwood trees around the courthouse square began to bud, but Jim still had winter in his soul. Caroline had been gone over three months now and still she hadn't written. And Louisa . . . well, Jim kept seeing her with Roger around the mill and at the boardinghouse. Although Jim had chosen Louisa in his mind that fateful day in February, the fact that Caroline had walked out of his life without even a good-bye rankled at his insides.

The higher Jim's frustrations, the smaller the room he shared with Arthur seemed. These best friends had moved easily into their living arrangement last summer but now the cordiality of their friendship had begun crumbling.

Their half-and-half arrangement with the dresser and chifforobe vanished in the face of Jim's growing selfishness. He appeared as if he *tried* to make Arthur give up and move out. Arthur sensed the changes in Jim but didn't know quite what to do about it.

~ ~ ~

Jim and Arthur dressed for work. "Callaway, I need your part on the April car payment."

"Don't have it."

"But it's due on Monday."

"Bones, I can't help you, not today."

"Well, when can you? By Monday?"

"Maybe . . . I'm pretty stretched out. I'll see."

"Jim, *I'll see* won't work this time. We pay by Monday or they'll come get the car." Arthur finished tying his shoes and stood to face Jim. "What's the matter, Buddy? Where's all your money goin'?"

A spasm of irritation crossed Jim's face. "What does it matter to you what I do with my money? I earn it, I spend it!"

Surprised again at this *new* Jim, Arthur stood his ground in silence.

"Here and there, Bones. My money goes here and there." He gave Arthur a dark, smoldering look. "I'm still paying on Caroline's Christmas present and I got me a credit account over at

Montgomery's Dry Goods. How'd you think I got these proper clothes for my new job? By the time I pay my board to Mrs. Hall, I'm spent out."

"Well, you're not spendin' anything on Louisa, that's for sure. You haven't gone by Miss June's in weeks. You tell me you're too busy, but I can see you're not. You're crazy about that girl and now you won't go near her."

"She's not missing me. Roger, from the mill, sees to that. He's always hanging around Louisa."

"How would you know that?"

"I know, Bones. I see them at work." Jim didn't mention that he stood up the street from the boardinghouse every Saturday when Roger picked up Louisa.

"Are you throwin' your money away on other women?" Arthur hesitated before asking his next question, but for Jim's own benefit, he asked anyway. "Jim, are you wastin' your money on liquor, like your poppa?"

Arthur hit a nerve with that and Jim turned toward him, hands balled into fists at his sides. His lips curled in disgust and anger's fire flamed in his dark eyes. "Don't you ever compare me with Poppa again!"

Jim jerked his coat from the chifforobe and pulled it on.

"Well, if you're not drinkin' up your money like John Lee Callaway, then give me your part of the car payment!"

"I'd rather be dead as be like Poppa," he spit out at Arthur. "I'm dating some, Bones, and that takes money," Jim lied.

He reached to open the bedroom door to leave for work.

"Jim, I mean it about the money. Get me your part by Monday. You hear? Monday!"

Jim slammed the bedroom door shut behind him and stomped down the stairs.

Bones stared at the door. *Lord, what's happenin' to my friend? Please reach down and rescue him from his selfish ways. He's followin' after the wrong things. Bring him back to You, Lord.*

~ ~ ~

When Jim had finished supper the next evening, Arthur had already left for Miss June's and his date with Callie. He hadn't mentioned the car payment again, but the matter hung heavy over Jim's head.

Alone, Jim paced his room and the floorboards squeaked with every step. He pondered the mess he'd made of everything.

He did have a job though, and a good one. He hadn't even been busy anymore since last month's purchase orders had dropped off. Yes, he had a job, even if he did come by it by lying about his age. And even if his promotion did come at Caroline's urging.

The room closed in on him, and Jim made his way downstairs and outside for a breath of fresh air. He found his landlady idly gliding back and forth on the front porch swing. The sweet perfume of honeysuckle climbing along the trellis behind her swing filled the night.

"Join me, Jim. I got out of the hot kitchen for a spell. Enjoying this first hint of spring in the air."

Jim walked across the porch and leaned his hands against the railing, looking out across the yard and toward the street as dusk approached.

"The first lightning bugs of the season have arrived. Look at them floating over the yard with their soft yellow blinking."

Jim remained silent, continued to face the yard. The shrill night song of katydids filled the early evening air. Across the street the Williams boy pushed his lawn mower toward their open garage, clickedly-click. The strong smell of freshly cut grass mingled with that of the sweet honeysuckle.

"Jim, what's bothering you?"

He turned around to face her. "How do you and my momma always know when I'm troubled?"

"When you draw those heavy eyebrows together, I know something's brewing with you and it's almost always bad."

"Well, you're right, and this time it's about as bad as it can get."

"Suppose you tell me, Jim. We've got some catching up to do. I've been missing our talks in my kitchen for a good while. Tell me. Then I'll decide how bad it is."

Jim knew that her concern for him was genuine. He realized then that he'd shut her out of his life too, along with others who cared for him.

He sat down beside her on the porch swing and began. He told her all about Caroline's leaving with no word. About Louisa being so distant to him now. That he hadn't visited his family since Christmas and admitted that it all was his fault alone. His best friend even tried to stay out of his way lately. And, on top of everything else, where was he going to get up enough money by Monday to pay on the car?

"And you're past due on your room and board too," Gertrude reminded him, her laughter deepening her crow's feet

"I know, I'm sorry. You going to kick me out?"

"If it would help you come to your senses, I might. Instead, I'm going to treat you like I'd want you to treat me if I was on hard times. Although it seems you've brought all your troubles on yourself. I'll loan you money for your car payment."

"I'm much obliged, Mrs. Hall." He turned on the swing to face her. "I'll pay you as soon as I can get straightened out."

"Seems to me you need a little help there, Jim."

"I'd appreciate all the help you can give me."

"Not help from me. You need a stronger source of help than what I can give you."

Jim left the swing and resumed his pacing across the porch.

Gertrude patted the swing beside her. "Jim, come on back and sit down. Hear me out. Sounds like you've tried just about everything else. Now listen to my suggestions."

He joined her on the swing again and looked out toward the street. Maybe another dressing-down from Mrs. Hall would help.

"Jim, you came through my front door about a year ago carrying your belongings and your dreams in a burlap sack. I was mighty pleased to have such a nice young Christian boy move into my house. You still minded your mother's good raising and prayed some fine blessings at the table. Past eighteen you are now, nearly a man by all rights."

At that Jim allowed a smile to cross his face in spite of all that bothered him.

Gertrude continued. "But, Jim, you've mixed up everything around you. To get what you wanted you've swapped your honesty for deceit. You've been careless with the affections of those who care for you. You've separated yourself from all that ever mattered to you and exchanged it for the lure of empty success. You've chased after success as the world claims it to be." When Jim moved to leave the swing again, she laid a gentle hand on his arm.

"Jim, like trying to push a chain, you have made a jumbled mess of your newly gained *success* and it's all caught up with you. It appears to me you've left your first love. Oh, you went to church with me a few times. But now you've strayed from God and His ways. Deep in your heart you know what pleases God. And that should be the first thing on your mind, pleasing God. When you do that then all these other things will fall into their proper place—your family, your girlfriends, even your money problems. You don't give God His part of your paycheck. Maybe that's why your money won't do for you what you want it to do."

Familiar words rang loud in Jim's soul as clear as the courthouse clock striking the hours: *But seek ye first the kingdom of*

God, and his righteousness; and all these things shall be added to you.

"Your circumstances are heavy on you, Jim," Gertrude continued. "Now, God may not change things the way you want Him to. He will be with you, though, in your circumstances and give you His grace to help you get through them.

"With God's help you can work on making some of these things right. He can help you let go of what you can't change. God's right there at your heart's door waiting for you to invite Him back in. He didn't leave you, you're the one who went away. It's past time you came back." Gertrude spoke from her unsinkable spirit.

"I don't know, Mrs. Hall. You make it sound so easy. It's not easy to solve my problems."

"You think about it, Jim. Pray about it. I'll be praying for you too."

~ ~ ~

When Gertrude stepped into her foyer the next morning on her way to church, Jim and Arthur stood at the top of the stairs outside their bedroom door. Broad smiles stretched across their faces.

Arthur had attended church every Sunday with her since last summer, but Jim's presence on this Sunday morning surprised her. Her face beamed when Jim bounded down the stairs dressed in his new suit Caroline had bought him last Christmas.

"Did I get my necktie right?"

Gertrude adjusted his necktie. "My, don't you boys look nice."

"I didn't sleep much last night, thinking about our talk. I figured if I was going to get back in good standing with God, the best place to start might be in His church house."

He bent his elbow and offered his arm toward her. "Can I escort you, ma'am?"

"It will be my pleasure, sir." She took his arm and Arthur's too. Down the porch steps the three of them went, arms linked: the tall, lanky boy on her left confident in the Lord, the muscular handsome young man on her right in search of solutions, and their motherly landlady, thanking God for answered prayers.

~ ~ ~

The sermon picked up where Gertrude Hall had left off the evening before. How could the preacher know he'd be here? He could listen to Mrs. Hall when she tried to help with her thoughts but he wouldn't have come to church if he'd known the sermon was the same.

A soft, clear voice echoed in Jim's mind: *I knew you would be here. He that hath ears to hear, let him hear.*

Jim listened to the message, his eyes riveted toward the pulpit and his heart receptive. The preacher read aloud from the Bible: *Remember therefore from whence thou art fallen.*

"You who have received Christ in your heart," the preacher spoke to the congregation, "you were on a mountaintop high with the joy of your new salvation. The Bible calls on those who have strayed away from God to remember how high on that mountain you reached before you fell back into your sinful way of living. Back then at first you took time to talk with God and obeyed His Word. At first you let Him direct your ways and have control of your life. What controls your life today?"

It was hard for Jim to think about giving up his new independence, of turning over control of his life. He wasn't ready yet.

Chapter 31

Leaving the mill office the next afternoon, Jim looked again back toward the parking lot next to the loading dock. Every day when he left work, his longing for Caroline compelled him to look that way. He imagined Caroline's little sedan waiting there, her running across the parking lot to embrace him. But she was never there. No word from her. Mr. Jacob never mentioned her name.

He looked away and started for his own car. Then he looked again and thought he recognized the figure coming his way. Yes, it was Poppa.

"Jim," John Lee reached for Jim's hand.

"Poppa." Jim shook his poppa's hand. "What're you doing here on a Monday? What's wrong at the farm?"

"Nothin' is wrong." He jerked his head back toward the dock. "I was watchin' for you to come out over there. You don't look like you're wearin' clothes for loadin' work. How come you came out up at the front?"

"I've got a promotion since I was home. I'm Receiving Manager. I handle the paper work on all the production orders. I work up front here now." Jim motioned toward the front of the mill.

Now that the small talk was out of the way, an awkward silence settled between them.

"Jim," John Lee ventured, "I need to talk to you. I kept waitin' for you to come back around the house. You didn't and, well, I've come to you. Where can we light a spell and talk?"

Jim led his poppa back inside the mill to the deserted lunchroom. They sat across from one another at a scuffed up table. John Lee scooted the half-filled glass salt and pepper shakers around on the tabletop, his eyes not meeting Jim's.

"Jim," his poppa began, at last facing Jim. "I've always loved you and the whole family. Now I'm a changed man and I wanted you to know. I've found Jesus and I've turned my life around."

Jim looked at John Lee in disbelief. Could Poppa be changed?

"It's the truth." John Lee couldn't keep from smiling. "Orrin helped me understand God's Word and His redemption for me. I've turned my life around," he repeated.

"Poppa . . ."

"No, let me finish. You and your momma have known Jesus for a long time. I was bitter and stubborn. Now I've seen the Light and I'm tryin' to do what's right in the eyes of the Lord."

John Lee pulled his ever-present crumpled handkerchief from a back pocket and dabbed at his eyes. "Son, I wronged you more times than I want to recollect. God has forgiven me for that and for all my sins. I need your forgiveness too. I've come to ask you to forgive me."

Could Jim forgive him? For the way he'd treated him? And the kids, and Momma? He called him Son. Who was this mild-mannered stranger?

"Will you forgive me, Son?"

A soft voice whispered to Jim: *Even as Christ forgave you, so also do ye.*

"Will you, Jim?"

Jim sensed God's words in his heart. *Forgive, and ye shall be forgiven.*

"Jim? Son?"

Jim couldn't wrap his mind around his poppa's words.

"Jim? Son?" John Lee repeated.

Jim struggled to escape the fog this conversation had put him into.

"Jim? Son?"

But if you forgive not men their trespasses, neither will your father forgive your trespasses.

Jim had trouble seeing through the blur of moisture in his eyes. He didn't remember standing or even walking around the table. While his poppa held him close, Jim heard the wrenching sobs of release pour from John Lee.

"Yes, Poppa, I forgive you."

"Thanks be to God! I love you, Son."

After John Lee shared some more with his boy and talked about the rest of the family, he left Jim at the mill and returned to the farm. But not before Jim promised to come soon for a visit.

~ ~ ~

Unsettled by John Lee's visit at the hosiery mill, Jim fought his nerves at the supper table. Each time he glanced toward Gertrude seated at the head of the long table, her eyes held hints of their earlier conversation on the front porch. He figured if he ate or if he didn't eat at all, either way he would be sick to his stomach. He couldn't keep his mind on the table's conversations, and soon made his way upstairs to his room.

Jim walked past Arthur and Gertrude, his face a study of desolation and his eyes haunted by pain. God was working on him, had been working on him since he and Gertrude talked on the porch the day before yesterday. Jim would have a hard time staying put until he settled things with the Lord.

Once in his room, Jim was drawn to the dresser where he pulled open the top drawer. He withdrew his Bible from underneath scattered underwear where it had lain untouched for a year now. He let the pages fan across his fingers.

What did that preacher say yesterday? . . . hear from God through Scripture. He fanned the pages again.

"Let me hear from you, God." Jim spoke out loud. "My life's miserable. It's all a mess. What do you want me to do? Help me, God!"

The Word came to Jim, stirring his spirit: *If my people, which are called by my name, shall humble themselves, and pray, and seek my face, and turn from their wicked ways; then will I hear from heaven, and will forgive their sin.*

Jim took his Bible to the desk and collapsed onto the chair, putting his face into his hands. His muffled cries went up to God. He smeared the tears across his cheeks with the backs of his hands and again started reading from the pages of his Bible.

Thou shalt have no other gods before me.

Remember the sabbath day, to keep it holy.

Honour thy father and thy mother.

"I'm real sorry . . . all the lives I've torn apart . . . I didn't put You first . . . I forgot Your commandments . . . I broke them all," Jim looked up as he called out.

He turned more pages and his eyes found the revealing Scripture: *But this shall be the covenant that I will make . . . saith the Lord, I will put my law in their inward parts, and write it in their hearts; and will be their God, and they shall be my people.*

Jim put his face down on the open Bible and continued to call out. "Oh, God, you wrote Your Word in my heart. I've buried it deep behind my selfishness. I was bound to do things my way, the wrong way. Forgive me, give me another chance. Take control of my life right now. You are my first love, please let me come back to You."

Jim raised his head and looked toward heaven. "Can You hear me, God?"

Just then, Arthur, who had finished supper and climbed the stairs, opened the door to their room and heard Jim crying out to God.

"God, people who loved me tried to help but I wouldn't listen. I was having too good a time. I filled every day with my own selfish ways, ignoring all your warning signs. Why change when I was having so much fun! But, Lord, today everything that's been fun doesn't make me laugh anymore. I want to renew my life, bring it in line with Your purposes. Please restore my soul! I can't do this alone. Please forgive me for being so stubborn. Thank You for loving me enough to lift me up and hold my hand as I start my way back.

"Will you take me back, Lord? Let me be Your servant and You be my King. Will You please come back to Your rightful place in my heart? Please forgive me! Have mercy on me!"

~ ~ ~

Arthur eased the door closed and rushed back downstairs, into the kitchen. "Mrs. Hall, Jim's praying! He's crying out for forgiveness."

"Praise the Lord!! An answer to all our prayers! Let's pray right now, Arthur."

They bowed their heads there in the kitchen amid the dirty dishes and leftovers and Gertrude prayed out loud. "*Our Gracious God, we praise Your faithfulness,*" Gertrude prayed. "*Thank You now for working in the life of our friend, Jim. He stands at another crossroad, needing Your guidance. Let him know that You will forgive him of all of his shortcomings. Draw near to him, God. Help him love others with Your unselfish love. I pray that You will finish the good work You started in Your child, Jim. Amen.*"

~ ~ ~

Again, a soft whisper filled Jim's mind: *Humble yourselves in the sight of the Lord, and he shall lift you up.*

"I'm humble, Lord. I want to return to Your presence. I want You back in my life."

Draw nigh to God, and He will draw nigh to you.

"Here I am, God."

Submit yourselves therefore to God.

Choose you this day whom ye will serve.

"I'm Yours, God . . . my life . . . my all . . . take control as You will."

~ ~ ~

Jim bounded into the kitchen, energized, invigorated. The joy and peace of the Lord spread across his face.

"I've come back home."

They understood.

"Can you both ever forgive me for my selfish attitude, my–"

He never got to finish because Gertrude pulled him against her ample body in a hug of love and thanksgiving. Arthur clapped him on the back over and over again.

Chapter 32

When Miss June came to tell her she had a visitor, Louisa wondered who it could be on a Monday evening. Her sister sat with her in their room or she would have worried Miss June had bad news about Callie. When Louisa had walked half way down the stairs, she saw Jim standing inside near the front door. As she approached, he shifted from one foot to the other with a smile on his face.

She laid a hand on his arm. "Jim, what are you doing here? It's almost eight o'clock and it's a work night."

"I couldn't wait till tomorrow." He looked around the foyer at the polished wall clock and the heavy-laden coat rack standing in the corner. "Can we go into the parlor? I want to talk private to you."

Seated on the stiff mohair-covered sofa, Jim reached for Louisa's hand but she held back. "Please." He reached again. She laid her hand in his and he covered it with his other hand.

He swallowed to push the lump back down his throat. "Louisa," he began, "you know you told me a while back about being careful what choices we make?"

Louisa nodded and he went on. "Well, I've made two very important choices I need to tell you about."

He told her about how the Lord had dealt with him over the last few days. Louisa sensed that God had answered her prayers and had led Jim back to a right relationship with Jesus. She reached out to him, placing her other hand on top of his.

Jim related how he had turned over control of his life to God and opened his heart to Him again. He told her about the change in his poppa. He told her he would be going to the farm Saturday to make things right with all of his family.

"And, now." Jim grinned from ear to ear. "Let me tell you about another choice I made. I've been stupid with love for you. I tried to slow up—you were so young—but ever since that night at the county fair, my love's been yours. I just went about it all wrong and got things all mixed up. Can you forgive me and give me another chance?"

When she started to speak, Jim held up his hand. "Not yet. Let me finish. With God's help now, I'm going to work on the mess I've made of everything. I'll love you for the rest of our lives. You *are* my life here on earth."

Louisa had waited so long to hear Jim say those words, she almost couldn't believe her ears. She pulled her hands away, clasping them beneath her chin as a tear rolled down her cheeks. She remained quiet in her joy.

At her silence, Jim's heavy brows knit together and confusion settled in his eyes. Not willing to give up this time, he gathered both of her hands back in his. "Have I waited too late, Louisa? Have you already started something serious with Roger?"

"Roger?"

Jim dropped his head. "Yeah, Roger, who works in the packaging room. I know about him." He searched her face again. "But, if you'll have me, I'll make everything up to you. I love you, Louisa!"

"Jim, my sweet, sweet Jim." She moved her hands up to hold his face. "There's nothing with Roger. You are my life too. I thank God for bringing you to me. Yes, of course I'll have you. I want you. I love you."

"Marry me, Louisa. I want you to be the mother of my children. Will you marry me?"

"Yes, Jim. Yes, yes. What took you so long to ask?"

Jim pulled her closer and kissed her forehead, mindful of her innocence. Then for the first time, he kissed her lips, careful to be gentle.

He drew back and looked into her blue eyes, the eyes that had captured him over a year ago. Jim's dark eyes that had been troubled so long now shone with love—love for his God and for Louisa.

~ ~ ~

Sixty miles north of Miss June's Boardinghouse, a new baby boy nuzzled his mother's breast. His tiny fingers closed around her thumb and his dark eyes tried to focus on her. Fingering the tiny garnet necklace hanging around her neck, Caroline looked down at her beautiful son. *Thank you, God, for this precious miracle.*

"Why was that doctor angry and shocked when I refused to give you away? My darling, you're looking at the only Mother you'll ever have. Your daddy's not here but with God's help, we'll do what we must do. We'll be fine, Baby. Yes, we will."

Chapter 33

The two o'clock wedding of Jim and Louisa highlighted spring activities for those who lived at Miss June's Boardinghouse and at Gertrude Hall's. It had been easy enough for the couple to get off work Friday afternoon. Work orders at the mill had slowed to a trickle. The simple ceremony took place in the judge's chambers at Sanford County courthouse. Arthur stood up for Jim and Callie for her baby sister

Jim's chin quivered with unconcealed emotion when he first saw Louisa. She wore a white satiny sheath dress that fell a little below her knees and with both hands at her waist she held a small nosegay of yellow buttercups resting against a circle of white lacy paper. Finger waves flowed from a side part in her blond hair and lay free beside her face. Jim wore his suit, striped tie, and white shirt—the clothes Caroline had bought him to wear last Christmas to her parents' party. Today Jim didn't remember that night.

Aaron and Mavis Johnson had brought their buggy into town and had signed permission papers for his daughter to be married since she was underage at only sixteen. Jim was pleased to see that Aaron wore his best to the wedding and minded his good manners that Louisa had been helping him with.

Jim and Louisa listened closely when the judge read the vows. They repeated them in a confident, loud voice without much faltering. As he held Louisa's hand, he sensed her raw emotions getting the better of her. He squeezed her hand and smiled encouragement down at her. After being nervous at the beginning of the ceremony, he soon forgot anybody was in the room with them. Jim remembered that they both had traversed some rough spots to get where they were today. This was important to them and Jim took the wedding vows as serious and meant what he said.

After the wedding, families and friends made their way to Mrs. Hall's house for Jim and Louisa. She loved Jim Callaway and embraced his new bride with equal love.

The long dining room table, covered with Gertrude's finest lace tablecloth, displayed every imaginable finger food. A large round punch bowl balanced each end of the table. The number of friends and family, congenial all around, watched the young married couple.

Jim couldn't stop grinning and never left Louisa's side until late in the afternoon. At last, Jim followed Louisa to the foot of the stairs and watched her go up to his room. When Louisa returned downstairs she had changed into a casual dress of pink floral print and more comfortable shoes. Jim took the stairs two at a time to his room to get out of his suit. Jim soon returned, dressed in a pair of laundered and pressed denim pants, the collar of his dress shirt loosened. He carried their two suitcases. Arthur took the suitcases from him and hurried to put them in the car.

The small crowd became silent, expectant. Mrs. Hall herded them all to the front yard. Mavis whispered to Louisa, telling her about throwing her bouquet. Louisa and Jim stood on the top porch step. Louisa aimed her throw toward Callie who caught the flowers and right away looked toward Arthur. The boys clapped Arthur on the back, kidding that he was next.

Jim couldn't be too upset when he noticed rusted tin cans tied to the back bumper of the car. At least they hadn't dirtied it up. Yesterday Jim had cleaned their Ford Model A until he could just about see himself in its shiny red surface. He'd taken the car over to the Texaco filling station and told the boys there to give it the works: fill up the gas tank, check the oil and water, and make sure the tires had enough air pressure. He'd saved money from his last few weeks' paychecks to buy gas and have some spending money for the honeymoon he and Louisa would have. He wanted the trip to be the best she'd ever had, something she would remember for the rest of her life.

The young couple climbed into the Ford for a weekend trip to the Great Smoky Mountains, near Knoxville. They neither one had been that far from home and looked forward to the outing, pushing their apprehensions aside. They both wondered where their future would take them, certain all their days would be good and all their dreams of a happy life together would be fulfilled.

Settled in the car, Jim inserted the key and pressed the starter button. While the V4 warmed up, he looked over at Louisa with tenderness in his heart. She returned his glance with all her love showing in her eyes. They drove away from Mrs. Hall's, not noticing the hoots and shouts from the folks standing in the front yard or the clanking of the tin cans trailing behind them.

Chapter 34

On their drive to Gatlinburg Louisa bounced around on the passenger side of the car seat, looking this way and that. The trip also had Jim keyed up but he had to keep his eye on the road and his mind on his driving.

"Jim, how long will it take us to get there?"

"I'd guess less than three hours, I hope. We should get there before dark."

"Where will we stay?" She blushed as soon as she realized what her question inferred.

"I don't know. But Martin Roberts at work told me we wouldn't have any trouble finding a place with a vacancy. There aren't too many places to rent but not many folks visit there."

They rode on, staying on Highway 411. They left Monroe County and crossed over into Blount County, passing the county seat of Maryville. From there Jim turned onto Highway 321. As he drove through Walland and then Townsend, lush mountains sprang up on both sides of the road. The air cooled the farther they drove. Entering Sevier County, they passed the huge, square courthouse in the middle of the little town.

When he passed through Pigeon Forge, Gatlinburg was near, witnessed by roadside signs advertising businesses and some lodging places.

"Jim, there!" Louisa pointed to a sign. "That sounds like a nice place we could stop and stay for the weekend."

"What's the name of it?"

"I didn't catch it all. Maybe we'll see another sign up the road."

And they did. Miss McCauley's Boardinghouse. "The sign says they have five guest rooms, each with its own bathroom." This intimate talk caused Louisa to blush again and duck her chin. But although they were married now and could talk of such things, it would take some getting used to.

They found Miss McCauley's right away, nestled on a wooded hillside two blocks off the main street that slashed through

Gatlinburg. Jim pulled the car into the parking lot and Louisa spotted the *vacancy* sign hanging beside the door. While Jim stepped out of the car to go find the office and ask about a room, Louisa took in the surroundings. The lodge, a plain, brown shingled rectangle teeming with a splash of eight single hung shutterless windows facing the street, rose three stories above the car. The hillside appeared to hug the building to itself to prevent it sliding down the hill. Jim vaulted a dozen or more broad rock steps, taking them two at a time to reach the office.

Within minutes Jim returned to the car smiling and nodding his head. He leaned into the car window. "We got us a room," and dangled the key in front of her.

As Louisa gathered her things to get out of the car, Jim lifted their suitcases out and met her in front of the car. They climbed the same steps Jim had just travelled, reaching the office area. Miss McCauley, skinny and angular, sat perched on a high stool behind a polished counter. She gave them a broad smile. After her years of running the boardinghouse she could recognize newlyweds with no trouble.

"I've put you two in Room Three on the upper level. You'll have a pretty view of the Little Pigeon River," Miss McCauley chirped. "The stairs are around the corner there," she pointed to her right.

Jim and Louisa both mumbled a thank you.

"Have you had supper?"

"Yes, ma'am, we stopped in Pigeon Forge for a bite."

"Well, I only serve breakfast here but plenty of little eating places are on the main street in town. You won't have any trouble finding something to eat tomorrow. And everything's in easy walking distance."

"Thank you," They both spoke in unison.

"Now, in the mornings I serve breakfast from eight-thirty to ten o'clock. Come hungry because we start off with fresh fruit, warm bread, coffee, and juice. Then I serve biscuits and sausage gravy, cinnamon-apple pancakes or French toast. I always have country-fried potatoes, eggs to order, and sausage. Like I said, come hungry, but everybody leaves the table full."

They stood in front of her counter, Jim still holding their luggage, which wasn't too heavy, but he was anxious to escape Miss McCauley. She loved to talk as much as Mrs. Hall.

"Well, you two run along. You've got everything up there you need, but if you think of anything else, just hop on down here and ask."

They climbed the two flights of stairs, almost giggling, relieved to get away. Jim unlocked the tall door and set the suitcases just inside. He turned with a grin at Louisa and swept her up in his arms and walked into the room.

"Oh, Jim, what are you doing?" She put her left hand around his neck.

"I am carrying my wife over the threshold. You know like they do in the moving picture shows."

He reached back and pushed the door shut with his foot but continued holding Louisa in his arms. Their faces were close, their breath mingling. Louisa touched his cheek with her free hand then pulled his head toward her until her lips found his.

"Wow, where did that come from?"

Her eyebrows reached toward her hairline and she gave him a comical look. "Same place you carrying me over the threshold, I guess."

They both laughed, releasing the tension in the air.

"Oh, Jim, I do love you."

He let her legs ease from his hold until they touched the polished hardwood floor then wrapped both arms around her, pulling her close. Their kiss this time was longer, deeper and when they drew back to look at each other their wide smiles returned. At that moment they had no doubts their future would be a *happily ever after* one.

~ ~ ~

The next morning Louisa woke rested and relaxed. She yawned, stretching her arms above her head in the mahogany four poster bed. She smiled, remembering the night before and looked beside her at her gorgeous husband. *Husband!* She heard the rushing river in the distance and smelled biscuits baking and coffee brewing drifting up from downstairs. Jim lay facing away from her. She turned toward him and dared to scoot closer. She softly laid her arm over his waist and moved nearer. How could she ever be this bold?

Jim breathed with a slight snore, which stopped when her body touched his. He stirred awake, took her hand that was around him and brought it to his lips. Turning onto his back, he kept her hand and pulled her even closer. They couldn't curb their delightful smiles, the same ones they had drifted into sleep with.

Louisa tapped the end of his nose. "Good morning, sleepyhead."

"Good morning. How long you been awake?"

"Not long. I just enjoyed looking at you."

"Not fair. I'll be sure to wake first tomorrow."

"Are you ready for breakfast? I smell the coffee and I'm sure Miss McCauley won't save anything for us after ten o'clock." She threw back the covers, stood on her side of the bed and padded in bare feet to the bathroom.

Later they dressed, trying to give the other a little privacy in the big bedroom. As they started down the stairs they noticed the quiet. No cars travelled past the lodge and just one other room was occupied. When Jim and Louisa entered the dining room, the other couple that had stayed the night before already had their breakfast before them. They looked up and smiled. Miss McCauley was topping off their coffee cups and talking like she hadn't paused since last evening.

"Sit anywhere you want, folks. Over here by the windows you can see a little bit of the river."

Jim and Louisa sat at a square table covered in a rose colored tablecloth laid with matching linen napkins. Those eight windows Louisa had seen last evening from the car now stretched across the long side of the dining room, morning sun exploding through them.

"These folks here are the Wilsons. And these young people are the Callaways. Newlyweds." Miss McCauley didn't notice the uncomfortable color on both their faces.

Mr. Wilson spoke first. "Good morning, there. How long are you staying in Gatlinburg?"

And the two couples and Miss McCauley chatted throughout breakfast. Excitement crackled in the air as the Wilsons spoke of exploring the mountains above Gatlinburg. Talk turned to discussion about the mountains becoming the Smoky Mountain National Park.

~ ~ ~

After breakfast at Miss McCauley's, Jim and Louisa walked down the inclined street two blocks toward town. Holding hands, they inhaled the cool, clear air. Having grown up in the foothills of their Southern Appalachians, the majesty of God's nature in the Smoky Mountains didn't surprise them. Except here they were much closer to the hazy mountains, Gatlinburg sitting in a flat area hemmed in on all sides by high ridges. They walked by a few small craft shops, looking in the windows at the local artistry. They took their time meandering along the sidewalk the length of the small downtown area. When they crossed the street to explore the shops on the opposite side of the street, the noise from the river grew louder.

Jim led Louisa across a large undeveloped area between buildings and walked toward the sound of moving water to find the Little Pigeon River. They walked onto an arched wooden footbridge across the river and stood at midpoint looking down at the moving currents, their noise the only thing interrupting the quiet of this peaceful place. Later, Jim and Louisa bought hot dogs and soft drinks from a walk-up window alongside the sidewalk in town and returned to the little bridge to sit and have their lunch, dangling their legs over the edge.

Being used to hard work at their homes and then at the mill, Louisa and Jim enjoyed this chance for idleness. As they ate, they exchanged glances, those perpetual smiles lighting up their faces. Jim reached toward her chin.

"What?" Louisa moved out of his reach.

Jim laughed. "Hold still. You've got mustard on your chin." He dabbed it away with his paper napkin then continued looking at her, growing quiet.

"What are you thinking about?"

Jim continued looking at her another minute. "You. You and me."

"What about you and me?"

"How lucky I am that you and God took me back."

"Jim, you came back to us. We were both just waiting."

"Yeah, I'm sorry it took me so long to come to my senses."

Louisa laid her head against his arm for a moment then sat up, looking at Jim. "I'm the lucky one because you did come back. I'm so happy we're at last together. I love you, Jim."

"I love you, Louisa. I told you that you're my life here on earth and I mean it. I'm going to make a proper living for us and give you a good life. I promise." He reached around her shoulders and pulled her close.

The newlyweds lazed away the day drinking in one another, desire shining in their eyes. They found a small café where they ate supper then returned to the lodge. They spent some time with Miss McCauley in the rustic common room with its knotty pine walls, open beam ceiling and wood burning fireplace. Soon they called it an early evening and started up the stairs to their room.

The next morning it was Jim who woke first. He turned toward his sleeping wife and bent his elbow to prop his head on his left hand. He soaked in her beauty, her goodness, again thanking God for bringing Louisa to him. A gentle breeze of cool mountain air pushed in through the open window and across the bed. Louisa shifted, opened her luminous blue eyes that had captured him over a year ago and discovered Jim staring down at her. She smiled and moistened her lips. They bumped heads and laughed as they snuggled down deeper beneath the covers.

After another of Miss McCauley's fabulous breakfasts, Jim and Louisa left the lodge and drove down the hill and through Gatlinburg.

"Thank you for a glorious weekend, Jim"

"You're welcome. I plan to give you many more enjoyable things. We're going to grow old together and each day will be better than the one before."

Chapter 35

Jim parked at the curb in front of Mrs. Hall's and he and Louisa gathered their things from the car. By the time they started up the short sidewalk, Mrs. Hall pushed open the screen door and met them on the front porch with open arms. She hugged them both.

"I've been watching for y'all. Did you have a good trip, Louisa? How was Gatlinburg?"

"Yes, ma'am, we did."

"Gatlinburg sure was nice."

They all went into the house and Jim started up the stairs with their luggage.

"No, no, Jim. I've fixed up one of my spare bedrooms down here for you two."

"Downstairs? What's wrong with my room upstairs? Didn't Bones get moved out?"

"I decided your pretty wife needed more privacy than being upstairs with all the other men boarders would afford her. She doesn't need to share a bathroom with a bunch of guys. Don't you agree, Louisa?"

"That sounds good, Mrs. Hall, but I can stay in Jim's room. Whatever you say, though. I appreciate you doing this."

"Well, okay. I'll get started moving my stuff down."

"Jim, I've had Arthur helping me. He has all your things already moved. Come on, you two, let's see how this room does for you."

Jim and Louisa shared a glance and followed Gertrude down the hall, passing the kitchen on the left and to a door on the right. The bathroom stood between her bedroom and theirs. Sure enough, there were Jim's things laid out on the dresser and as he set down their suitcases he noticed his clothes hanging in the chifforobe.

"I'll have to thank Bones for all this. Is there anything else I can do, Mrs. Hall?"

"No, Jim, I think not. I believe everything is taken care of.

Well, I'll let y'all get settled. Bless your hearts, I'm sure glad you're back safe and sound."

~ ~ ~

After supper, Louisa and Jim drove over to Miss June's Boardinghouse with Arthur to visit Callie. They found Callie waiting in the April sunshine on the porch steps. The sisters hugged each other with all their might, squealing with delight. Callie and Arthur fired off questions about their trip and Jim and Louisa were glad for the chance to talk about their weekend. When they described the lodge where they'd stayed and the river and crafts shops, Arthur and Callie kept sharing timid glances. Then Jim figured it out.

"What's up with you two? It's almost like you have a secret and you want us to guess what it is."

Arthur put his arm across Callie's shoulders and tugged her close beside him on the porch swing.

"Callie said yes . . . I asked her to marry me and she said yes." Arthur's voice held thick excitement and his eyes sparkled as he spoke.

Jim let out a whoop, jumped up from the porch steps to pump Arthur's hand and patted him on the back. Callie rose from the swing to meet Louisa in another hug, this one filled with as much fervor as their first one minutes ago.

"You *did* catch my bouquet after the reception Friday. I guess it's true that whoever catches it will be the first one to marry next."

"When, Bones?"

"When, what?"

"You know, when are you getting married? Have you set a date yet?"

"We would have done it yesterday, but we wanted to wait for you both to be there with us when we get married." Callie paused a second. "It wouldn't seem right if you weren't."

Arthur jumped into the conversation with a goofy grin on his slim face. "So, we think maybe next Friday or Saturday. We haven't told our folks yet, but we'll get word to them before next weekend."

"We thought we might go to Gatlinburg after we're married too," Callie added. "Tell us more about where y'all stayed and what all y'all did there."

Jim saw that the double meaning of her words caused a heat of blush to creep across the girls' faces. The boys looked at their shoes.

"We'll tell you all about the place," Jim offered. "And where we stayed . . . you can tell Miss McCauley we sent you."

And so, the following Friday, Louisa's sister and Jim's best friend married in the courthouse and Gertrude outdid herself again with a nice reception. As the couple drove away, the same crowd as last week waved them good-bye.

"Well, Jim, I guess you'll have to help me move Arthur's things. I've got one more spare bedroom downstairs and I suppose that will be their new home when they get back. This marrying thing sure was highly contagious."

"Yes ma'am, looks like it was. I'd say it's the best thing Arthur and I have ever done to get these two Johnson girls to promise to put up with us." Jim pulled Louisa to his side.

Chapter 36

"What did Daddy say?"

"Well." Aunt Martha hung up the telephone. "Your daddy's as obstinate as he ever was. He won't permit you to come home if you bring the baby. He insists that you give it up for adoption."

"Aunt Martha, I can't do that. I *won't* do that."

"Fred also said that the family name had better not be on that baby's birth certificate or be used as his last name—ever."

Silence rattled around the spacious living room and against the glass window lights on either side of the front door. The echo was deafening, each woman deep in thought. Caroline was fighting the tears that pooled in her eyes. She rocked the baby with more determination, as much to comfort herself as him.

"Caroline, I've been thinking about this. Now, please don't stop me until I'm finished. Because you're keeping your baby, your daddy has in essence disowned you and your child. He says he and your mother never want to see you again because you have brought shame on them. He won't permit your return to Newton under any circumstance."

The tears found their way down Caroline's cheeks. She brushed at them with her fingers before they could drip onto the baby's face.

"Now, the way it seems to me is you need a place to raise that sweet child. You're welcome to stay here with me—forever."

"Oh, Aunt Martha . . . "

She held up her hand, palm toward Caroline. "No, don't talk, please. Since your daddy is being so stubborn, and unfair I might add, you also need a new last name for yourself and your child. My husband has been dead for eight years so I don't have to ask for anybody's permission to give away my last name. My girls are married and have other names now. They would have no right to argue with me on this. If you want it, the name is yours. Your baby can be James Hensen and you can be Caroline Hensen. We can go to the Probate Judge and have the change made legal and have another birth certificate issued for James."

Martha rose from her wing chair, crossed the hardwood floor, and took James from Caroline who was overcome with emotion. She sobbed out loud, her shoulders shaking, as the covered her face with both hands. "Oh, Aunt Martha, why would you do this? Why would you be so kind to me? No one has ever been as good to me as you've been."

In the end when Caroline looked up through her tears of joy, she smiled at her aunt, who returned her smile. Caroline left her rocking chair and wrapped her arms around Martha, sandwiching little James between them.

Chapter 37

The following week after returning to the mill, Jim made fewer trips across the production floor to take papers to the loading dock. And when he did, he didn't hear the ear-shattering noise of the clanking machines as he was used to hearing. Workers stood around mumbling, worry etching their faces. Jim asked Ginger in the office how things seemed to be going for the mill but could get little information from her. He understood her necessity to be loyal to Mr. Jacob and not talk about the mill's business or lack of it.

After work each evening at home he learned from Louisa that she and Callie were gradually less busy at work. Not as much product came to them for sizing and boarding as usual. They sent fewer and fewer finished hosiery to the packaging room.

"Are you worried about the mill, Jim?"

"I've not been before but now I wonder. I see in the papers how bad off folks are around the country. More and more folks are without work and income and in the big cities unemployment is so bad they stand in line for food at soup kitchens. I didn't think this depression thing would get down to us here in Tennessee. You know, we don't depend on a lot of commerce coming out of the north. Well, not much anyway." Then second thoughts entered Jim's mind . . . the mill did depend on some materials being shipped in and any replacement machinery had to be ordered from up north.

"I know Callie and I haven't been as busy in the Boarding Room. It seems a little scary when I read those newspaper reports you're talking about."

"I reckon we'll just have to keep at it until we learn something more."

And three weeks after they'd returned from Gatlinburg they did learn something more. Callie and Louisa arrived at the car before Jim did on that Friday after work. Jim approached from the front of the building walking slower than usual. He got in the car, shut the door and sat still, looking out the windshield. At long last he turned toward Louisa beside him on the passenger seat and also glanced toward Callie sitting on the other side of Louisa, against the door. Who would speak first?

"Jim . . .?" Louisa said.

"Louisa. Callie."

Then they all three knew. They'd each received a lay-off notice when they'd clocked out of work today. In the same envelope containing their paycheck for the week. When would they receive another check? Three of the four close friends had no more money coming in. Just Arthur still had his job. Or so they hoped. They expressed none of this aloud. There was no need for explanation, they just knew.

They drove home in fearful silence. Jim parked in front of the house and they all three remained in the car. They just sat there. After a while, they forced themselves to get out and make their way toward the house. They could push themselves no farther than the front porch. The girls took the swing and Jim leaned against the porch railing, each deep in consuming thought.

Gertrude came through the front door. "Why are y'all so quiet? You didn't bound into the house with renewed energy just to be off from work."

Off from work. They all looked up in unison.

"What is it? You're scaring me. What's happened?"

"We got laid off. We just drew our last paycheck."

Gertrude went still. Her silence signaled to them how serious she deemed this news because not often did Gertrude get this quiet.

About that time Arthur walked up the street from the store and onto the porch. "Hey, everybody. What's goin' on?"

Jim explained again to Arthur what the day had brought them. Arthur went at once to stand beside the swing and took Callie's hand. What could he say?

Gertrude couldn't undo the bad news the young people had received and did the only thing she knew to do: pray. *Lord, please help these young people. They've received bad news today. Please work Your good will in their lives. Help us all to get through this. Amen.*

~ ~ ~

Into the next week, Jim saw that their combined paychecks from last Friday wouldn't last long. After they paid Gertrude their weekly rent and paid the lady who did their laundry, little remained. And that was only one week's expenses. What about all the weeks to follow?

Louisa and Jim sat on the porch swing contemplating their situation. Jim left the swing and walked back and forth across the porch.

"Louisa, I'm going to have to look for a job someplace even if I have to leave Newton."

"Jim, no." Louisa followed him to the other end of the porch and grabbed him by the sleeve. "Please, no. Please don't do that. I'd miss you awful bad. You don't want to do that, do you?"

"No, I don't. But, Louisa, *any* money would be good money when we don't have more coming in."

"Jim, please. I don't want to be separated from you. Are no jobs close around here?"

"Well, yeah, the state's doing some road work on four-eleven down toward Chattanooga. I hear that won't last very long, though. And I don't even know if I can get hired on there."

Louisa gripped Jim's shirt sleeve in her fist and clung to his arm as if doing so would prevent him leaving her. They had just begun their life together at last and being separated would be miserable. They looked at each other, willing the other to come up with a solution.

"If I had to work away from you it wouldn't be worth the trade-off. That's the truth, Louisa." He took her by the shoulders and turned her toward him. "But, look, if I can't find a job around here, I've got to do something."

Louisa laid her head on Jim's chest and he held her there. In a few minutes her body began to tremble as she cried, trying to smother her sobs against his shirt. This abrupt change in their *happily ever after* jolted them back into the abyss of reality.

"Louisa, I'll try to get on with the road crews on four-eleven. I'll leave at daybreak in the morning and go down toward Chattanooga to see what I can find out. Sshhh, now, it won't be too bad. Everything will get better before long."

~ ~ ~

The state hired Jim. He worked twelve-hour days, six days a week. It was hard work and it was hot work. Using pick and shovel, Jim and the work crews leveled ground to improve the shoulders at both sides of the highway. Next the dump trucks spilled rock gravel over where they'd leveled the shoulders. When the huge blackened trucks poured steaming asphalt on top of the gravel, the men had to monitor its movement to prevent it from overrunning it specified area. They used long handled brooms and some had straight blades with which to push the asphalt into its proper borders. Keeping the steaming asphalt on top of the gravel was a tedious, back-breaking job. Jim learned that if you made a mistake and stepped in the poured asphalt you might back away with a melted shoe sole. He caught on real fast how close you could come to the hot mixture.

Jim returned home exhausted and ate the plate of food Louisa had saved from supper, which helped to rejuvenate him. The first week of working on the road Jim came home excited with all he'd learned each day about working with asphalt concrete. He talked about each step of the work and how each layer wouldn't work if the one before wasn't done right. After supper he often fell asleep in their room while resting on the bed. Then Jim used their Sunday afternoons to make up for the lost week days together.

Arthur told them the hardware store was just hanging on but old Mr. Henderson wanted Arthur to stay around to help him. Mr. Henderson couldn't pay him as much as before but he did pay him some. He wanted to keep the store open, even selling on credit to the customers who had no cash to spend. Arthur said Mr. Henderson had no doubt saved every penny he'd made since he built the store and could stay open using his own money to pay his expenses. But once the store's inventory was depleted, would Mr. Henderson be able to replenish it? And what would happen then? Would Arthur also lose his job?

~ ~ ~

But everything didn't soon get better as Jim had told Louisa. The Depression lingered—banks closed, unemployment kept rising, soup lines in big cities grew longer. People sold their cars for $15 to those few who hadn't lost all their money. The country was in a long dark tunnel with no visible light at the other end.

But that marrying thing remained contagious: Despite the promise of hard times, Jim's sister Shirley Ann married Henry Frank soon after they finished high school in May, which was no surprise to anyone.

"Well, my sister and Henry Frank have been keeping company for three years and it was bound to happen. They went to live with Henry Frank's parents so that he could continue to help his folks work the farm."

Louisa thought about this new information. "Looks like that arrangement will work out well for them. Shirley Ann fits right in with his parents and they love her, approving of the marriage."

"Henry Frank's family, living on their own land and growing food for just their own table, the Depression hadn't hit as hard as it did those on jobs in town." Jim pulled his eyebrows together and continued. "But big-time farmers who sell their products to make a living have been hurt by the Depression because prices of farm goods have fallen to about half as much as they're worth."

Jim missed a fun-filled summer. Fred Jacob gave no July Fourth mill picnic.

Jim wasn't prepared for the harder blow that hit. And then another. That winter an outbreak of influenza spread across the mountains from lower North Carolina and down through the Southern Appalachians. Arthur and Jim accompanied Callie and Louisa up into Maple Hollow when they got word that their dad and stepmother had succumbed to the disease. Their deaths hit the girls hard. They were crazy about their dad.

"Now, now." Jim wrapped his arms around Louisa, trying to console her. "We just have to go on with this." Jim watched as Arthur tried to help Callie. The glow of being newly married dimmed in the wake of such a loss.

In just a few days Elizabeth and John Lee Callaway became sick. Shirley Ann told Arthur's sister at church and her mother had gone to check on them. Mrs. Gray tried to make her good friend and her husband comfortable and cooked meals for them but neither were well enough to eat. One morning when Mr. Gray brought his wife to the Callaways in the wagon, she found them worse and out of their head with fever. "Take the wagon on into town to get the doctor and Jim and bring them back," Mrs. Gray told her husband.

By that evening when Mr. Gray brought Jim and Louisa on his wagon from Newton and Dr. Blount following in his car, it was too late. Jim's momma and poppa had died soon after Mr. Gray had left for Newton that morning. Mrs. Gray had sent The Twins down to Maynard Junction to get someone to phone the funeral home. The undertaker had brought caskets, prepared the bodies and now they lay in the front room, against the wall where little Ollie had lain a year ago. Food already covered the dining room table and two ladies from church were busy in the kitchen. Shirley Ann and Emmajean stood close to Mrs. Gray crying, with tears streaking their faces. The Twins stood off to themselves showing no emotion.

When Jim and Louisa walked into the front room, all four children rushed to Jim. As tired as Jim was from work that day, he mustered a reserve of energy and tried to comfort them.

Emmajean cried, holding Jim around the waist.

Shirley Ann's cheeks were wet with shed tears. "It happened so quick, Jim. I didn't know they were that sick. You know how both of them worked so hard. I thought they were just tired and then they got awfully sick."

The Twins stood near and looked at the floor.

Jim stooped down, level with Emmajean. "Now, now, Squirt, please quit crying. Settle down, now." He pulled his baby sister into a fierce hug, which made her cry more.

"She's been that way since they . . . passed away. I can't get her to stop," Shirley Ann said.

"Let's go over here." Jim took Emmajean's hand in his and led her to a chair. He sat and pulled her onto his lap where she threw her arms around his neck and folded into his chest. "I'm here with you. You can quit crying now." He patted her back and smoothed her hair back from her face, smeared with tears. Her sobs began to subside and Jim looked toward Louisa. She sat down beside them.

"There, Emmajean, do you feel a little bit better? Would you like a drink of water?"

Emmajean nodded her head against Jim's chest, still clinging to his neck. Louisa started to get up to go get the water but Shirley Ann put her hand out. "You stay with her, I'll get the water."

Returning with water for Emmajean, Shirley Ann handed it to Jim who offered it to Emmajean. "Here you go, Squirt." Jim helped her with the glass.

Henry Frank came to stand behind Shirley Ann, putting a comforting hand on her shoulder. No one spoke. What could they say? The Callaway family had lost its foundation. What would they do now?

Chapter 38

Jim inherited the position as head of the Callaway family, a chilling job for an almost-twenty-year-old with his country in the midst of a frightful economic crisis. Even before the burial of their parents, Jim steered the Callaway children, Henry Frank and Louisa in planning for their immediate futures. "The Twins can live with me and Shirley Ann. On the farm they can help out and we can feed two more mouths better than you and Louisa can," Henry Frank offered.

"We will take Emmajean with us. She won't move two inches away from Jim."

So, early in their married life Shirley Ann and Henry Frank became *parents* to two twelve-year-olds and Jim and Louisa the same to a clinging ten-year-old girl.

"Henry Frank, reckon you and your daddy could use our two mules?"

"Yeah, I guess so. I'll see if he can give you a little money for them."

Shirley Ann grabbed Jim's arm. "This is about more than I can take." At the burial for their Momma and Poppa she and Emmajean wept aloud, even Robert and Richard shed a silent tear or two. As a reflex Jim moved through his duties as the oldest, trying to calm them all. The preacher said his last words over the Callaways at the gravesite, praying for God's comfort to help the family to get through this loss and to ease their burden.

As he watched the two caskets lowering into the ground, Jim heard his momma's words as clear as the day she said them to him after he'd moved to Newton: "God may not change your troublin' situations, but He will give you strength and guidance to get through them. He'll help you, but you must ask Him and have faith in His love for you." *God help me with Your strength and guidance to do what's before me. Amen.*

~ ~ ~

That evening after the funeral, Gertrude stood at her kitchen window and saw the doctor's car pull up to the curb in front of her house. She was relieved to see Jim and Louisa step out of the car, glad they had finished their unpleasant business at the Callaway place. Then she saw them turn back to the car and begin helping a child out of the car. They shut the car door and waved to Dr. Blount as he drove away. Curious to find out what this was about, Gertrude met them on the front porch.

"Well, hello there, little lady. What's your name?"

"Emmajean."

"Mrs. Hall, this is my baby sister. We brought her into town with us."

Gertrude noticed then that Jim carried a paper sack that looked like it might contain clothes for the child. "Well, bless your heart, I'm mighty proud you're visiting with us. Come on in the kitchen with me and we'll look for some fresh-baked sugar cookies."

Jim and Louisa followed them as Gertrude in her inimitable way made Emmajean feel at ease. Gertrude noticed the relief on Jim's face, as if some of his new heavy responsibilities had been lessened.

While Emmajean sat at the kitchen table and ate her cookies and drank her milk, the grown-ups stood by the window to talk. Gertrude learned of all the decisions the family had made while at the farm and that Jim would now be looking after his little sister. While they talked, Gertrude worked out something in her mind.

"Well, Jim, you can't take care of your sister in that one room you and Louisa have. We'll have to work out something better."

"I'm not sure how we'll get all this done, but she'll be fine in our room."

"No, I'll figure something out. Now, Emmajean, do you want more milk? Or cookies?"

Emmajean shook her head and yawned, her eyes heavy.

"Emmajean, come with me and we'll find a place for you to sleep." Louisa took the paper sack from Jim and she and Emmajean left the kitchen to go to their bedroom.

Jim started to follow when Gertrude called him back.

"You know, all my boarders left after that last big lay-off at the mill. All those rooms are empty upstairs now. Looks like we could make a better arrangement than we have now. Let me think on this tonight and we'll do some shifting around tomorrow. Jim, do you think the three of you can rest tonight in that one bed in your room?"

"My goodness yes, Mrs. Hall. I grew up sleeping three in a bed with my brothers. We'll make it tonight just fine. So, all the boarders got laid off?"

"Yes, they did. And they've all moved on, looking for other jobs. Everybody's having a hard time, Jim. The papers are blaming President Hoover for the mess everything's in and nobody sees it getting better anytime soon."

"That's what I hear."

"You look tired, Jim. You go on to your room now and watch after Emmajean and Louisa and get some rest. You've had a rough few days."

"Yes, ma'am, I have. I didn't get back to the farm much, but I'm sure going to miss Momma and Poppa. I'm going to have to hold on tight to the words Momma always told me about from The Good Book. I didn't always pay attention to what she said, but I know now she told me all those things for my own good. I'll need all the help God can give me now." Jim turned to leave the room. "Well, good night, Mrs. Hall."

"Good night, Jim."

Lord, you heard your child say he needed You. Please stay close to him in the coming days as he and Louisa work through the things thrust upon them. Watch over them and Emmajean too. Amen.

~ ~ ~

Everyone remained quiet at breakfast the next morning. Arthur, Callie, Jim, Louisa, and Emmajean remembered the funeral yesterday. Even Gertrude's eternal laughter was missing. She'd put a big breakfast on the table, but they all looked down at their plates, picking at the food.

"Well, you boys going to work today?"

"I'm taking one more day off," Jim glanced at Emmajean. "Try to take care of some things. How about you, Bones?"

"I'm goin' on down to the store after a while. Not that it will be busy, though."

"I've been thinking about things around here and I've come up with a suggestion."

That caught all their attention and they looked up with bated breath.

"If possible, you married people need some privacy and Emmajean here needs a room to herself." A broad smile spread across Emmajean's face. She'd never had a room all her own.

"I don't know about that, Mrs. Hall." Jim patted his sister's back when she looked up at him.

"Well, *I* know, and this is how I think it will work. Since all my boarders have left, and if Arthur and Callie agree, they can move upstairs and Emmajean can have their room right next to Jim and Louisa. There's no sense in even thinking of putting this child upstairs all by herself." Gertrude looked around the table for their responses.

"Folks, what do you think? Arthur, Callie?"

They didn't hesitate. "Sure, Mrs. Hall, we'd be glad to do that. When I get home from work I'll get our things moved up there."

"Since Jim will be here today, we might all pitch in and help Callie with the moving. That way, everything will be all set by nightfall and everybody will be where they need to be."

Nods and murmurs of agreement passed among them. With that settled, all their appetites renewed, even Emmajean's.

"One other thing," Gertrude said.

Huh-oh. They all looked at one another. What had they done, now?

Gertrude chuckled. "I wish you could see yourselves. Y'all look like you just got caught doing something you shouldn't be doing."

"What is it, Mrs. Hall? What did we do?" Both girls asked, a little fearful.

"Well, as hard as things are now on everybody with this Depression, I've been thinking about the rent you pay me."

They all exchanged glances again. Both couples were behind on paying their rent.

"Let's see if this works. Forget about paying me rent. If you boys can rake up enough money to help me with the groceries and the electric bill, we'll do that and see how it goes."

"I can't believe your generosity. That's good for us, but what about you? Do you have enough money to carry us like that?"

"Well, Arthur, I've never told y'all this, but when Arliss was alive he didn't believe in banks. Never put his money there, always kept it here in the house. So, I do have a little money the Depression can't touch. I can always dip into that if I need to. Y'all just help me to buy food and to pay the electric bill like I said and I think that'll work out."

The relief and smiles around the breakfast table excited Emmajean. This would be fun living here.

Lord, thank you for Mrs. Hall, Jim prayed, *and for watching over my new little family of three. Please never let me forget Your love for me. I trust You to straighten out the road ahead of us. It's not going to be easy . . . people are hurting all around us. But I trust You. Amen.*

Chapter 39

"Jim, I have something to tell you," Louisa hesitated. It was the summer of 1931, the country still held in the jaws of the continuing Depression.

"What is it?"

"I'm going to have a baby. I know we hadn't planned to."

Jim grabbed her by the shoulders, a wide grin on his face. "We hadn't planned *not to*."

~ ~ ~

Louisa had consuming morning sickness every day for a few weeks.

"I can't leave you like this, Louisa."

"You have to go to work." Gertrude pushed him on his way. "I'll take care of Louisa."

When Jim returned in the evening from work, Louisa felt and looked much better than that morning. "I'm glad you feel better than this morning."

"Jim, I'm sorry I'm being such a burden on everybody."

"None of that, now. You're no burden. I just want you to feel better."

~ ~ ~

When Louisa's labor started, her pain twisted his heart. He wanted to lessen her pain or bear it himself. But all he could do was stay by her side.

Dr. Blount came to the house late that evening. After he checked on Louisa, he spoke to Jim "I'm going to stay here tonight. The baby might come before morning. Gertrude did as he instructed, almost as if Louisa had a private nurse at her disposal. Sometime late that night, Dr. Blount went upstairs to rest in one of the unused rooms, instructing them to call him when the time came.

Jim stayed by Louisa's bed all night and about daybreak, Louisa began to thrash about. He took her hand and she reached and claimed his and didn't let go. "Louisa, what is it?"

When a contraction began she squeezed his hand and as the pain pushed down through her abdomen Jim witnessed strength in her hand he didn't imagine she possessed. But he didn't flinch even when he thought it was quite possible she might break some of his fingers. Louisa twisted among the bed clothes.

Louisa continued to writhe and squash his hand but didn't utter a sound or a word. With a soft cloth Jim wiped away the perspiration glistening across her forehead.

"Louisa, go on and holler or scream if you want to. It's okay. Go on and maybe it will help you with the pain." But she didn't. She continued gripping his hand.

"I think it might be time," Gertrude said. "I'll go get Dr. Blount."

So it was that a baby girl entered the world around eight o'clock in the morning. At long last, Louisa stilled and a smile settled over her damp face when she held the baby. Emmajean and the rest crowded near the bed to glimpse the new baby.

"Do y'all have a name picked out?" The doctor stood in the room, filling out some papers.

"Yes," Louisa answered with a weak voice, "it's Lynn Elizabeth. My middle name with Jim's momma's name."

"Lynn Elizabeth it is." Dr. Blount noted the name on his papers and put them in his black bag. "I'll get these all filed at the courthouse and get the birth certificate to you."

"Thank you, Dr. Blount." Jim walked the doctor to the door. "What do I owe you?"

"We'll settle up later. You just take care of that wife and baby girl."

~ ~ ~

"Look at you, you beautiful little girl." Jim made Lynn the center of attention at the Hall house.

"Yes, Lynn, we'll all take care of you." Gertrude acted just like a grandmother. "You sure behave well for such a little girl."

Jim, not Louisa, proudly carried her into the church on Sundays, basking in the admiration of the congregation. Lynn was the delight of her parents and the image of her mother, blond curls and bright blue eyes that drew everybody's love. Jim worked on a regular schedule with the state and their little family was whole. Finally, they had their *happily ever after.*

Chapter 40

After Lynn's second birthday celebration, Jim noticed that Louisa's face became paler and paler. Spring had come but Louisa hadn't responded to the sunshine and flowers.

After supper one evening Jim tentatively asked Louisa, "Let's go for a walk around the block and get some fresh air."

"Oh, Jim, maybe not tonight."

"Emmajean's playing with Lynn. She'll be fine, let's go."

"Maybe I'll sit on the porch swing with you."

Jim pushed the swing back and forth a few inches at a time. He took her hand. "Louisa, how do you feel?"

"I'm so tired. I don't seem to be able to snap out of it."

"Why don't you go see Dr. Blount? Maybe you need something to build up your blood."

"I don't think it's anything I need to see the doctor about. It'll pass."

"Okay, but if you don't get to feeling better soon, you might should go see him."

When Louisa didn't get to feeling better but stayed tired and run down much of the time, Jim continued to insist that she see the doctor. She gave in and Dr. Blount gave her a tonic, told her to finish it and come back if she didn't improve. Soon on Sunday mornings by the time she got Lynn ready for church Louisa was too tired to get herself ready.

"Jim, you go on to church. Take Lynn, she's already dressed to go."

Jim let her talk him into going. "You rest until we return."

Louisa finished the bottle of tonic the doctor had given her and still dragged herself around, overcome some days with fatigue. When Jim and Arthur were away at work, Louisa battled her symptoms of a cold. Doing the least bit of work around the house left her short of breath until she had to sit down for a while.

One night while they were sleeping, Jim woke to find Louisa shaking.

Jim turned and leaned over her. "What's the matter, Louisa?"

"I'm really cold. I'm so cold."

He got up, found a quilt in the chifforobe and spread it over her. How could she be cold in June when the house was so stuffy? As he tucked the covers around her neck, his hands touched her skin. It radiated heat. She shook with cold but her skin sizzled. Jim went to the bathroom and returned with a cool, wet washcloth, placing it across her forehead. He moved barefoot, not wanting to wake the baby. Louisa continued her shaking chills.

"I'll be right back, Louisa. You stay right there. Be still."

Jim hurried to Gertrude's bedroom door and tapped. No sound came from the other side of the door. He tapped again, this time a little louder. Then he heard movement in her room as she opened the door.

"Jim, my goodness, what is it?" As she asked him, she grasped the situation from the fear covering Jim's young face. "Is it Louisa?"

"Yes. She's got the chills but she's burning up. Please come and take a look at her."

Gertrude turned back into her room and returned, pushing her arms into her long yellow chenille house coat. She brushed past Jim and turned toward their bedroom. For a minute she looked down at Louisa then laid her hand on her forehead.

"She has a high fever. Jim, take the baby to Callie. She doesn't need to be in here with her mother this sick." She pushed Jim toward the baby's bed while at the same time stripping away the quilt he had just put over Louisa. She took the washcloth off Louisa and went in the bathroom to rinse it with cool water again. She'd just returned to Louisa when Callie and Jim entered the bedroom.

"Where's the baby?" Gertrude asked.

"Arthur has her. She didn't even wake up. She's in our bed."

"Good. Bless her little heart."

"Mrs. Hall, what's wrong with Louisa." Callie smothered a sob at the back of her throat.

"I don't know. I took the quilt off. I'm afraid covering her up will just raise that fever."

"But, Mrs. Hall, she said she was cold."

Louisa stirred and looked up at them. "Please give me some cover. I'm freezing."

Jim, Callie, and Gertrude exchanged glances. "Jim go to the bathroom and get the aspirin bottle in the medicine cabinet and bring a glass of water."

When Jim gave Louisa two aspirin, she took a couple of swallows of water and tried to smile at them. "I'm so cold and my head hurts. I ache all over." Louisa lay her head again on the pillow.

"These aspirins will help. You just rest." Jim sat on the edge of the bed holding her hand.

Jim sent Callie and Gertrude back to their bedrooms and he stayed the rest of the night beside Louisa.

By daybreak the aspirin hadn't helped. Louisa's head was hotter than it had been a few hours earlier. She stirred, coughed and moaned.

Jim thought she was waking. "Louisa, are you feeling any better?"

When she didn't respond, he touched her shoulder. She didn't move or open her eyes.

"Sweetheart, talk to me. How do you feel?"

Her silence scared him. "Louisa?" Again, no reply.

Jim rushed to Gertrude's bedroom and pounded on the door. Gertrude swung open the door, already cinching the belt to her house coat.

"Mrs. Hall, Louisa won't talk to me. She won't even open her eyes. Can you do something?"

Gertrude fussed over Louisa, who didn't acknowledge that anyone was even in the room. She refreshed the washrag on her head, knowing it was a futile attempt. Her fever had gone up.

"Jim, get Arthur to go for the doctor." When Jim simply stood by the bed, Gertrude pushed him toward the door. "Go, Jim! Get Arthur to fetch Dr. Blount."

Within thirty minutes the doctor arrived. Callie took Lynn to the kitchen to feed her breakfast. Arthur was in the way in the small bedroom and left to join Callie in the kitchen. He fixed the coffee percolator, turned on the burner and set the pot on it. Soon the coffee was bubbling up into the glass dome on top of the percolator. Worry etched Callie's face.

"Here, let me finish with the baby. You go see about Louisa."

Grateful, Callie kissed Arthur and the baby on their cheeks and went toward her sister's sickbed. She stood in the doorway. The doctor was questioning Jim and Gertrude about Louisa's symptoms. Their answers were what Callie would have said. Dr. Blount removed his stethoscope from his bag, pressed it several places against Louisa's chest and listened. He lifted her eyelids and looked inside with a small flashlight.

"I'm afraid Louisa has drifted off into a coma. The high fever has taken away her consciousness."

"What's wrong with her, doctor?"

"Jim, I can hear coarse breathing and crackling sounds when I listen to parts of her chest. I think she may have pneumonia. A lot of folks have come down with it between here and Knoxville. It's a rough thing to have."

"You can help her, can't you, Dr. Blount?"

"Jim, ladies, I can give her a shot. It might help her and it might not. She's in a coma. We'll have to wait and see if she wakes up."

"But, if you don't give her the shot, what?"

"Jim, without the shot she won't have a chance to come out of the coma. Even with the shot I can't promise you she will. It's going to be a waiting game."

After he gave Louisa the shot, the doctor left saying, "I can't do any more, but I'll come by this evening.

Jim didn't leave Louisa's side except to go to the bathroom and eat a bite in the kitchen. But even then he had to be sure somebody would be beside her. If only her fever would break. But it wouldn't. Gertrude and Callie tended to Louisa's personal hygiene and continued to wipe her face and arms with a cool cloth, trying to bring down the fever.

Dr. Blount came by that evening and the next morning, but there was no change in Louisa's condition. Her fever had not come down. He left and returned that evening and again the next morning. Two days Louisa had lain in the coma that robbed her body of knowing what and who surrounded her. Except for the flush of fever on her cheeks, she lay on her back, pale and lifeless. Late in the afternoon of the third day, Louisa's breath became shorter. By the time the doctor arrived after his office hours, he could hear her coarse breathing while standing in the hallway outside her door. Dr. Blount took his stethoscope from his bag and listened again to her chest. He stood.

"I'll wait a while and check her again." He went into the kitchen where Gertrude fed him supper, along with Callie, Arthur, Emmajean, and Lynn.

Jim eased onto Louisa's bed and laid his head beside hers on the pillow. Her frail body scorched his skin as he snuggled up against her. He touched her cheek then laid his hand on her shoulder.

"Louisa, please wake up. Can you hear me? Listen to me, now. Try your best to get better. We need you, Louisa. I love you. You know you're my life. Come on, open your eyes. Talk to me, Louisa. Please!" He didn't know what else to say, what else to do, so he lay with her, willing her to come back to him. Weak light slanted in across the bed from the hall.

Lying beside Louisa, Jim drifted off, his body giving in to his fatigue. When the others found them asleep, they tiptoed out and let them rest. Just about dark, Louisa's labored breathing fell quiet. Jim lay, asleep, his hand still on her shoulder.

Sitting around the kitchen table, the others sensed the quietness drop around them. They all stood together, Gertrude holding Lynn. The doctor moved first, the others following. Inside the bedroom, Dr. Blount assessed the circumstances in a moment. When he leaned down to the bed and put the stethoscope to Louisa's chest, Jim woke and looked up, met the doctor's eyes. The doctor straightened and motioned for Jim to move off the bed, and they walked across the room. Dr. Blount faced Jim and looked up at him. The others stood in the doorway and saw the doctor shake his head.

Jim heard the doctor's words but refused to believe them.

"No! . . . No! She's not dead! She can't be dead!"

When Jim started toward the bed, the doctor moved to stop him. He jerked from the doctor's hold and fell on his knees beside the bed, his head once again on the pillow beside Louisa. "No! No! No!" He kept repeating and repeating. His sobs echoed through the big house. It pained them all to witness such sorrow. Callie screamed her sister's name. Emmajean started to cry.

After a few minutes, when Jim's crying didn't stop, Dr. Blount motioned for Arthur to help him get Jim to his feet. As they pulled him up and away from the bed, he reached frantically toward Louisa, only grabbing the air in his fist. As young and strong as Arthur was, even with Dr. Blount's help, it took Herculean effort to get Jim out of that room.

Dr. Blount spoke to Gertrude, "Please get me my bag."

By the time they held Jim down lying on Emmajean's bed, Gertrude's trembling hands held out the open bag to the doctor. He quickly prepared a syringe and gave Jim a shot. They had to hold him down for a few more minutes before the shot took over his body, forcing him to calm down then close his eyes.

The doctor looked up. "He was hysterical. I had to give him that." The others nodded.

Dr. Blount returned to Louisa's bed and pulled the covers over her face. He pulled his pocket watch from his vest, checked the time and wrote it on a notepad in his bag.

Callie had fallen apart when she saw the doctor shake his head at Jim. After Arthur helped the doctor get Jim to bed, he sped to Callie's side. She turned toward him, dissolving against him as he held her close.

"I'll stay around and see how Jim is when he rouses up."

~ ~ ~

When Jim woke from the induced sleep, he took a minute to get his bearings. Realizing he was in Emmajean's bedroom, he remembered. "Louisa!" he cried out and ran from the room. Just a few steps took him up the hallway and to his own bedroom. He pushed open the door. The bed was empty and properly made up. The window shade had been raised allowing afternoon sun to stream through the window onto the bed where Louisa had lain earlier. He turned around in the room, looking for . . . what?

"Louisa!" he shouted again. "Louisa!"

Arthur hurried into the room, went to Jim and put his arm around his shoulders.

"Jim, Louisa's not here. Settle down. Let's go on outside."

"No! Where's Louisa?"

"She's not here, Jim. Louisa got real sick. She's . . . dead. Come on." Arthur tugged on Jim's arm, trying to get him to leave the room.

"No, she can't be. She wouldn't leave me and Lynn. Where is she?"

"The undertaker came, Jim. He took her to the funeral home."

Jim was still a little groggy from the shot Dr. Blount had given him. "The funeral home?"

"Come on, Jim, let's go outside on the porch."

"No," his voice rose. "No. I want Louisa."

At the commotion, Dr. Blount came into the room. He motioned for Arthur to leave and shut the door.

Gertrude met Arthur in the hallway. "How's Jim doing?"

"Pretty bad."

"Let's let the doctor be with him a while. Dr. Blount deals with folks who've lost loved ones. Maybe he can talk to Jim and calm him down." Gertrude wiped her nose and she and Arthur returned to the kitchen across the hall.

A couple of hours later, Jim and the doctor exited the room. Dazed and his hair disheveled, Jim walked like a frail old man, broken, hopeless. Staring at the floor, he allowed the doctor to lead him into the kitchen where he sat at the table. Gertrude placed a glass of water in front of him, and he emptied the glass without stopping. Then he looked up at them standing around the table.

"Louisa's gone. Did you know she's gone? The pneumonia fever took her away." He began to sob, Louisa's absence distorting his handsome face. Seeming to have just remembered, Jim called out, "Where's Lynn? Where's my baby?"

Callie stepped toward Jim, tears streaming down her face and the baby in her arms. Jim stood and lifted the baby to him. "Lynn, your mother's gone. She won't be coming back." He wept out loud and hugged Lynn against him so tightly that it frightened the child. His sobs shook his shoulders, and he squeezed Lynn tighter to his chest. Gertrude pulled the baby away from him and left the room trying to calm her crying, Emmajean following close behind. Jim continued to weep.

~ ~ ~

For weeks and months after Louisa died, Jim questioned God. "Why did Louisa die? Why did God take the baby's mother away? Louisa was my life, why did I lose her?"

Gertrude tried to help him the best way she knew. "Jim, you can't find answers to your questions. But you can find comfort in the Bible. Listen to these words spoken by God through Jesus. Now, listen and know that God is speaking them to you: *Fear thou not; for I am with thee: be not dismayed; for I am thy God: I will strengthen thee; yes, I will help thee; yes, I will uphold thee with the right hand of my righteousness.* Take comfort in those words, Jim. They won't bring Louisa back, but they will help you if you'll receive them."

Looking into Jim's eyes she saw his yearning for understanding and comfort.

"Listen to these other words from the Bible, Jim. *Come unto me, all ye that labour and are heavy laden, and I will give your rest. Cast thy burden upon the Lord, and he shall sustain thee. Casting all your care upon him; for he careth for you.* And the apostle Paul had enough faith in God to say this, *'I can do all things through Christ which strengtheneth me'*. Believe what God says. Jim, take Him at His word like your momma taught you."

Eventually Jim leaned on God more than he ever had, laying his burdens down before Him. Jim wished he could have died with Louisa. He would have begged God to take him on if it had not been for Lynn. He wanted to care for Lynn as her mother had, but how in the world would he raise a child with the necessary attention when his every thought brought to mind Louisa and not the child?

Callie and Arthur had helped Jim to raise Lynn. Shirley Ann and Henry Frank had also been available when Jim needed them. In addition, each of them needed help coping with their own personal needs. Loss had touched them all—loss of work and income, loss of loved ones, loss of innocence, and loss of *happily ever after.*

PART TWO
1950

Chapter 41

Twenty years later
Fall, 1950

Jim Callaway and his daughter Lynn rode in painful silence, so painful that both hardly kept their tears in check. Jim Callaway wanted Lynn to have a future neither he nor her mother had had, one where her education could take her through doors they never had dreamed of entering. So, Lynn was going to college and Jim was driving her from Newton to Knoxville to settle her in at the University of Tennessee.

"Daddy," Lynn began. "You don't have to give me a college education. You and Mother didn't go, and you both turned out fine. I can work in Newton without a college education. I could even work for you in the mill. Well, maybe not *in* the mill, but in the office." She gentled her determination, but still it reminded Jim of her mother at that same age. And he remembered when he first saw Louisa at the county fair, when her light blue eyes had touched his soul.

"You don't need to get stuck in Newton. You've lived there all your life. You need to see other parts of the country. In Knoxville you'll be near enough so that if you need me I can get to you right away."

Jim could leave the mill whenever he wanted. He had owned Southeastern Hosiery since Lynn was eleven years old. Jim remembered when soon after Mr. and Mrs. Jacob had died in an evening's fiery car crash with a Red Star Lines bus heading to Knoxville, Jim had been summoned to the lawyer's office. There Jim learned that the Jacobs had provided for him in their wills. Since they had no child, at least not one they acknowledged, they had left their beautiful brick Federal-style home, some money, and the hosiery mill to Jim.

He had never heard from Caroline Jacob since that Christmas Eve party at her parents' house in 1929. Mr. Jacob had explained her continued absence by saying to all who asked that she had married a young man she'd met in Atlanta and they had moved to his home in Texas.

After a complete closing of Southeastern Hosiery in the 1930s during the Great Depression, Fred Jacob was able to reopen the mill after the United States entered World War II in 1941. The mill was needed to fill generous orders from the government for military socks to issue to the growing numbers of soldiers. He had asked Jim to come back to the mill. He trusted Jim and depended on him to help him keep all operations running well. At Mr. Jacob's death, the mill had gotten back on its feet and had returned to its earlier dominance in Newton's business community.

"But, Daddy," Lynn broke into Jim's thoughts, "I'm going to miss you. Who will take care of you when I'm not at home?"

"Lynn, that should not be a worry of yours."

"But Mother is not there to help you," she said with compassion, yet as determined as her mother had been during the short time her parents had been together.

"Your mother would be proud of you getting accepted into UT. She'd want you to do this. I do too. It's all going to be fine. You just jump right in there and do your best and you'll do great." As he drove, he glanced at his daughter and smiled at how much like her mother Lynn was, in her disposition as in her appearance. Lynn kept her blond hair shorter than Louisa had and brushed away from her face, giving her sky-blue eyes their rightful prominence that gained her attention from the boys and envy from the girls in high school.

Lynn leaned back against the passenger door and looked at her daddy's handsome profile, stunning dark eyes and straight black hair. She watched the muscles move in his jaw, a tightness she had learned meant that he was under stress and doing some deep thinking. She would miss her daddy. She wondered if she would make friends, be able to find her way around or get lost the first day, and would she like her teachers. Nevertheless, Lynn was buoyed by the encouragement from her daddy and the assurance he gave her by saying that her mother would agree to this move to college. Turning to look out her side window, Lynn saw a road marker that showed them coming close to Knoxville. A wrench of apprehension but also a rise of excitement flooded through her.

~ ~ ~

"There, now, have we carried everything upstairs, you think?"

"Yes, Daddy, we have. And, thanks for the Coke. I'll remember where we got it so I can go there again."

"Well then." Jim struggled for conversation and cleared his throat.

They each held the other's gaze, neither wanting to say good-bye. The specks of white at Jim's temples flashed in the sunlight. Jim had never recognized how much Lynn looked like her mother than standing there in the late September sun, her blond hair shining.

"Well then," Jim repeated. This was more difficult that he expected it would be. He was leaving his only child in a strange city sixty miles from home. "You be sure to get in touch with me right away if you need anything."

"I will."

"If anything gets too rough for you, you let me know. You don't have to stay if you think it's not right for you."

"I know."

"Well, Lynn." Jim stepped forward and held her by the shoulders. "You be a good girl and study hard." He kissed her forehead.

She slung her arms around his neck and held on, not wanting to let go. "Daddy, take good care of yourself. Let Aunt Callie and Uncle Arthur know when you need anything."

"I will." He turned and walked toward his Pontiac. Lynn followed.

Jim looked back at the girls' dormitory. It was bigger than Miss June's where Louisa had lived, and housed some 200 college girls on three floors. Ivy climbed the brick walls up to the top floor. Girls and boys sat on the low brick wall bordering a front patio. He hoped Lynn could make friends and soon be comfortable with such a group.

"You'll be safe here. Make you some friends and the time will pass better."

"I will." Her eyes glistened with unshed tears.

"Well then." Searching for words, he opened the car door. He slid under the steering wheel, and started the engine. "Good-bye. I love you more than anything on this earth, Lynn."

"Daddy, I love you more than anything."

Driving away, Jim watched in the rearview mirror as Lynn and the dormitory became smaller and smaller. He thought about turning the car around and rushing back to Lynn. But he knew it would be best for her to try this out.

Lord, stay close to Lynn in this new venture. Guide her in Your ways and keep her safe. Amen.

Chapter 42

No boy had ever broken her heart. But now Lynn's heart hurt. It was homesickness but she didn't know that. She just knew she was miserable.

A month ago, her daddy had helped her move into her living quarters just at the edge of the UT campus. Preparing for classes and going to them had become mechanical, something she forced herself to do. She didn't want to disappoint her daddy. She knew he worked hard at the mill to make the money it took to pay for her to attend college.

The weather didn't help her misery. The brightness of the day her daddy left her in Knoxville had given way to colder days. And today the dark clouds were heavy with snow. "Just what I need to make my day better," she groused out loud but to herself.

Lynn had returned many times to have a Coke at Sharp Drugstore where her daddy and she had gone that move-in day. Today, after class and before returning to the dorm, she stopped by the drugstore for a cup of hot chocolate. She saw a vacant swivel stool at the food counter near the far end and made her way toward it. Someone sat on either side of the empty stool. She inquired of them both if the stool was being used.

On the left sat a boy wearing a football jacket boasting a prominent letter T in the school's unique golden orange color. He shook his head without a word. The boy on the right of the empty stool turned his head toward her. Lynn looked at him and pointed to the empty stool.

"No, it's not, please, have a seat."

So impressed was Lynn with his polite words, she chanced a glance at him as she slid onto the backless stool. He was engrossed in a textbook laid open before him and drank hot chocolate.

When Lynn ordered hot chocolate from the waitress behind the counter, the polite boy overheard and looked at her with curiosity. Most students, trying to appear sophisticated, drank coffee, inferring that to drink anything less would be childish.

As Lynn waited for her order, she pulled off her thick gloves, removed the wool scarf from around her neck, and stuffed them all into the pockets of her full-length royal blue coat. She took a textbook from the stack in her lap, opened it on the counter, and began to read. When her cup was placed in front of her, she paid for it and stirred it with a spoon to cool it some.

"You don't like coffee?"

"No." Lynn was surprised that the boy had spoken to her. Then she ventured, "I don't drink coffee but I've loved hot chocolate since I was a little girl. In fact, my daddy doesn't even drink coffee. I see you don't either, or not this morning anyway."

"Nothing's better in this cold weather we're having. Looks like more snow will be falling on top of what we already have."

"Yes it does." Lynn was delighted with the conversation but was at a loss for what else to say after talking about their drinks and the weather. In the lull she looked him over. Straight, black hair. The blackest eyes she'd ever seen besides her daddy's. And was he good looking!

"My name is James."

"Hey. I'm Lynn."

An easy smile slipped across both their faces. His onyx eyes flashed and Lynn sensed an eternal spring had melted all the snow outside. Suddenly the day brightened and her hurting heart began its journey back to wholeness.

"What year are you."

"This is my first year. How about you?"

"I'm a junior. What are you going to major in?"

"I don't know yet. What's your major?'

"I'm not sure yet either, but I'm thinking about law school." He was mesmerized by her light blue eyes and the blond hair with the side part that framed her face.

They talked and scrutinized one another until their cups of hot chocolate were no longer hot. James had to get to class on the hill in Ayers Hall. "Can we meet here again tomorrow?"

Lynn smiled, tucked her chin as her mother had done at her age, and agreed. *Of course*! "Sure. What time? I get out of class earlier tomorrow, at one o'clock."

"I'll be here by one thirty waiting for you."

"Great. I'm glad."

Bundled again in their coats, they walked out of the drugstore together, turning their separate ways after saying good-bye with smiles they couldn't keep inside. As she walked away,

Lynn chanced a look over her shoulder at James. He was looking back at her.

And that's how James and Lynn began.

~ ~ ~

James and Lynn met at Sharp Drugstore the next day, and the next day, and every day. They compared their class schedules and spent any free time together. They took their books and studied at the Hodges Library. They browsed the University Bookstore. On days when the sun shone and melted the snow, James drove them to the agriculture school area on Neyland Drive where they perched on a picnic table beside the river.

The sizable UT campus spread to the circling banks of the Tennessee River as did the east side of Newton rest along the meandering Caney Creek.

One afternoon James and Lynn sat at their favorite picnic table. "Your Tennessee River looks dangerous. So wide and its waters move strongly east to west. If a person fell out of their boat here they could drown in a minute before they could swim to the bank.

James looked toward the river. "Yeah, a few accidents have happened here, but not lately that I've heard of."

"Our Caney Creek at home is peaceful and safe. Nothing bad has ever happened there."

They continued looking at the moving water.

Lynn turned toward James. "Do you ever think where all this water comes from or where it's going?"

"I guess it runs into another river and they keep running together into others and then spill out into the Gulf of Mexico. Have you ever been to the Gulf of Mexico?"

"Yes. The sugary-white beaches around Pensacola, Florida are beautiful. Did you know the sand there is made up of fine quartz that has eroded over time from granite in our own Appalachian Mountains?"

"No. How do you know that?"

"I've read that rivers and creeks carry the sand from up here and deposit it there on the shore. Just think—this water we're looking at probably has some of that white sand in it and headed for the beach someplace along the Gulf."

They sat without talking for several minutes watching the busy river. The hum of traffic moving on the nearby elevated UT Bridge spanning the river didn't interrupt their silence but played as background music.

"Maybe someday we can go together to the beach along the

Gulf."

His comment held an intimate hint and Lynn blushed. "Maybe."

~ ~ ~

One afternoon James took Lynn to the Tennessee Theater in downtown Knoxville. When they walked into the grand lobby, its splendor took Lynn's breath away. James waited for her to take it all in. She looked up at the ornate ceiling that she guessed was five or six stories high centered with an elaborate fresco and large carvings at its junction with the white marble walls. The floors were an extension of the gleaming marble and echoed their every step. They walked almost to the base of a curved and carpeted stairway hugging the wall and leading upward. A matching stairway did the same on the other side of the lobby. Ahead of them were splendid dark red velvet curtains drawn across a tall entryway.

"Do you want to sit downstairs or in the balcony?"

"I don't know. Where do you usually sit?"

"I like the balcony."

"Fine."

They climbed the nearest stairway, up, up, close to the ceiling.

They sat in the front row of the balcony. Lynn noticed James's wide smile. She had no clue what he was up to.

"Hear the music? Look over to the left near the stage."

Sure enough, a small part of the floor had opened and an organ on a platform, with a man playing the keyboard with gusto, rose little by little into the cavernous room. The music filled the elaborate theater all the way to where they sat. Lynn clasped her hands beneath her chin in her excitement.

Leaving the theater, Lynn and James turned left when they reached the sidewalk, walked to the corner and stopped.

"Lynn, have you ever eaten a square hamburger?"

"A square hamburger? No, we eat round hamburgers in Newton." She punched him in the arm. "Have you?"

"Yeah. Let's cross the street here. I want to treat you to something new."

James took Lynn's hand and led her across the street and back up the sidewalk to the right until they were across the street from the theater.

They walked underneath a sign that read Krystal and slipped inside a food place. Lynn saw that the room was not much more than ten feet wide by twenty-five feet long, a cooking area along the length of the left wall with a serving counter between it and the crowd already there. She liked the décor of black, white and chrome, which carried over to the round swivel stools. People sat on every stool with more people standing along the right wall waiting their turn for a vacated place to sit.

"Let's pick two stools where it looks like the folks are almost finished eating."

They did and planted themselves right behind them, marking their territory. When the two places became available, they sat and in a second or two a waitress in a white uniform appeared in front of them with her order pad. James ordered for Lynn and himself and paid the bill. The waitress had no more than turned toward the cooking area, when she reappeared and placed their food in front of them. Each inexpensive porcelain dishware held two square hamburgers, some skinny French fries and a chocolate-covered cake doughnut.

"That's your Krystal. A square hamburger on a square steamed bun."

Lynn pointed to one of the burgers. "This is a Krystal?"

"Yeah. Want some ketchup or mustard?" James passed both bottles to her.

"Okay, I'll try some."

Lynn bit into her burger and rolled her eyes heavenward. "Oh my goodness. This is delicious. Fresh and steamy. Wow, what a treat for just seven cents each."

Going back to her dorm afterwards, neither could have told anyone about the movie they'd seen. Their attentions had been on each other. They had held hands all through the movie and exchanged numerous glances. And Lynn still marveled about the square hamburgers.

~ ~ ~

On one of their afternoons sitting by the river, James couldn't take his eyes off Lynn. He studied her face so he would never forget her.

"What?"

"Nothing."

Lynn smiled. "You're staring at me."

"Lynn, I'm happy when we're together. You make me so comfortable just being with you. I don't know how I moved around the campus before you came along. You make my life just perfect."

She ducked her chin and blushed.

"I'm sorry. I've said the wrong thing."

"No. No, you haven't. I've been thinking the same thing, James. What did I do before I met you?"

James smiled. "You bring sunshine into my life even when it snows."

Chapter 43

Fall days dragged on, colder and brutal. Near the Tennessee River and in the shadow of the Smoky Mountains, frequent snows blanketed the UT campus. And not just snow flurries—snow at least above boot tops. Such nasty weather hampered travel so Lynn's daddy didn't drive to Knoxville frequently. He and Lynn wrote often and sometimes spoke by telephone. Lynn had adjusted well but still looked forward to quarter break at Christmastime when she could go back to Newton for a few weeks.

The friendship between Lynn and James grew stronger as the weeks went by. She had learned that he lived in the city with his mom, that his father died when he was a baby and he was an only child as she was. They arranged to meet between or after classes when possible and helped each other to study for tests even though they were not in any of the same classes. And they continued to enjoy hot chocolate at Sharp's, their most likely place to meet.

Lynn liked being with James. She could talk to him about almost anything. And he seemed to be comfortable with her. He had an easy laugh that compelled her to smile along with him.

One day James and Lynn walked around the campus "Lynn, I'm glad we have time together. You're not like other girls. You act natural, not stuck up. Not thinking you're better than anybody else. I like the way you stay so casual and don't get up tight about little things that bother other people."

"It's because I like being with you. All my troubles and stress seem to fall away when we spend time together."

"Lynn, would you, uh, would you like to have supper sometime with my mom and me? At our house?"

"That sounds great. Sure." *Absolutely*!

"I'll check with Mom to set a time."

"Just let me know." *Any time*!

~ ~ ~

The next Friday, James drove off the campus, out Cumberland Drive toward the Sequoia Hills community. Lynn watched through the windshield as the campus buildings and stores gave way to old estates, not unlike the house she and her daddy lived in. But here the large homes were numerous, compared to the few in Newton. The day was blustery, but the skies had cleared to an appealing bright blue following two weeks of snow. As the late afternoon sun dipped overhead, clumps of melting snow slipped from the bare tree limbs and splattered to the ground.

"It's beautiful here! The homes are spaced so far apart, with lots of privacy. I like that. At home our little town is so small and most of the houses are so close together that everyone knows everybody's business."

James laughed. "Knoxville's growing, but this part of town has been here a long time. The homes sit back from the street. Some homes you can hardly see through the mature landscaping."

Lynn wondered which one would be James's home. Maybe it was on one of the side streets. Or did it face this main street?

James turned left into a driveway leading to a square, two story red brick house. He drove past the circular drive and pulled the car to a stop on the brick driveway in front of a detached garage. "This is it. I know Mom's watching for us. Ready?"

James made it sound ominous, as if she were about to face a firing squad. She had not been nervous about meeting his mother until now. Ready? *Sure,* she guessed. *Of course. Why shouldn't she be?*

~ ~ ~

James went around to the passenger side and helped Lynn out of the car. He placed a hand at the small of her back, guiding her penny loafers around spots of snow still on the sidewalk and toward the front door. They stamped their wet shoes on the welcome mat, James used his key in the door and they stepped inside.

"Mom! We're here," James called. He helped Lynn out of her coat, took off his, and hung them in the foyer closet.

A beautiful woman with smooth milk-white skin rounded the corner into the entryway, beaming toward her son. Lynn took in her strawberry blond hair pulled sleek back from her face into a French twist low on the back of her head and the tiny garnet stone she wore around her neck. Lynn fleetingly decided that James's daddy must have had dark hair for James's to be so black. He and his mom hugged until James broke away and turned toward Lynn.

"Mom, this is Lynn. Lynn, this is my mom."

"Hello, Lynn. I'm so happy James has brought you to our home."

"Thank you, Mrs. Hensen. It's a lovely place. I know you must enjoy living here." Lynn was drawn to Mrs. Hensen's intense sapphire eyes. "When James parked the car I noticed the river running by out beyond the garage. The east side of our town borders on Caney Creek, but it's not as impressive as your Tennessee River."

Caney Creek? Could there be another Caney Creek? Caroline shook the questions away and spoke to Lynn. "Yes, fall and winter subdue things a bit, but spring's flowers, the dogwood trees, and azaleas will burst into bloom to brighten our days. We will be awash in a sea of pinks, whites and reds. Come into the living room and be comfortable."

They moved underneath an archway over the broad entrance to the living room leading off the left of the foyer. A fire blazed in the tall fireplace on the opposite wall. The furniture covers and decorative pillows pulled their colors from the mixture of navy blues and golds in the area rug. Some of the furniture appeared to Lynn to be antiques but the room looked cozy and inviting. A portrait in gilt-edged framing hung over the fireplace and showed James's mom as a younger woman, her glossy hair loose, complementing her classic beauty. Lynn took a seat on the sofa and James sat beside her. His mom sat in a wing chair facing them. Conversation flowed without effort between the three of them. Encouraged by his mom, they spoke of their school matters at length. Then, eventually, James and his mom talked about their years in Knoxville, filling in Lynn on James's life. She learned that his dad had worked for the railroad, they had purchased this house, but he had died when James was a baby.

No mention from his mom that her Aunt Martha had deeded the house to her as she grew frail in her last years. Neither of the aunt's daughters ever came to visit their mom and Martha decided that she owed them nothing. Hence, the house now belonged to James's mom. Aunt Martha had arranged her copious financial matters so that James's mom would never have to work if she chose not to.

James and his mom gave Lynn a tour of the house, ending at the elegant dining room, where they took seats at the polished cherry table. James's mom sat at the head of the table, with James and Lynn at either side of her, underneath the ornate chandelier. Mildred, a plump middle-aged woman, served their meal. Fragrances from the kitchen trailed her when she approached the table.

~ ~ ~

"I liked your mom. Thank you for taking me to meet her."

"She liked you."

"Do you think so?"

"Yes, I do. I could tell."

"Oh, I hope so."

"Lynn, would you like to go to church with Mom and me Sunday?"

"Really? I'd love to . . . yes."

"Great. We'll pick you up at the dorm about ten thirty Sunday morning"

Evening ushered in the night as they drove. They rode in silence for most of the short way back to campus. James walked her to the door of her dorm. He took both her hands in his then leaned down and kissed her cheek. Lynn blushed with the newness of that intimate move.

"Well then, goodnight, Lynn."

She looked into his beautiful dark eyes. "Goodnight."

~ ~ ~

When James returned home after leaving Lynn at her dormitory, he bounded up the stairway before realizing that his mother sat in the living room on the sofa, an open book on her lap.

"Did you get Lynn back safely to her dorm?"

He went in to join her, sitting across from her.

"Yes. Isn't she something, Mom?"

"She's a pretty girl, James. You met her at a drugstore?"

"Mom, she's great! We get along so well. We can talk about anything. I feel so comfortable around Lynn. She's not like any other girl I know. It's like she's part of the family. She's beautiful, but she's not stuck up like other girls are. I enjoy being with her!"

"Do you two have any classes together?"

"No. Mom, I invited Lynn to go to church with us Sunday. I hope that's okay. And, Mom, she's invited me to join her over Thanksgiving break. Could I please drive the car and take her home for one night—that Saturday night?"

"I'm glad she's going with us Sunday. As for the Thanksgiving break, we *might* arrange that. But you will be here with me on Thanksgiving Day?"

"Sure! Would it be okay with you if we invited Lynn here for Thanksgiving dinner?"

"James, you don't know her all that well."

"It's like I've known her all my life, or at least like she's the one I've been looking for all my life. Mom, she's great! You did like Lynn, didn't you?"

"I welcomed her into our home. She is pretty and very well mannered. Let me think about Thanksgiving dinner. What do you know about her home, her family?"

"Not much, I guess."

"Where is Lynn from?"

"She's from Newton. That's down toward Chattanooga."

Hearing the word Newton heightened Caroline's senses like a dash of cold water.

"Tell me about her family. What is her last name?"

"Her last name is Callaway. Her daddy owns a hosiery mill there. Her mother is dead."

Callaway. The hosiery mill. My daddy's hosiery mill? Caroline didn't have to ask what Lynn's daddy's first name was. It was Jim. Her Jimmy. The past smashed against Caroline, leaving her breathless. She remembered everything about those days with Jimmy. Their Sunday afternoons spent in a cozy booth at The Evergreen Café. How handsome he'd looked in his new suit, the last time she'd seen him the night of her parents' Christmas Eve party. That summer on the mossy bank of Caney Creek. All sensation drained from her body; she felt faint.

"Mom? Mom! What's wrong?" James moved to sit beside her on the sofa. "Mom, are you sick? Can I help you?"

Caroline tried to pull herself from her thoughts of Newton and Jimmy. Oh, and Lynn. If her daddy was indeed Jimmy then she and James were half brother and sister. What a mess love has caused . . . at this late date! How could she be sure that Lynn's daddy is Jimmy? Until she could be sure she wouldn't mention any of this to James. He was so enamored with Lynn, she couldn't dampen his spirits.

"No, James. Thank you. I guess I'm just a little tired. I think I'll go on to bed now. Lock up and turn out the lights, would you please?"

"Sure, Mom, let me know if I can do anything else for you."

What else can he do? What can anyone do? It may all have been done twenty years ago. If so, her dear son and her first love might be destroyed by this revelation.

James told his mom goodnight. She noticed that he couldn't stop grinning. She took her time ascending the stairway to her bedroom, carrying the weight of twenty years on her shoulders.

~ ~ ~

Sunday morning dawned bright and clear. Before she opened her eyes, Lynn stretched the length of the bed, a smile curving her lips. She lay among the tangled covers, thinking of her time spent with James. Lynn jerked herself from her early morning daydreaming. She had to get up so she would be ready when James and his mom came by to take her to church.

The First Baptist Church on West Main Street loomed above the sidewalk, fronted all across by a dozen wide concrete steps. After James parked the car, he guided his mom and Lynn up the steps, past the huge white columns and through the ten foot high heavy wooden double doors. The organ prelude permeated everything—the dark paneling and pews, the color-splashed stained glass windows, the pulpit standing high on a podium, and Lynn's heart and soul. The pastor conducted the service with dignity and empathy for his congregation. Lynn especially enjoyed the choir music. The choir members almost outnumbered her Newton church's entire crowd on a Sunday night.

The experience buoyed Lynn's spirits. She remained bathed in the impact of the church service well into their noon meal at the Regis Restaurant. The fanciest place to eat in Newton was The Blanchard Hotel dining room. It would be unfair to try to compare The Blanchard to The Regis. Opulence was the best word Lynn could muster to describe The Regis. Its dignity equaled that of James's mom who appeared so at ease in their surroundings. Even James seemed comfortable but in a more relaxed mood than his mom.

Chapter 44

November 13, 1950

Dear Daddy,

Hope these few lines find you well. I know you have those large orders from the government to fill, but don't work too hard. I'm sure our soldiers in Korea will appreciate the fine socks from your mill. I wrote Uncle Richard and Uncle Robert to wear their uniform socks with pride and tell all their buddies their big brother made them in his mill.

The weather has been so bad for a while and I've missed seeing you up here. I've been thinking, could I bring home a friend with me over Thanksgiving break? Maybe on Saturday, for just one night? My friend is a boy, Daddy. He's a gentleman and I think you will like him. He lives with his mom here in Knoxville. He plans to spend Thanksgiving Day at his home and has invited me. Then we would come down there on Saturday. I hope this sounds okay with you.

Are Aunt Callie and Uncle Arthur going to be with you for Thanksgiving? They're probably fixing the turkey and all the trimmings because you could not possibly do that without help. Ha. If it's okay that I bring James home, maybe you could save us some leftovers.

Daddy, let me know what you think about James coming home with me. He has a car and he'll be driving us down, if you let us come. Let me hear so I can let him know. I'll do whatever you say.

I miss you and I love you.

Love,

Lynn

Chapter 45

Lynn being away at school left Jim alone in the house. It seemed larger to him each time he entered it after work. Way too much room. Jim sometimes found himself reminiscing about the first time he had walked into this house. He remembered how fantastic the house seemed to him when he entered it that Christmas Eve. It was the Jacob's Christmas Eve party in 1929. That's when Mrs. Jacob had to appear to accept him because he was with Caroline. The last time he had seen Caroline. Not one word from her since that day. Her daddy said she'd moved to Texas. But she never came home even for a visit with her parents. Her absence remained a mystery to Jim. He tried never to dwell on it.

Jim aimlessly roamed the sizable house. His footsteps echoed through the rooms until he stopped at the French doors. He stepped out onto the patio and looked across his backyard, barely blinking. Hands thrust into his pants pockets, he stood ramrod straight. He squinted through his foggy mind to see Caney Creek, which marked his lot's back border. The creek bubbled on its continual trek to the Big Stone River. Caney Creek. The Fourth of July. That ill-fated day he had crossed the line into immorality with Caroline. Jim had long ago asked and received God's forgiveness but at times like this, alone in the house, that day haunted him. God forgave him but Jim couldn't forget.

Caney Creek, so much a part of his life for years. Where had the time gone? Lynn in college and bringing home a friend—a boyfriend—Saturday. He shook his head to scatter the cobwebs and walked toward the kitchen for a glass of water.

Having lived in the Jacob home seven years, Jim knew he was a fortunate man to have been named in the Jacobs' wills. The home continued to impress him, but he slowly came to acknowledge that it was truly his home and Lynn's. But the spacious house needed family and friends to fill the rooms, and they would on Thanksgiving Day. Only Lynn would be absent, but she would be coming down the following Saturday. He was anxious to meet Lynn's friend, James. Jim wondered just how serious she was about liking this boy. And how serious he was about her. He hoped this James boy wouldn't break his daughter's heart—like his own broke twenty years ago.

~ ~ ~

"So, Lynn's bringing a friend home Saturday?" Callie watched as Jim carved the roasted turkey. "What do you know about him?"

"Not much. Except Lynn is excited. When I called her to tell her it was okay to bring him, she was bubbling over! Sounds like they've been spending a lot of time together."

"Jim, what did she say about him? About his family?"

"Bones, I guess we can quiz him when he gets here. About all she said was that he lived with his mom in Knoxville. Maybe we'll find out more while they're here." Jim called Arthur by his nickname from long ago. Arthur still had that gangly way of walking but he had filled out some, carrying the extra weight well.

"Are you goin' to let us come by and meet him?" Shirley Ann asked.

"Yes! Everybody come back Saturday and help us eat leftovers. Looks like we'll have plenty to go around. Just look at all the food you ladies have prepared. Let's bow our heads and give thanks." They all joined hands. "*Lord, we do thank you for our blessings; for our family at this Thanksgiving bounty. Continue to bless us and keep us close to You. Amen.*"

Conversation was exchanged around the table as the five adults and five teenagers filled their plates.

"Shirley Ann, how're things over at the hospital? Many sick people these days?" He looked toward his sister, who had remained the black haired beauty and had maintained her figure after the three children.

"Well, you know, the patient numbers do drop off around holidays. Most of the folks in the hospital now are really sick. As usual not much elective surgery got scheduled this week. That's how it was easier for me to get off today. Only a minimum nursin' staff works today and through the weekend."

"You still like your nursing job after all these years?" Jim swallowed a big chunk of roll.

"Sure do. I can't imagine myself doin' anything else."

The turkey, sweet potatoes, cranberry congealed salad, corn on the cob, scalloped potatoes, and fluffy yeast rolls made the rounds for everybody to serve themselves.

"Bones, you haven't changed the name of that store of yours yet?"

"Nah, I'm leavin' it alone. Everybody knows the store as Henderson's General Store. If I changed it to Gray's, nobody would know what it is. Since the A&P opened up on the outskirts of town, I think I'll stop carryin' any groceries. Probably change the name to Henderson's Hardware."

"Bones, you're lucky Mr. Henderson took a liking to you and sold off small pieces of the business to you along. When he retired, you held a majority of ownership and stepped right into the running of the store."

"Yeah, with you ownin' and runnin' the Southeastern Hosiery Mill, Henry Frank ownin' his own car place and me runnin' Henderson's, we're great examples of home town boys doin' good."

Callie jumped into the conversation. "Henry Frank, is your car dealership doing a good business now?"

"Yeah, it is." He drank some sweet iced tea and continued. "These new '51 Fords comin' out now are really snazzy. And the colors! That new peachpuff color with the white top sure is popular with the buyers these days. I might need to get Shirley Ann one."

"Oh, Henry Frank, I'm just now gettin' used to the 1950 you gave me. Don't you go bringin' home another car and take away the one I'm drivin' now."

"I know you like that car but how would it look if the Ford dealer's wife didn't drive a brand spankin' new car every year?" Henry Frank gave his wife a broad smile, his ears still standing out from his head.

They all chuckled, enjoying the moment at Shirley Ann's expense.

Henry Frank looked toward Jim. "What do you hear from your twin brothers?"

"Richard and Robert? They write when they can. They make it sound like Korea is a hard place to be right now. They don't much like it that they're America soldiers at a time when the United Nations is so involved."

"Yeah, this is the first war when a world organization like the United Nations has played a military role. But at least General Douglas MacArthur is the commander in chief of the UN forces."

"Robert and Richard have been in the military since they volunteered at the beginning of World War II. I just wonder when they might decide not to reenlist when their tours of duty come up for renewal." Jim held his fork full of turkey mid-air.

"You think they might just stay in and make the Army their lifelong careers?" Callie glanced up at Jim and her blond good looks again reminded him of his deceased wife, her sister.

"No telling. Oh, they also wrote about General MacArthur leading the Allies in the capture of Seoul, the South Korean capital toward the end of September. Robert and Richard were in that bitter battle. Thank God they survived."

Jim looked around the table. "And how about our teenagers here? Are y'all about to take over Newton High School?"

Some inaudible grunts and syllables passed between the young folks as answers. You couldn't coax much talking from the teenagers with adults present. But, typically, when they separated themselves from the grown-ups, the discussions flowed.

Jim knew they were all good kids. Arthur and Callie had done a pretty fair job raising their two, especially the girl. She was a sweetie, making good grades and having friends from fine families. But their boy, Art, was another thing. Jim had listened to Arthur when he talked about Art's less than stellar grades, which was not unexpected because he exhibited such a cavalier attitude about school. Jim agreed with Arthur that being a high school senior he showed very little maturity toward school or life. His tardy and absent days were always just within the bounds of required attendance to pass from grade to grade. Jim sympathized with Arthur and Callie who had little success in pinning Art down about where he was when he should have been in school.

Jim was proud of the three teenagers, all girls, that belonged to Shirley Ann and Henry Frank. They'd done a good job of raising them so far. Jim thought one of them looked just like his momma, the auburn hair and apple-green eyes and very much like their Aunt Emmajean. When Jim looked at Shirley Ann's daughter, he couldn't help but think of his baby sister Emmajean.

Now thirty, Emmajean had lived in Atlanta since she finished high school. She wrote Jim about her work in the fashion world of the big city. But Jim missed seeing her. She only came to Newton to visit maybe once or twice a year. Despite Jim's urging the last few years, she hadn't been coming home at all. She claimed her career had really taken off and she just couldn't get away, even on weekends. When Jim would write about visiting her, she strongly discouraged him, saying if he did visit, she wouldn't have any free time to spend with him. So, Jim and the folks had to be satisfied with occasional letters from Emmajean.

After perfectly baked Thanksgiving pumpkin pie, the adults stayed around the table, still talking. The teenagers—Callie's two and Shirley Ann's three—had long ago left the confines of the formal dining room, and sounds of the television and laughter drifted in from the old sewing room in the back of the house.

"Jim, do you know where The Twins are in Korea? Will they be able to enjoy a good dinner today?"

"Bones, I don't know. Haven't heard from them for a few weeks. They must be in the thick of it. I pray they're safe."

"We pray and trust they are," Callie said. "And, Jim, what about Emmajean?"

"I can't get through to her. I get no answers to my letters I write to her and she's never home when I call her place. The roommate never knows when to expect her back in."

"We may all have to go down to Atlanta and jerk some sense into her and convince our sister to come back home to Newton."

"After Momma and Poppa died during that pneumonia outbreak and Emmajean lived with us at Mrs. Hall's and then in that little house I rented, she grew up into a high-spirited girl. You couldn't tell her a thing. She always had all the answers. She was hard to reason with. I just hope that personality hasn't proved trouble for her down there."

Jim downed the last of his sweet iced tea as silence engulfed those at the table. Finally Shirley Ann spoke into the quiet.

"Jim, you're still alone in this big house. I worry about you bein' lonely and not eatin' right. You need a wife."

Callie took a chance and added, "And I believe Louisa would want you to find someone to share your life with. She loved you with all her heart, but it's been sixteen years. You can't turn back the clock."

Jim stared down at his empty plate. "You girls mean well, but it's not going to happen. No one can take Louisa's place in my life." He raised his head and looked around the table at them all. "I've said it before, but again I'll say I appreciate y'all helping me to raise Lynn. I think we all did a good job of that, don't you?"

Nods of agreement circled the table.

Shirley Ann broke the silence. "So, that's settled . . . once again. Let's get this table cleared. Everybody carry somethin' to the kitchen; then Callie and I will wash the dishes."

Chapter 46

The bed shook all over. Was it an earthquake? In Georgia?

"Emmajean," the perplexed voice shouted as the bed continued to shake.

"Huh?"

"Come on, get up. You'll be late."

"What?"

"Emmajean, get up. It's past six."

Bolting from the pillow, Emmajean looked at Angela from vacant eyes.

"What are you doin' up in the middle of the night?"

"It's not the middle of the night. It's daylight. Why didn't you get up when you turned off the alarm clock?"

"I turned off the clock? Not me. I just got to bed. What's your problem, Angela?"

"My problem is you. I don't see why you have to work on Thanksgiving. Nevertheless, Mr. Baker won't be so happy when you stroll into the diner late for work."

The mention of work spurred Emmajean from the bed. She hit the floor and made it to the bathroom in two leaps. Soon the shower turned on and Emmajean began banging around on the other side of the door.

Combing through her shoulder-length tangled auburn hair, Emmajean flung clothes around until she found the least wrinkled uniform. Arranging herself and taking one last glance in the dressing table mirror, she made her way to the door.

"Why didn't you wake me earlier?" she fused.

"I've been trying to wake you but you wouldn't budge. What time did you get in last night, anyway?"

"What, are you my momma now?"

When Angela backed off, holding her arms up palms forward, Emmajean continued a little calmer. "I don't know what time it was. Barry wanted to go out last night since today was a holiday and he didn't have to work. Then he wanted to stay out later than usual."

"Emmajean, what in the world do y'all do all hours of the night and where do you go? I still can't understand what you find to do around here in College Park. It's not Buckhead, after all. The sidewalks here practically roll up at dark."

Gathering up her purse and coat, Emmajean wondered just how dense her roommate could be. Of course, nothing happened in College Park past decent bedtime. But activity in Buckhead was a little rich for her and Barry. No, they didn't spend time in Buckhead. But pretty close. Wherever the customers caroused at night, Emmajean found them. Or rather Barry did and he and Emmajean delivered to them.

"Emmajean, you need to take time to eat some breakfast. You'll be on your feet for several hours and you'll run out of energy."

"I don't have time to eat, I'm goin' to be late as it is. I'll grab a coffee at the diner."

"You need to eat better and more. Your face is pale and look how skinny you are, Emmajean."

"Like I said, Are you my momma now?"

"I worry about you—out half the night then working every day."

"Angela, you know I failed at the fashion industry. Well, I really didn't even get into it enough to not make it. My high school teachers said I had artistic talent, but I just couldn't ever fit in here in the big city."

"Emmajean, for eight months now I've been asking you about where you and Barry take off to at night."

"Sometimes I wonder about what I'm doing too. But the good money Barry gives me sure does boost what Mr. Baker pays me or the tips I get at the diner."

"You make it sound so mysterious. Why won't you tell me?"

"If you want to know what Barry and I do, I'll talk to you about it when I come home from the diner. I don't have time now." She grabbed her purse. "I'll be lucky to get there for the breakfast crowd as it is. We'll talk then." And she hurried out the door.

~ ~ ~

That afternoon Emmajean poured iced tea for Angela and herself. Sitting across from each other at the kitchen table, Emmajean told Angela about her evenings with Barry.

"Angela, it's simple. I go with Barry on weekends as he drives north of downtown to a drive-in restaurant then parks in a space away from the buildin'."

"Why does he park there instead of parking up front?"

"Just wait . . . I'll tell you. Barry watches for certain cars that are meetin' him. Then Barry gives me a small paper sack to take to that car. He says I make a prettier delivery girl than he could and besides, he says, guys liked seein' a good lookin' redhead like me."

"What's in the sack?"

"I don't know. Barry tells me which car to take it to but not to look inside the sack or I'd be embarrassed. I think it might be guy stuff so I just deliver it and take their money back to Barry."

"It almost sounds like maybe he's using you for something illegal."

That scared Emmajean. "I don't think so. I hope not."

"Well, he's using you to do something he doesn't want to be seen doing. You'd better quit running around with Barry. He sounds to me like he could be trouble for you."

"If I quit Barry, I couldn't pay my half of the rent on this apartment."

"Well, I want to get far away from whatever it is Barry's up to. I'm moving. I'll be out before the weekend."

"Angela, you can't do that! I can't pay *all* the rent."

"Get another roommate." Angela went to her bedroom to begin packing.

~ ~ ~

When Emmajean asked Barry if he could pay her more, so she wouldn't lose her apartment, his solution was for her to leave her apartment and move in with him at Cabbagetown. Barry worked days at the Fulton Bag and Cotton Mill a few miles down the eastern rail line from downtown Atlanta. The mill owner, Jacob Elsas, had built a community of simple frame "shotgun" and cottage-style houses flanking the mill. Everyone living in this community worked in the mill, and Barry occupied one of the cottage-style houses.

"Barry, I can't live with you. I won't do that."

"Just as friends. You'd have your bedroom, I'd have mine."

When staring at the possibility of being kicked out of her apartment because she couldn't pay the rent, his offer seemed attractive. "If you're sure that's the way it'd be . . . okay. Can I move in this comin' weekend?"

Would she let her family know her new address? She'd been successful all these years to keep them from visiting her, giving various lame excuses. Her old standby explanation was she was so busy with her career she wouldn't have time to visit. The same excuse went for not ever going home. If she didn't give them her new Cabbagetown address or Barry's telephone number, she wouldn't have to continually lie her way around her family. But wouldn't not telling them she had moved be yet another deception in her long list of lies?

She weighed her two options and decided to not tell them she'd moved. Doing that, they wouldn't be able to contact her. Maybe soon they would forget her. She was a failure anyway so why would they even want to keep contact with her. Especially Jim. He'd become a successful businessman in Newton, and she would surely be an embarrassment to him if he knew the truth about her. It would be better if he didn't know.

Chapter 47

Caroline, James, and Lynn sat at the long dining table for the Hensen's Thanksgiving Day dinner. The same plump woman served the turkey with all the traditional trimmings—cornbread dressing, fluffy mashed potatoes, sweet potato soufflé, green bean casserole, deviled eggs, cranberry sauce, and delicious-smelling yeast rolls. The chandelier twinkling overhead reflected in Lynn's light blue eyes. Caroline watched the consuming attention James gave across the table toward Lynn. Her son had never told her he'd been in love before, but now Caroline feared he was falling head over heels for Lynn. And she seemed just as captivated with James.

Caroline decided that Lynn didn't look like Jimmy and her mother must have been that girl who worked at the mill and watched Jimmy like a hawk. Louisa, that was her name. Caroline vaguely remembered she had blue eyes as Lynn did and she was about the same size, young and slender. And she had the same blond hair.

"Lynn," Caroline ventured, "James tells me your daddy owns a hosiery mill in Newton?"

"Yes, ma'am, he does. Southeastern Hosiery. He used to work there; now he owns it. The former owner, a Mr. Jacob, and his wife died in a car crash with a Red Star Lines bus on their way to Chattanooga. Their wills left the mill to my daddy. They also left him their home. We live there now on the East side of town on the border of Caney Creek."

Her parents both dead! When did that happen? Caroline was glad to be sitting. How many more bolts of lightning could she endure? Where will all the surprises end? *Every time this child visits, more is revealed about her hometown and about Jimmy.*

Caroline's color faded and she grew silent.

"Mom, are you sick? You're as white as this tablecloth. What's wrong?"

"Oh . . . nothing. It just felt a little warm in here. Isn't it warm in here?"

"No, Mom."

"I'm sorry . . . Did I say something wrong, Mrs. Hensen?"

"No. No, Lynn. Of course not, dear. Who wants seconds on turkey or dressing?"

Caroline busied herself with the food, trying to let her emotions subside to normal once again. She found that impossible. Her hands shook when she passed the rolls. What must she do? Could she allow James to go to Lynn's home Saturday? To refuse him after she'd given permission for the trip would cause a terrible argument. She would let him go. None of the folks in Newton would know whose son James was. After all, his last name is Hensen, a name they don't know. For now she'd keep quiet and contemplate her options. Did she have any?

~ ~ ~

Saturday finally arrived. Lynn bounced on the front seat with excitement about the trip to Newton to see her daddy and her family. On the other hand, James dreaded the trip. James's mom was the only person Lynn had had to meet. Now he was being thrown into a covey of relatives. And in a strange place, away from his home turf. Nevertheless, as he drove, some of Lynn's enthusiasm flowed over James and began to cover his apprehension. Lynn jumped around in her seat, telling James once again about her family, especially her daddy, her hero.

"My Aunt Callie, mother's sister, married Daddy's best friend, Arthur. And then Daddy's sister, Aunt Shirley Ann, married her high school sweetheart Henry Frank Stevens. They'll all be at my house, along with their five teenagers, my cousins. My Aunt Emmajean, Daddy's baby sister, lives in Atlanta, but she won't be coming up. We don't see her much. I don't know why. And my daddy has two younger twin brothers, Uncle Richard and Uncle Robert. They're both in the army and in Korea. All my grandparents are dead. So . . . that's who my folks are.

"It's easy to get to Newton," Lynn continued. "We just follow four-eleven and it takes us straight there. You'll have to go through a few little towns on the way. Well, not any smaller than Newton," she smiled. "I told you we're having leftovers from Thanksgiving, didn't I? I'm sure my aunts prepared enough food on Thursday to feed several families, so you don't have to worry about there not being enough to eat. Are you anxious to meet my folks?"

"Sure. I'm looking forward to it." And he was. They were Lynn's family, important to her.

~ ~ ~

"Here they are," called Callie from the living room window as James pulled the car into the driveway of Lynn's house. "Oh, he's a handsome young man."

They all rushed out of their chairs and joined Callie at the window to peek out at Lynn and James.

"Get back," yelled Jim. "Poor boy, he's probably already nervous. Don't let him see y'all! He'll think we're a bunch of hicks who never see anybody pull in our driveway."

Jim met the two young people at the door, throwing it open. Lynn jumped into his arms. He still savored her little-girl hugs. Suddenly he didn't want to share her with anyone, especially not this good looking boy.

"Daddy, this is James. James this is my daddy."

James offered his hand to Jim. "Good to meet you, Mr. Callaway." Jim appreciated the boy's strong handshake.

"Oh, hey, everybody, here y'all are," Lynn noticed her folks in the living room. They had withdrawn from the window and politely remained in the living room while Jim had greeted the youngsters in the foyer.

~ ~ ~

Talk flowed all around the table during their early supper. James appeared at ease and fielded their many questions good-naturedly, satisfying everyone's curiosity. Jim was thinking of his twin brothers in Korea when he asked James how he had escaped the military draft.

"Since I'm a full-time college student the government granted me a 2-S deferment so I can finish my studies," James explained.

They wanted to know what he was studying and seemed satisfied when he told them he was thinking about pre-law but might change to business and go for a MBA degree later.

During all the conversations, Jim noticed Callie watching Lynn and James from down the table. What was she thinking?

Jim had noticed James's striking black hair and ebony eyes. Even his heavy eyebrows. He'd tried to gain more information from James about his family. But all he could learn was that he and his mother lived together in Knoxville and that his father had died in a railroad accident when James was a baby. No mention of aunts or uncles or even grandparents or distant cousins. It sounded to Jim that James and his mother were well situated financially and the boy spoke as if he was a product of proper upbringing. But when Jim looked more closely at the boy, it was almost like looking into a mirror. He didn't know any Hensens in Knoxville, though. Jim had never known any Hensens anywhere else, for that matter. Jim tried to dismiss these thoughts, to push them to the back of his mind.

~ ~ ~

"Arthur, what did you think of Lynn's friend?" Callie ventured as they drove home.

"James?"

"Yes. Did you like him?"

"He had a good handshake. You know, a man needs a good sturdy handshake to stand his ground in this world. People think better of a man if he does."

"Anything else?"

"Callie, what are you fishin' for? What else do you want me to say? He's a nice lookin' boy, he speaks well of his mother, he seemed at ease around all of us."

"Yes, he did. Almost like he was one of us, family. Did you think he looked like anybody we know?"

"What do you mean?"

"Arthur, think real hard. Who do you think he looks like?"

"Well, come to think of it, he has black hair like Jim, he's as tall as Jim. You thinkin' he looks like Jim?"

"Yes, it just struck me at the table. James and Lynn looked like a young Jim and Louisa."

"Callie, don't let your imagination get the better of you. James is just a nice, likable kid. I don't believe Jim has any kinfolks by the name of Hensen."

Callie looked out the passenger side window. "If you say so, Arthur."

~ ~ ~

In their bedroom while she dressed for bed, Shirley Ann kept running the supper at Jim's through her mind. Was it just her, or what?

"Henry Frank, what did you think of James?"

"He's a nice kid." Henry Frank sat and took off his shoes.

"That's all?"

"Well, he was easy to talk to even if he is a college-educated guy. What did you think of him?"

"I just wondered if you thought he looked like anybody we know."

"Well, maybe."

"Who?"

"Well, he looked a little like your brother. What do you think?"

"I think so too. The black hair and dark eyes. And he's tall like Jim."

"Yeah, you're right. How about that?"

As she slipped into bed, Shirley Ann sank into her pillows and pulled up the covers. They'd never known any Hensens, especially not any in Knoxville.

"Finished with the light?" Henry Frank was ready to crawl into bed.

"Hmmmm." Shirley Ann snuggled against Henry Frank.

~ ~ ~

Caroline had already gone to bed when James returned home late after he and Lynn came home from Newton on Sunday. She heard him make his way to his bedroom.

At breakfast Monday morning, Caroline wanted to know about his trip without seeming to pry. She asked gentle questions and leaned in anxiously for his answers. Caroline gave James her undivided attention as he described Lynn's home and her thoughts took hold as she could remember being in those very rooms James had been shown. That's where she had grown up and she couldn't even tell her son.

"Mom, you should see Newton. It's a neat little town, laid out around the courthouse square. And then the houses on the east side of town are bordered on the back of their lots by Caney Creek. Its water is clear and bubbly, so peaceful."

There it was again. Caney Creek. Caney Creek would forever bind her to Newton. And to Jimmy. Does Jimmy ever think about that July Fourth, what with Caney Creek always running behind his house? Yes, James, Caney Creek is clear and so very peaceful. The rippling sounds of its bubbly water had helped her to fall asleep many nights.

"Mom, are you okay? You drifted away there for a minute. You've been doing that a lot lately."

"I'm okay. Just thinking of how you enjoyed your trip. What did you think of Lynn's daddy?"

"He was nice. Made me feel welcome. They all did. Her Aunt Callie looked at me pretty strong at the dining table, though. But I guess maybe she just wanted to size me up to make sure I was good enough for Lynn. You know, since Lynn's mother is dead maybe her Aunt Callie steps in to do the things a mother would ordinarily do."

"Yes, you may be right." Caroline remained fairly certain that Louisa had an older sister who also worked at the hosiery mill her daddy had owned.

"Mom, what do you think about inviting Lynn and her daddy here sometime during our Christmas break?'

"Oh, James, I don't know . . . ."

"Please think about it. We can talk about it later. I've got to run to class. See you this afternoon."

Jimmy here?! How could she get around this? Did she want him to visit them? Caroline wanted to see him so badly she ached all over. But, did she dare, did she dare impose into his life? Now? Tell him he has a son? And that her son and his daughter are fast moving into a relationship? Maybe Jimmy could help her diffuse this situation better than she could do it alone. *Would* he help her?

Chapter 48

Caroline was torn between inviting Lynn and her daddy to her home and refusing James his request for the Christmas season. She wouldn't explain why she was hesitant, and he couldn't understand her. Caroline had used every reason she could think of not to have them in her home. All her excuses floundered when James continued to beg her to relent. She'd never denied him much that he'd asked for over the years. He was a good kid. But this recent request of his had Caroline stumped as to what to do.

She supposed he was so adamant about having Lynn and her daddy in his home because he'd grown up with no family, just him and Caroline. He said Lynn's folks made him feel like family. Since he's never had a *family,* he might be inventing his own with the Newton folks he met over Thanksgiving.

"Mom, we have so many bedrooms there wouldn't be a problem to have them stay a night or two. And it wouldn't be extra work for you, Mom. You have Mildred to do all the cooking and cleaning."

"James, I just don't know . . . . "

"Why can't you make up your mind on this? I've never seen you like this."

Of course he'd never seen her like this! She'd never been like this! After twenty years she had a chance to see Jimmy again. What would his reaction be? When he saw her would he leave or would he stay? Oh, just to see him again. Her daddy had sent her to Aunt Martha's and she had no chance to explain to Jimmy what was happening. She'd never tried to contact Jimmy. She didn't want to disrupt James's life by having to tell him the identity of his real father. Maybe now she wouldn't have a choice. There's only one way to learn the outcome of this mess. Invite him here.

"You're correct, of course. Tell me when you would like for them to be here, and I'll have Mildred ready their rooms for two nights. Will they come before or after Christmas?"

"I'll talk to Lynn and we'll work it out." He went to her and gave her a tight hug. "Thanks, Mom. It'll all work out fine."

She certainly hoped so for all of them, especially for her son and Jimmy.

Chapter 49

"Mrs. Hensen, what is the matter with you?"

"Mildred, nothing is the matter with me. Why do you ask?"

"Mrs. Hensen, pardon me, but you have paced all over this house for a few days and you're checking and rechecking everything. I've been with you since James was a small child and I've never seen you this restless."

Caroline looked at Mildred. Was she that transparent?

"I'm finished in here. I'll leave you to yourself then."

Alone in the kitchen, Caroline began pacing again. What had she opened by inviting Lynn and Jimmy here for two days? Had she lost her mind? She shouldn't have done it. She should have left well enough alone. After twenty years, everyone in Newton had forgotten her, even Jimmy. What was she thinking?

James entered the kitchen. "Mom, you look beautiful."

"Thank you, James. Do you think this emerald silk blouse and velvet skirt are too much?"

"No, of course not. You look radiant. Your eyes even sparkle."

The brightness in her eyes probably came from the bouts of tears that she couldn't stem every time she thought about what she was about to do. James left to go to the front of the house to watch for Lynn and her daddy.

Since James had been born, Caroline had never done anything spontaneous or foolish. But today would make up for all that. She'd never been as unsure and uncertain as today. Using poor judgment as she had that day on the mossy bank of Caney Creek, today would at least equal that foolishness. Surely the consequences of today wouldn't sprout tentacles as far-reaching and life-changing as those of that one day twenty years ago.

"Mom," James called from the living room. "They're here."

Caroline froze. She was unable to move forward yet unable to retreat farther into the back of the house.

~ ~ ~

James opened the door for Lynn and her daddy, took his hat, their coats, and then showed them to the living room.

"I'm glad you finally got here." James couldn't stop smiling. "Excuse me, I'll go get Mom."

"It's a lovely room, isn't it Daddy? Warm and toasty with the fireplace blazing."

Lynn walked toward the fireplace and Jim's gaze followed her. Then his eyes rested on the portrait above the mantel. What a beautiful woman and she looked familiar. The hair, the sapphire eyes, the ivory skin. Jim wondered if the girl in the picture was Caroline Jacob. No that was impossible. The girl in the portrait could be a sister to Caroline, but some of Caroline's sauciness was missing in the girl's face. Wait . . . what's that around her neck?

Studying the portrait carefully, Jim didn't hear James say, "Mom will be here in a minute."

Jim turned away from the fireplace just as Caroline rounded the corner of the archway and entered the room. A blow hit the center of his chest and sucked his breath away. Then the dizziness moved upward into his head. The room whirled around him and he became mute. Jim turned to look at the portrait above the fireplace once again and then back at Caroline. When his eyes met hers she nodded. It *was* Caroline. Just as beautiful as the first time he'd seen her, coming out of her daddy's office at the mill in Newton. She'd had on a green blouse that day and had had a similar effect on him. She had her strawberry blond hair pulled away from her face and looked like royalty with it in a French twist resting low on the back of her head. And there was the garnet lying at her throat.

~ ~ ~

Caroline had made it to the living room and then had frozen again. Her feet would not move. She couldn't utter a word. It *was* her Jimmy. He was the same. Tall and handsome with that dazzling black hair and those amazing eyes as dark as the night. He had replaced the middle part in his hair with a neat side part. He looked so nice in his suit and wide red necktie, but he still hadn't mastered tying his tie just right. Her heart pounded in her ears as their eyes held each other's. Twenty years! And she had been unable to let him know about James or her location. Could he ever understand even if he gave her a chance to explain? How quickly would he leave now that he was there?

Caroline opened her mouth then closed it because she couldn't find her voice. But remembering her manners, she finally spoke. "Please, Mr. Callaway, you and Lynn have a seat."

"Jimmy. Please, call me Jimmy."

"Fine. Call me Caroline."

James and Lynn stood on the periphery of this emotion-packed scene surrounding their parents. Neither of them could comprehend what they were witness to, what exactly was transpiring.

In the living room Jim and Lynn took the sofa across from Caroline, and James sat in the side chair near Lynn's end of the sofa. Conversation between Jim and Caroline was next to impossible. How could they bridge twenty years with mere words? Lynn and James picked up the banter while their parents contributed one-word responses here and there. Caroline noticed Jim chancing glances at James with a questioning look and a furrowed brow. Had he guessed that James was his son? He couldn't know for sure unless she told him. Tell him? Of course she'd tell him! She must! The pretense had gone on far too long.

James ventured to break the reason for the difficult conversation, whatever it was. "Mr. Callaway, I'll go out to your car to bring in your luggage and take it upstairs." He and Lynn left the room and soon returned to climb the stairs leading to the second floor. Almost immediately they returned to the still-silent living room.

"Mom, Lynn and I are going to watch the television in the back."

"Yes." She silently thanked James, for sensing that the grown-ups needed some time alone. Even if he didn't have a clue as to why.

Silence fell hard in the large room. Only the sound of the crackling fire embraced them. Jim leaned forward, his elbows on his knees and his chin resting in his hands. He closed his eyes and covered them with his fingertips. The image of Louisa's sweet face swept through him. Here he sat within two steps of Caroline, his lost love, and he couldn't push Louisa out of his thoughts. All these years after Louisa had died, Jim still remained loyal to her. She was his life. He'd never sought to replace her. Her love for him had been enough. And now here was Caroline.

Finally finding her voice again she implored, "Jimmy, please let me explain."

"Explain?" Jim stormed to his feet. "It's been twenty years since you just waltzed out of my life with not even a note to say where you went and now you want to explain? No, Caroline, it's too late for that!"

Jim started for the door then turned toward the back of the house to find Lynn. Caroline bolted from her chair and reached him before he could call out to Lynn. She placed her hand on Jim's strong arm. He looked down at her hand, the heat of her moving through his body.

"Jimmy, please give me a chance to tell you what happened that Christmas Day I left."

"I don't want to hear . . ."

"But you must hear me out. Sit down. Please," Caroline begged.

~ ~ ~

Jim was torn between his years of questioning Caroline for what she had done to him, and now a chance to hear her try to justify herself. After all the years of absence, they stood together in the same room, a room foreign to him but one that held the presence of his former love. He moved to the sofa and sat. She went to the chair across from him.

"Now, Jimmy, please don't cut in. You deserve to know what happened, so let me tell you. That last Christmas season, I found out I was pregnant . . . No, don't, just let me finish. When I became sick on Christmas morning, at the breakfast table, I hurried upstairs to my bedroom. Mother followed and I had to tell her why I was sick . . . nausea plagued me for over five months, all day long. Of course, she called for Daddy. He demanded I tell him who the boy was. When I wouldn't give him a name, he sent me here to Knoxville to Aunt Martha's and told me I was to have the baby and give it up for adoption. Daddy demanded that Aunt Martha intercept any letters I might receive and any that I might try to mail. I couldn't use the telephone without my aunt knowing. I couldn't get in touch with you. I wanted to, but it was impossible.

"When I had the baby, I *couldn't* give it up for adoption. Aunt Martha telephoned Daddy and told him that, but he wouldn't permit me to come home if I brought the baby. Daddy also told Aunt Martha that the Jacob name had better not be on my baby's birth certificate or be used as his last name—ever."

Caroline paused to brush tears from her cheeks with her fingertips and gather her courage to continue. Jim saw her glance at him, but he showed her no hint on his face of his thinking. He wondered at what bravery she must have had to go through everything all alone.

"Daddy basically disowned me and my child. He said he and Mother never wanted to see me again. I had disgraced them. He wouldn't permit my return to Newton under any circumstance." She sobbed out loud, her shoulders shaking, as she covered her face with both hands.

Jim didn't move toward her, didn't rise from the sofa. He hadn't stopped her, as she'd requested. He didn't have appropriate words for the situation. Were there any?

"Aunt Martha was kinder to me than my own parents." Caroline continued this impossible explanation. "She invited me to stay here with her as long as I wanted. And, Jimmy, she talked to me about God and led me to His restoration." Jim couldn't keep his lips from curving in a slight smile at that. "Aunt Martha also said that since Daddy was being so stubborn and unfair that I needed a new last name for myself and my child.

"Her husband had been dead for eight years so she didn't have to ask for anybody's permission to give away her last name. Her girls were married and had other names. They would have no right to argue with her on this. So she declared that if I wanted it, the name was mine. I could be Caroline Hensen and my baby could be James Hensen. We went to the Probate Judge and had the change made legal and had another birth certificate issued for James. Aunt Martha helped my situation tremendously by doing that."

Caroline stopped talking. She had no more that she could give Jim to help him span the last twenty years. She stood, approached the fireplace, and punched the logs around with the poker. She didn't look at the sadness and questions Jim now had on his face. She turned her back to him and stayed at the fireplace. Jim thought she was probably waiting for him to say something. Anything. She waited.

When Jim finally stood, wiping his palms on his pants legs, he didn't approach Caroline. He feared what he might do if he was within arms' reach of her—hug her, sympathize with her over what she had been through alone, say he was sorry for thinking badly of her, or ask if James was his son.

He took a few steps toward her, struggling for the right words. "Caroline, did you and James live in this house with your aunt?"

"Yes. She died several years ago and left the house to me. She also left me well off financially. I'll never have to work unless I choose to. And, Jimmy," she continued, "after Aunt Martha died I wanted to try to find you. But I decided that if I could have found you, I would have been so embarrassed for you to know about me. I figured you had a family of your own by then. But, when James began telling me about this girl he'd met . . . and that she was from Newton . . . and when he went down there and visited . . . it all came together."

"Caroline, I'm so sorry for all you've gone through alone these past twenty years. I wish I would've known. Your daddy said you married a boy in Atlanta and moved to his home in Texas."

Caroline wiped her cheeks again and turned to face him. "I've thought about you every day. You and James have been my life."

"Caroline, is James . . . ?"

"Yes," Caroline answered quickly to relieve his discomfort. "He's your son. He's *our* son."

No wonder Jim had imagined he was looking in a mirror when they met at Thanksgiving. The boy had to be his son. That July Fourth beside Caney Creek.

"Oh, Caroline, why couldn't I have known?"

He started toward her just when the kids entered the room, full of chatter.

"Mom, Mildred says dinner is ready whenever you want it served."

"Thank you. Fine. Well then, let's move to the dining room." Her voice trembled and she shivered as she walked past Jim. Their eyes met, but they couldn't continue their conversation. She clasped her arms across her chest to help calm herself. Jim dutifully followed them into the dining room. Caroline, James, and Lynn took the same places they'd sat before when Lynn visited. The only extra place setting was at the other end of the table, opposite Caroline.

It was a most trying meal to get through. The food was delightful, but eating was difficult for Caroline and Jim who could barely swallow past the tightness in their throats. Caroline had never had a gentleman friend in her home and Mildred smiled at her each time she came into the room.

After dinner, James and Lynn went out to get ice cream although they had eaten heartily of Mildred's chocolate cake. After Mildred finished up in the kitchen, they heard her car leave the driveway. They looked at one another. The first time in twenty years they had been alone. Who would speak first? Or make a move toward the other?

"Caroline, those kids are crazy about each other. We can't let them continue to spend time alone together without knowing the truth. They must be told they're half brother and sister."

"Well, who's going to tell them? It will break their hearts. I know what a broken heart feels like. I can't tell them."

"I've had a broken heart too. When I couldn't find you."

She moved to sit on the sofa next to Jim and laid her left hand lightly on his right hand. With his other hand he slowly covered hers. They looked down at their touching skin. Caroline's breath became shallow and Jim thought she could probably hear his thundering heartbeat. With her other hand Caroline reached for his cheek and turned Jim's face toward her. He searched her eyes and discovered love for him sparkling there.

~ ~ ~

The front door swooshed open, bringing in the cold December air. Jim heard James and Lynn in the sizable foyer hanging up their coats in the closet. What a knack the kids had at fortuitous intrusion at awkward times. Jim moved away from Caroline, pretending to do anything except what their children had disrupted.

"It's beginning to snow hard and we decided we'd better get back. I guess we can find some ice cream in the kitchen." They walked past the living room. James smiled at Lynn. "And also fix some hot chocolate."

They vanished in the direction of the kitchen. Jim looked at Caroline. So much to discuss and decide. So much between them that had to be resolved before they could go on. *Could* they go on? Could they again be part of each other's life? He turned toward Caroline to speak, when James appeared in the archway.

"Mom, you and Mr. Callaway want some hot chocolate?"

She consulted him and he shrugged okay.

"Sure, James, thanks for asking. A mug of hot chocolate will help ease the chill in the air." Caroline again hugged her arms across her chest trying to get rid of an unwelcome sensation of cold.

After James returned to the kitchen Jim rubbed a hand up and down Caroline's arm, the silk of her blouse smooth to his touch. She shivered, and he went to the fireplace, bent over and added another log. The fire spit, caught and claimed the new log, engulfing it with flames. He stood to look back at her only to find that she had followed him and faced him when he turned around.

Jim stepped around her. "Caroline, we can't chance the nearness. Even if we want to and I'm not sure we should want to. Not yet . . . if ever. The kids wouldn't understand."

"Here we go. Hot chocolate all around." Lynn followed James who carried the tray covered with a linen cloth, sporting four steaming mugs and some cookies.

When they each held their mugs, James raised his mug. "A toast to our guests!"

As they raised their mugs, four swirls of steam reached upward to the ceiling and vanished, not to be retrieved. Was this what all their dreams would do—vanish before they had a chance to grab them? Jim wondered what the future held for them all.

~ ~ ~

After James and Lynn went to bed at separate ends of the upstairs hall, Jim and Caroline sat at the kitchen table gazing at the melting ice cream in their bowls. They had more questions than answers and cast the other bewildered looks. Jim thought about his past and speculated on his future.

Finally, Jim spoke. "You haven't asked about what became of me during the last twenty years."

When she didn't reply, he continued. "I married Louisa Johnson. Caroline, I loved her. She was my life and an excellent mother to Lynn. Louisa died with pneumonia when Lynn was only two years old. When she died I begged God to let me die with her, I was lost without her. But then I knew that wasn't to be, I had Lynn to take care of. I didn't know how I was supposed to do that, but I leaned on God to get me through. My sister Shirley Ann and Louisa's sister Callie actually helped me to raise Lynn from that point on. I sometimes wonder where Lynn and I would be had they not been around."

Caroline nodded.

He had to say it. "Caroline, I didn't know where you were or if you were coming back . . . I didn't know. Then when Lynn was eleven your folks died in a car wreck with a bus and left me the mill. And their home. I'm living in your parents' house."

Caroline nodded again. "I know. I've heard most of this in conversations with Lynn and James. I guess I put the rest of it together, about Louisa." She reached across the table and laid her hand over his. "Jimmy, I'm sorry for your loss."

Jim smiled, withdrew his hand and stirred his melted ice cream. He forced his thoughts to the present, to Lynn and James.

"Jimmy, tell me about my parents' accident."

"Oh, well, they were driving to Chattanooga and collided with a Red Star Lines bus headed to Knoxville." He paused to gauge Caroline's emotions, talking about the deaths of her parents. "The sheriff's office never determined who was at fault, but . . . your parents died instantly from the impact. They didn't suffer."

Caroline nodded. "Thank you for telling me, Jimmy."

Jim sought to turn the conversation around. "What about this? Lynn and I will leave for home tomorrow to separate the kids for a while."

"And separate us again." Caroline said.

"No, Caroline. Now, wait. They have a few more days of Christmas break. I'll tell Lynn I have a business trip for the mill that can't wait until after the holidays. She can stay with her Aunt Callie or Aunt Shirley Ann. They'll think my trip is for business too. Then I'll drive back up here and somehow we'll meet, just the two of us. Do you think you can get away from James for an afternoon?"

"Yes, I believe I can arrange that. When will you come back? Can we pick a day now?" If they didn't set a day, would he come back?

"Caroline, I can see the doubt in your eyes. I *will* come back. If not for us then for the kids. We have to figure out how we're going to keep them apart, how and when we're going to break the truth to them."

"It won't be easy for us or for them."

"I know, but we can't let things continue as they are between them. They look so . . . comfortable together."

"Jimmy, that's the way we used to look. And we *were* comfortable together."

"Let's don't go there, Caroline. I think we have to get our kids straightened out first."

Chapter 50

Jim remembered yesterday driving home with Lynn when she'd asked him why they couldn't stay another day in Knoxville. She let him know of her disappointment.

Now he was driving alone on his way back to Knoxville. Caroline was to meet him for a late lunch at two o'clock at Regis Restaurant, downtown. What would they talk about? Would they talk about themselves instead of about the kids? No, their purpose for meeting today was to discuss the kids. And that's what they must do first. First things first.

Jim had never been to the Regis. When he entered the restaurant, its magnificence caught him off guard. But then he smiled to himself. The place was pure Caroline. Always sophisticated with a quiet richness. The lush carpet and upholstered chairs and banquettes were a proper backdrop for Caroline. Fresh flowers in tiny crystal bowls graced every table.

He checked his hat and overcoat with the girl near the front. "I'm meeting Mrs. Hensen."

"Right this way, sir." She led him straightaway to a table in an out-of-the-way alcove.

Caroline was already seated and glowed in her dark scarlet woolen suit. She smiled up at Jim as he approached, his long strides taking him to her table. Jim thought she looked even lovelier in this setting than at her home. She also looked a little more relaxed now that their initial meeting yesterday had passed.

Earlier luncheon diners still lingered over their food. Heads turned as Jim neared the table just as men diners had followed Caroline's entrance when she'd arrived earlier. Women smiled and whispered what beautiful children the couple would have together.

"Hello, Caroline." Jim took a seat across the table from her.

"Jimmy." Caroline smiled up at him.

The waitress arrived at their table with two glasses of iced water and laid menus on the table in front of them. They both busied themselves with reading the luncheon selections, neither of them sure of where this meeting would lead. They had to consider their children's future first but where were their own futures headed?

Caroline pointed to the different items listed on the menu. "The baked chicken is good here, or the steaks are also good."

The waitress appeared again and asked if they were ready to order. Caroline ordered the chicken with sweet iced tea. After pausing slightly, Jim ordered the same. He thought something light would sit better on his stomach with what may lie ahead of them.

"Jimmy, how was your drive up."

"Fine. Just fine. Caroline, have you given thought to how we're going to handle this situation between Lynn and James?"

"*Handle* it?"

"Yes, *handle* it. Somehow we've got to put the brakes on their budding relationship. Do you know how far James's infatuation with Lynn has gone?"

"No, not for sure. But James says he's never met a girl like Lynn. That she seems like family, he can talk to her about anything."

"That sounds more like a friendship that a relationship. Great. Now we just have to keep it from blooming into something more serious."

"I don't think James would be moving that fast with Lynn."

Well, his mother had moved fast enough with Jim. He remembered how he had loved every minute of her attentions.

Caroline reached across the table, laid her hand on Jim's, and smiled at him as if she read his mind, as if she had the same memories. Jim gently withdrew his hand out of her reach.

"Caroline, how does this plan sound to you?"

"Jimmy," she broke in, "wait. Why don't you relax and enjoy our time together. People are all around us. I'm not going to leap across the table into your lap." She smiled at him. "But I do love being with you."

"I'm relaxed. But I just want to get this settled about the kids."

Just then their lunch arrived and Jim and Caroline fell silent while the waitress placed their salads, drinks, and bread on the table. They ate for a few minutes without talking. When they both looked up from their plates, their eyes locked as if they were again at The Evergreen Café south of Newton. The noises from the surrounding people faded away and so did the problems involving their kids.

"Jimmy . . ."

"What?"

"Jimmy, can we ever be together again? What would it take?"

"Caroline, I honestly don't know. I've thought about it since I left you yesterday. I couldn't sleep, I couldn't keep my mind on anything else. But your home's here. It's all James has known and he's in school here. My home's in Newton where my mill is. Can either of us leave our places?"

Caroline gazed blankly at Jim and struggled for an answer to his question. She had none. She hadn't thought it through, only that she desperately wanted it to work for them again. When she didn't answer him, the quiet gave Jim time to realize that they needed to get back to their original reason for meeting. He cleared his throat and began.

"Caroline, let's get back to my plan. How's this? We must explain to the children the past that joins them together. When I get back to Newton I'll sit down with Lynn and make it clear to her about our past and that James is my son, her half brother. After I leave today, you do the same with James. Tell him I'm his father and that Lynn's his half sister. This won't be easy for either one of us but we have to do it. For the kids if not for ourselves. What do you say? Can you do that?"

She still didn't answer him. Jim didn't know whether to take that as a yes or a no. He waited her out until she finally answered.

She reached again for his hand and held on tightly. "I guess that's what we must do. I can do this if I know we will see each other again. James and Lynn will be shattered, but let's temper the news with a promise that we can all four get together often. James needs to know his father. I hope he won't hate us and that he will want to get to know you. And, Jimmy, I hope Lynn won't hate you or me and can be a friend to James. I can do this if I know you support me."

"We'll support each other. When do their classes start again?"

"January third."

"So, we don't have time to waste. As soon as I get back home I'll talk to Lynn. Maybe she'll be over the shock of the news in time to get back to school."

"Jimmy, when are you leaving for Newton?"

"Well, I told Callie and Lynn that I'd be back tomorrow so guess I'd better find me a place to stay the night and head on out in the morning."

"You can stay at my house."

He shook his head back and forth. "No, Caroline, I can't. James would wonder why I'm here alone and would be sure to tell Lynn he's seen me. No, I'll get someplace to stay. Where would you suggest?"

"We have a nice hotel at the east end of Gay Street, the Andrew Johnson, right on the river. . . . Jimmy, can we spend the afternoon together? I told James I'd be gone most of the day."

~ ~ ~

After finishing lunch they left The Regis Restaurant. "You follow me in your car to the hotel."

Jim secured a room for the night, left his car parked there and joined Caroline in hers. From there Caroline drove Jim around Knoxville and the UT campus—just like she had driven him around twenty years ago. It was an enjoyable time, neither pressuring the other for anything more than companionship. Maybe they *could* get together again. Maybe start as friends.

~ ~ ~

Now as he drove closer to Newton, Jim began to ponder his talk with Lynn. He had stayed awake most of last night formulating the conversation they must have. It was obvious that Lynn was delighted to have James's attentions and looked forward to time spent with him. Jim just wished he knew for sure how she would react to the news. She'd often mentioned that she would have enjoyed having a brother, or even a sister. But he was sure this was not the way she imagined getting one. Jim resolved to have their talk this evening. Lynn had to leave for winter quarter in a few days.

~ ~ ~

Lynn fixed a beef stew with potatoes and carrots for their supper. Her specialty. Her biscuits were light and fluffy and slathered with honey and butter, they were a delicious desert.

She washed dishes while Jim dried and put away, each lost in their own thoughts.

"Daddy, why did James's mother call you Jimmy?"

Their talk was beginning before he was ready. But what a way for Lynn to help him along.

He handed Lynn the dishtowel. "Lynn, rinse you hands and dry them. Come sit with me at the kitchen table."

"What is it Daddy? You look so serious. What's wrong?"

"You asked me a question. I want to try to answer you. James's mother and I knew each other twenty years ago right here in Newton. Her parents were Mr. and Mrs. Jacob who owned the mill. Mr. Jacob hired me on and I did good work for him. When they both died in a car crash, their wills left me the mill and their house, this house."

Before he continued, Jim reached for Lynn's hand and held it firmly to prevent her from leaving the kitchen when she heard what he was about to say.

"Mr. Jacob's daughter Caroline, James's mother, took a liking to me and we began to see each other. She had a car and would take me places. I liked her too. Besides, I was dating the boss's daughter and that made me think I was special. She didn't want to call me Jim like other people did, so she always called me Jimmy. She was a real sweet girl."

He could sense Lynn's hand trying to tug away from his grip. He gripped it tighter, with both hands.

"What about Mother? Were you dating both of them?"

"This is the part I'm not proud of myself for. My behavior was unforgivable. I was dating both of them at the same time. I had just come off the farm to Newton, a big city to me at that time. I already knew your mother when I met Caroline. But, you see, Caroline was away for college down near Atlanta. I would date her when she'd come home for the summer and at Christmas. That's about the time your mother moved into town and she finally told me I had to make a choice between the two of them. I chose your mother."

"So, what about you knowing James's mother? Is that it?"

Jim looked at his shoes for a while. "Well, no, it's not all. Caroline and I were indiscreet. One time. She got pregnant. Her daddy sent her to her aunt's in Knoxville and told her to give the baby up for adoption. If she didn't, she could never return to Newton. When she had the baby, she couldn't give him up and her daddy basically disowned her."

Jim held onto Lynn's hand although she half rose out of her chair. Pain twisted her face.

"Daddy—"

"Lynn, you are my daughter. You're mine and your mother's daughter. Caroline is James's mother . . . and I'm his daddy."

As she pulled and pulled her hand, trying to free herself from Jim, he rose with her from the table. To keep her from running away and to give her comfort if she'd take it, he enclosed her in his arms. She tried to resist him, beating his shoulders relentlessly, until finally he wore her down and her sobs began. Every time he thought she had cried herself out, he loosened his grip on her only to find that she began pelting him again.

Finally calmed down, they sat on the sofa with Lynn's head on her daddy's shoulder.

"Daddy . . . ?" she asked in a whisper, wiping tears from her cheeks.

"What, Sweetheart?"

"Daddy, is James my half brother?"

"Yes . . . . Yes, he is."

"Why didn't you tell me sooner? Why now?"

"After Caroline left town and didn't return, her daddy told everybody she had married and moved to Texas. I didn't know she was in Knoxville or that she'd had a baby. When we visited them after Christmas I saw her for the first time in twenty years. I guessed that James was my son and she confirmed it."

"Do Aunt Callie and Aunt Shirley Ann and everybody know?"

"I think when Aunt Callie saw him here after Thanksgiving she noticed the resemblance between James and me, but you're the first person I've told. Lynn, I hope you can forgive me for what I've done and not hate me. And not hate Caroline either. I hope you and James can remain friends. The four of us can get together from time to time if you want to."

When Jim looked at her, he saw a jumble of mixed emotions contorting her face—confusion, hurt, questions, accusation.

"Daddy, I'm really tired. I'd like to go to bed if that's okay with you."

"Sure. You go on up. I'll finish things in the kitchen. If you want to talk more, we can do it in the morning after you've rested." He kissed her cheek. "Good night."

"Goodnight, Daddy."

He watched her climb the curved staircase to her bedroom. Jim was bushed and as weary as she looked. Would they talk more on this? Was she satisfied with what he'd told her? Did he do a good job of telling her how the past had now tangled up the future for her and her daddy? What would tomorrow bring?

Chapter 51

The day after having lunch with Jim at The Regis, Caroline wandered through her house, from room to room. In college she was the calm one with chaos all around her, but not anymore. Not today. She reminded herself of what she'd done all by herself. Well, with Aunt Martha's help. She'd raised James and what a fine young man he was today. She'd managed her money well and kept her looks and figure. But in just a few days her life had been jumbled up like pieces of a jigsaw puzzle. Now she faced a new hurdle. James really did care for Lynn. Her news might devastate him. Would it ruin their past? Take away a pleasant future? Many parents didn't have a good connection with their kids. Would that happen with James and her? And if it did, would he hate his mom?

After dinner James had gone out with some friends, and Caroline had taken that time alone to prepare herself for her discussion with James.

"Hey, Mom," James called when he entered the foyer. Coming into the living room, he went directly to the fireplace where he rubbed his hands together to warm them. "It's still pretty cold outside. What've you been doing?"

She laid her book aside. "Reading. Can you sit with me a while?"

James joined Caroline on the sofa.

"What is it, Mom? What's wrong?"

"Nothing. I need to talk to you about something but I want you not to cut me short. Okay?"

"Okay."

"James, Lynn's daddy and I knew each other when we were very young. Twenty years ago."

"Why didn't Lynn tell me?"

"Lynn didn't know. I didn't know. But when Lynn and her daddy came here a few days ago we both recognized one another. We met in Newton, Lynn's hometown."

Caroline paused, not wanting James to speak, but giving him a chance if he had a question. He must have questions.

"Mr. Callaway and I spent a lot of time together while he worked at the mill and I was in school at Agnes Scott College near Atlanta. Daddy had bought me a little Buick two door sedan and all summer I would drive Mr. Callaway and me around everywhere. We agreed on just about everything. We had the best times." Caroline became misty-eyed and stopped to catch her breath.

She finished explaining her story to James. What life-changing news she'd laid on James. Why didn't he say anything?

"James, please don't hate me for what I've told you. For what I've done. And please don't hate your daddy. He didn't know where I was or that you existed until Lynn and he visited us a few days ago."

She could see questions lurking behind his dark eyes. Why was he hesitant to speak?

"James . . . Lynn is your half sister." Caroline waited for James to say something and when he didn't she asked, "James, do you understand?"

After a lengthy and quiet consideration, James met his mom's eyes. "Mom, remember when I first met Lynn I told you we got along so well together, that she seemed like family? That we could talk about anything? Well, that's what she is, family. My family. Now I have a sister."

"James, it looks like you two are crazy about each other." She hesitated then asked, "How far has your relationship gone?"

Caroline waited for his answer, but dreaded to hear it.

"Mom, I've kissed her on the cheek a few times, but that's it. Basically all we do is have fun together. Does Lynn know all you've told me?"

"Mr. Callaway is supposed to be telling her today."

"Why don't you call him Jimmy? Now that I know."

"Really? Thank you, James." A tear trailed down from her eye.

James gently wiped the tear away with his fingertips.

"Mom, thank you for telling me. I don't hate you or Mr. Callaway. I'm proud of you for raising me so well. I wish I could've known my dad earlier, but maybe we can be together now. Do you think we can all get together some"

"Of course, we can. If fact, Jimmy and I hoped we would. He wants to get to know you. I've been wondering, do you have plans with your friends for New Year's Eve?"

"No. Please see if they can come up. Or, we could go down there, couldn't we?"

What a joy James had always been to her. Especially right now. How had she been so lucky to have a son so sensitive and kind and mature?

~ ~ ~

Caroline saw Jim watching out a living room window. James held her elbow, careful of the icy patches from the recent snow, as they walked up the steps and across the deep front porch. Before they reached the door, Jim flung it open, a broad smile covering his face. Standing slightly behind him was Lynn, trying to smile. It was an awkward moment before Jim moved aside and motioned them inside.

Caroline noted the concerned look James gave Lynn. "Hello, Lynn."

"Hey."

Caroline glanced around the house she had been forced to leave many years ago. It was just as she remembered—the curved stairway, second floor balcony, tall ceilings, beautiful fireplace—and it appeared Jimmy had changed nothing since it was her girlhood home.

Jim watched her reminisce. "It's almost like you left it."

"It's good to come back."

"Lynn, please take their coats."

James stepped to her side. "I'll help you."

~ ~ ~

Jim and Caroline moved into the living room, leaving the kids in the entrance hall.

"Lynn, Mom told me about everything. How're you doing with it all? You going to be okay?"

"Sure, I guess. You?" They finished hanging the coats in the closet.

"Yeah. I knew you were special that first day I met you in the drugstore. You seemed like family from the start. I told Mom that. Now you are. Family, I mean." He opened his arms to Lynn. She hesitated before walking into them. She wrapped her arms around his waist and gripped the back of his sport coat in her fists. He hugged her gently, allowing her soft sobs to move her whole body.

"It's going to be okay. It's really going to be great. Nothing will tear us apart ever. We're family."

She pushed an arm's length away from him. searching his face.

"You're really okay with all this, aren't you?"

"Yeah."

"You don't hate my daddy?"

"No. It's all in the past. They were young . . . and in love from what Mom tells me. Do you hate my mom?"

"I guess I can't. For Daddy's sake, and yours. Do you think we can make this a *Happy* New Year's Eve?"

~ ~ ~

After an early supper at The Blanchard Hotel dining room in town, the four of them returned to Jim's. Much of their tension had gradually disappeared, the mood lightened.

They spent the evening talking, trying to catch up on one another's lives. Lively conversation filled the house where hardly any had been since Lynn was small. Jim loved to see his little girl laugh. Several times he chanced a glace toward Caroline from across the room and saw the pleasurable look on her face. Jim watched as Lynn warmed up to Caroline, passing and enjoying easy exchanges, not concerned with wondering if James could be her *boyfriend*. Jim was delighted to see their two children overcoming the obstacle their parents had unwittingly placed between them years ago.

"It's almost midnight, Daddy. How about we toast in the New Year with some hot chocolate?"

"Yes! Great idea. I'll help you."

"No, uh . . . Dad, I'll help her." They left for the kitchen.

Caroline and Jim met in the middle of the room. "Caroline, did you tell him to call me that?"

"No. And he didn't mention to me that he wanted to. Do you mind?"

"I don't mind. It will take some getting used to, though. Wonder how Lynn will like it?"

"Please don't push her to call me Mom. James has never had anyone he could call Dad, so it comes easier for him than it might for Lynn. She had someone she could call Mother. So, whatever she wants to call me is fine."

Jim took her hand and pulled her toward him. He could smell her shampoo, her eyes sparkled. "Caroline, thanks for coming down here today."

"There's no other place I'd rather be."

Jim and Caroline stood apart as the kids brought in a tray of hot chocolate.

"Just in time. It's almost midnight," Jim announced.

They raised their cups and waited for the clock to chime.

"Happy New Year, everybody." Jim again took Caroline's hand. "Here's to a wonderful 1951 with many more to come!"

"Happy New Year to our new family," James added. He looked at Lynn as he held her hand.

"Happy New Year." Caroline was lost in Jim's beautiful dark eyes.

"Happy New Year." Lynn looked at James, unable to restrain her smile.

After toasting with their hot chocolate, they placed their cups on the tray. James and Lynn turned to each other, sharing another hug. Still holding Caroline's hand, Jim gently tugged her a step closer. She turned her face up toward Jim and he brushed her lips with his. A tender kiss that challenged time and restored their love. Jim sensed a new and different beginning for them all.

Books by Jo Huddleston

<u>Nonfiction</u>

Amen and Good Morning, God: A Book of Morning Prayers
Amen and Good Night, God: A Book of Evening Prayers
His Awesome Majesty: Praising God's Greatness

<u>Fiction</u>

THE CANEY CREEK SERIES
That Summer

Other Books from Sword of the Spirit Publishing

2008

All the Voices of the Wind by Donald James Parker
The Bulldog Compact by Donald James Parker
Reforming the Potter's Clay by Donald James Parker
All the Stillness of the Wind by Donald James Parker
All the Fury of the Wind by Donald James Parker
More Than Dust in the Wind by Donald James Parker
Angels of Interstate 29 by Donald James Parker

2009

Love Waits by Donald James Parker
Homeless Like Me by Donald James Parker

2010

Against the Twilight by Donald James Parker
Finding My Heavenly Father by Jeff Reuter
Never Without Hope by Michelle Sutton
Reaching the Next Generation of Kids for Christ by Robert C. Heath

2011

Silver Wind by Donald James Parker
He's So In Love With You by Robert C. Heath
Their Separate Ways by Michelle Sutton
Silver Wind Pow-wow by Donald James Parker
The 21st Century Delusion by Daniel Narvaez
Hush, Little Baby by Deborah M. Piccurelli

2012

Retroshock by David W. Murray
Destiny of Angels by Eric Myers
It's Not About Her by Michelle Sutton
The Legacy of Deer Run by Elaine Marie Cooper
Decision to Love by Michelle Sutton
The American Manifesto by Steven Flanders
It's Not About Me by Michelle Sutton
It's Not About Him by Michelle Sutton
Will the Real Christianity Please Stand Up by Donald Parker
Amazing Love by K. Dawn Byrd